How the Eagle Dies

The Sparrow Duology

Book One: Why the Sparrow Cries
Book Two: How the Eagle Dies

How the Eagle Dies

The Sparrow Duology #2

By

Hope Bolinger

DEDICATION

To Twix, my faithful co-worker and fat cat. I do dearly hope you're around by the time this book releases. If not, at least I'll know I did have a chance to dedicate a book to you before you left us.

Future Author's Note: He wasn't around by the time the book released. However, I have two new rescue cats, Odin and Freya, to add to this dedication. Great reminders that out of tragedy can come something new and something beautiful.

CONTENT WARNING

This book contains violence, death, slavery, and some brief allusions to sexual assault that has taken place in the past for some characters. All of these issues were prevalent in the Greek Dark Ages, especially in wartime. I have done my best to touch on these topics with the utmost sensitivity, as many of these issues hit close for me as well as others, but I thought it would be wise to inform readers ahead of time before the story begins.

Part One – Life

"Any moment might be our last. Everything is more beautiful because we're doomed. You will never be lovelier than you are now. We will never be here again."

—Homer, *The Iliad*

Chapter One
How the Lightning Arrows Pierce

IF DEAD LANGUAGES DON'T KILL ME, this internet connection will.

I move my laptop to the other side of my bedroom. My boyfriend Homer's fuzzy face on the video call focuses. First the beard that decorates his sharp chin. Then his dark brown eyes and curly black hair.

I don't have the heart to tell him I don't love the facial hair. Two years ago, when I visited England and found our little time-traveler in the British Museum, he'd said he worked in an ancient temple, where they required all servants and priests to be clean-shaven.

But after I left, he stopped using Uncle Laran's razor. On one of our calls, he claimed Palikarians, the group of people he came from, viewed bearded men as, well, men.

"Let us try this again, Harper." He says this in his ancient tongue, a similar language to Greek. But Lord knows what happens whenever I compare Palikarians to Greeks in front of Homer. He gets heated.

I can't blame him. A friend of mine from Brazil does the same whenever high schoolers compare her with Spanish-speaking cultures.

"'The eagle clutches the snake in its talons,'" he says. "Repeat."

He gestures at the screen with a flourish. Sunlight spills behind him. Odd, because when we do the Palikarian portion of the call, I've just left school. Ten o'clock in the evening his time. Only in the summer do we see the sunshine on his end.

"The *até*." The second word trips over my tongue.

No idea why I can't get much of the Palikarian dialect down. You'd think that two years of calls like this would render me fluent.

After all, living in Arizona, I've already learned Spanish. But every once in a while, I can't nail a word. Like eagle.

I try again. "The eagle—"

A growl rumbles in my throat. Homer hides his laughter with the hoodie he has on, strange for June weather. Uncle Laran, who he stays with in England, doesn't even have AC.

I switch to English. "Homie, when is this ever going to come up in an actual sentence?"

"Ah, ah, ah." He wags a finger at the screen. "We already had our hour of English. Palikarian, please."

So goes the format of these calls. I dial him at five a.m. my time on school days when I get ready, and we speak in English. Usually, we go over what happened in the previous days and discover more about each other. Then, when I get back home from school, we do his language.

Took me a few months to be able to speak it. But after a few weeks, I could understand most of what he said.

My leg adjusts to the side of my bed, where I've moved my computer. My ankles knock against my suitcase. "Dude, I'm about to leave for the airport in an hour. Can't we wait to talk in Palikarian when I get there?"

Homer had planned for us to speak in his native language my whole two months in England. Because he only gets to practice one hour a day with me, he says he's lost some nuances.

Make sense. Whenever my Brazilian exchange student friend got on a call with her parents, her Portuguese would falter, since she didn't have many chances to practice or speak anything but English.

What's Homie going to do when I leave England? Will he remember enough?

I've saved enough for a two-month trip. Considering Mom footed the bill of the airplane ticket as a graduation present.

Speaking of Mom, I watch the woman outside my bedroom window place another stone in the spiraling rock garden her new boyfriend gifted her. Smooth stones whirl in the sand.

Man alive, I'm going to miss Zona's temps in England. Fifty percent of the contents in my suitcase are hoodies and sweatpants. I'll miss the scent of dry sunshine and heat, something no one has managed to make into a candle scent yet.

But for Homer, I'd suffer the tundra.

I return my attention back to the screen as Homer forms his hands into the shape of a bird. "Again, please."

"The eagle clutches the snake in its talons."

A twinkle ignites his pupils. "We will work on it." Then he frowns at the screen and switches to English. "You didn't dye your hair blue."

Blonde hair falls over my nose. I pinch the locks and flip them behind my ear. "Been dyeing too many people's hair. Decided to leave it as is." At least I'm sporting a similar length to last time.

Two years ago, I flaunted a blue pixie when Mom and I went to England for the summer. But dye cost too much, even when I retouched the roots myself instead of letting a hairstylist do it. I had to save everything for food and expenses. Even though my classmates asked me to touch up their roots and dye their hair, high schoolers can't afford salon prices. I'd get fifty bucks at most, most of which went to supplies.

I'd promised Homer I'd try to go blue again, for old times' sake.

So much for that.

Outside, Mom palms her forehead and pulls some blonde wisps behind her ears. She checks the watch on her wrist and her gaze roves the windows until she finds my face. She taps her device and twitches her head over her shoulder.

Got it. Go time.

"Homer, I'm sorry to cut this short, but Mom's weird about me getting to the airport early. I'll see you in about sixteen hours?"

He chews on his lip and then forces a smile. "Sure. Can't wait to see you, my love."

I blow a kiss at the screen and hit the red hang-up button before my gut can wriggle. The calls never last long enough. How will I survive when the trip to England ends?

Homework, proms, school pep rallies …I've had to do all these things without my boyfriend by my side. Two hours a day, and five to six on the weekend. Can we keep this up when I get a job? When I go to college? Will I up and move my whole life to England and forever spend my days there, since it would be difficult to get a man from a different time period a passport?

Gravity forces me to slump back onto my pillow. Gusts send pamphlets for schools in England circling and falling to my carpet. I pick up one for Oxford and sigh.

I knew I wouldn't get in there. Most schools in England expect some ridiculous requirements from the American students—impressive AP class test scores, high SAT rankings, GPAs that could kill—none of which I had.

Not to mention, I have no idea what degree I'd do.

Photography? Cutthroat, and I've scanned through galleries of even local colleges. My work doesn't come close to matching the quality of those photos. No way I can go into debt ten thousand a year before I know what I'll do with myself.

Maybe I could convince Laran to let me stay with him for longer. I could get a job at a coffee shop there. They did have one on every street corner in London.

But customs officers get weird about Americans. They'd make me leave every six months.

I clap the brochure that boasts old stony buildings back onto my nightstand. Then I heave myself up and fiddle with the contents inside my suitcase. This morning, I forgot to close the zipper, so now undergarments galore spill out of the bag. Glad Homer didn't spy any of that on the video.

As I stuff the lacy cloth inside the overstuffed luggage, I hear my phone buzz on my sparrow-decorated comforter.

We spotted the bedding on sale at a home goods store. It reminded me of him, my sparrow.

Homer had, in fact, come to us through a Palikarian sparrow ritual. Sparing myself from reliving the details of that gory ceremony, I let memories of Homer holding onto birds in Hyde Park flood my vision instead.

A text from my classmate, Dakota, flashes on the screen, pulling me away from my recollections.

Dakota: Hey, girl. Really appreciate you sending me the graduation photos.

Three dots surface in a bubble again.

Dakota: I also noticed you sent a Venmo request. Before I pay that, I have a few edits I'd really like for you to do. Hope you understand, girlie! Can't wait to see the finished product.

Anger bubbles in my stomach. She sends a screenshot with her list of demands moments later. Rocks sink into my stomach, pulling me closer and closer to my carpet. These will take hours to do. Days, maybe.

I rattle off a text to her and mutter, "Dakota, I'm giving you the best prices possible."

But I've gotten used to this. Last summer, I made a few extra bucks shooting weddings and grad pics of friends and family members. More than once, people sent back edits they wanted. If I calculated all the hours the revisions took, I was working far below minimum wage.

Harper: Hey. So I'm about to get on a plane. Any way you can pay me, and I'll get you the edits in a day or two after I land?

Should've done an upfront fee. I've seen some YouTube photographers explain the importance of charging this as a safety, in case someone refuses to pay you for your work. But all those people had degrees and professional classes under their belts.

What did I have?

A memory from yearbook auditions stings my skull. I sweep the thought away and return to my phone to spot the next text from Dakota.

Dakota: Sorry, but I really think these edits need to get done before I get you the money. Makes no sense to pay for a half-done job, you know?

Heat sizzles in my cheeks. Before I can even tap out a reply, she's sent another one.

Dakota: I could always have my cousin, Calian, re-shoot them. He has a pretty nice phone, good quality. Don't want to put too much on your plate, girlie!

The audacity of this girl.

I rattle off a text, venom coursing through my fingertips. Then I pause. Hit erase.

The one hundred dollars for her photos could go toward a day trip on a train with Homer. Maybe we could see a show together, or blow it all on churros, like we did two summers back. Well, we didn't quite spend $100 on churros. But in my opinion…if we had, it would have been well worth it.

Besides. I chew on my lips. *She's right. Your work isn't all that good, chica.*

Clouds fill my chest as I send my last text.

Harper: No problem :) I'll get those edits to you soon!

My phone drops to my carpet. But I swear it's marble, because I can hear the thud echo for a minute straight.

"About time."

I thrust my suitcase down in St. Pancras train station and bolt to Homer, who stands near a moving sidewalk.

"Hi, Har—"

An "oof" follows as I barrel into his belly, lifting him up in the hug. I drop him, and he wastes no time in lunging forward for a kiss. Warmth spreads in my insides. Tingling fills my gut.

This makes up for the fact that I went to the wrong terminal back in Arizona. That I almost stepped onto the wrong train coming here and seemingly couldn't do anything right today to get to Homie.

We've waited for this for two years.

Dizziness fills my skull when we pull apart. Who knows how long we'd held that kiss? Enough to send dopamine firecrackers exploding in my brain.

Homer grips the handle of my suitcase and motions to a bench. Good idea, I might collapse from the long plane ride followed by the hour-long train trek here.

We slump onto the seat, and I inhale the sweet, robust scent of coffee. A man on a nearby seat blows away steam from his cup. Where he got it, who knows? I scan the area for any open shops. All have closed, and only a few people mill the grounds with their suitcases.

My neck cranes toward the display boards with neon times of departures winking in and out. "I'm surprised they're still having trains run at this time."

Homer doesn't appear to hear. Instead, he stares at the lace fringe at the end of my dress. "You dressed up?"

"Changed between Heathrow and the train to Pancras." I shrug. "Figured you always see me in hoodies and could use a change of pace."

Plus, after Dakota's texts burned in my brain for the twelve-hour flight, I needed to wear something I know I can rock. A plus-size maxi with a floral pattern, and lace at the edges.

He kisses my forehead and makes me lean into his shoulder. "You look beautiful in anything." We sit in silence and watch passengers click their wheeled bags onto the moving sidewalk. "Besides, anything is a better sight to look at than Uncle Laran."

I snort.

We check in and wander about the station. A man in a

business suit rubs the stomach of a statue. Good luck, I suppose. We follow suit. Bronze shows beneath my fingertips.

"Speaking of Uncle Laran..."

Homer leads me to the train platform. He holds my suitcase, and I adjust my heavy backpack on my shoulders. Any more bags would've cost me a fortune. I'll have to do most of my shopping here.

"He has gotten"—Homer searches the skies for a word—"*obsessed* with sending me back to Palikari."

I frown and loop my thumbs through my backpack straps. "I thought time travel wasn't possible going backward."

My uncle explained the whole spiel to me in the British Museum shop. You'd have to go close to the speed of light to go *forward* in time. Backward? Out of the question.

"That's how you got here in the first place. Lightning struck a metal vessel, and it formed a wormhole."

We'd even attempted to replicate the experiment in the backyard of a tomb robber. Fear seizes me as the memories flicker across my vision. Even two years later, I can't erase the images of the knife, of the man drowning in the tub, of Homer emerging with a gouged leg.

Homer grips one of my hands, and I steady.

"Indeed." Ah, he does slip into British slang every once in a while. He doesn't speak with Laran often—owing to the fact my uncle teaches at University most of the time—but Homer's accent does flip somewhere between American and British.

He glances over his shoulder and then leans down to whisper, "But we're not including magic in the equation."

Something uneasy worms in my gut. We'd suspected that magic had a possible hand in getting Homer here in the first place, or some bad vibes from a Palikarian ritual. Human sacrifices have a tendency to evoke dark forces, after all.

Wormholes plus magic equal Homer's possible ticket home.

Unclenching my jaw, I force myself to relax. That could take Uncle Laran years. "So is he going to saw you in half or something?"

Homer sniggers as our train rolls up to the platform. We stay behind the line on the floor until the doors ding open. An arched glass ceiling above us reflects the yellow paint of our train. I imagine in the broad daylight, milky light would spill through those panes.

We step inside the train, and I notice no other passengers have entered. Unusual. Last time Mom and I came to this station, most of the seats had filled. But we'd arrived in the afternoon then.

Now, we're pushing the hours I used to call Homer after school, ten or eleven his time.

He slides into a seat, and I place my suitcase in a storage container near the doors of the train. Red carpet muffles my footsteps. Then I squeeze into the chair next to his. My stomach burns.

Homer must hear the rumble. "Get any food on the plane?"

I wrinkle my nose. "Sort of. They didn't really have many vegetarian options."

The sour aftertaste of my blueberry yogurt lodges into my throat. Maybe they'll have a rolling cart of food pass through these aisles like last time. I check the backpack on my stomach and breathe a sigh of relief when I open the top zipper. The money I exchanged for pounds sits atop my hoodie I scrunched in there.

Train doors slide shut. I glance behind me to make sure no one else will grab a seat. Then I place my bookbag on the chair in the aisle across from us.

A female British voice says we're departing.

"I wonder why there isn't anyone else on our car." I frown and fiddle with the lace at the end of my dress. "Did you see anyone else get on?"

Homer shuts his eyelids. Then they fly open. "I think I saw them get onto other carts. Just not this one."

Relief fills my gut for some reason.

I place my head on Homer's shoulder and clamp my eyes shut. Sleepiness overtakes me, and I cannot, for the life of me, pry open my eyelids. "Anyway, Uncle Laran is going to join Cirque du Soleil to get you back to Palikari. Tell me more."

Homer's chuckle bobs me up and down. Or maybe that's the steady rumble of the train tracks.

Speaking of rumbles, thunder utters a muffled growl outside. Dark clouds had filled the skies when I landed at Heathrow. A flash of light turns my vision orange. Confirmed, we have lightning.

"I don't know if he wants to replicate the ceremony per se." Homer pauses. "But he thinks something beyond scientific explanation got me here. That would be needed to get me home."

"He seemed pretty dead set on science last time I was here. The lightning, the metal container, the wormhole." I tick each one off my fingers. Then I let my arm drop. Too bad I can't see, because it hits something plastic, and pain shoots through my wrist.

Must be the armrest.

Orange light fills my vision again. Growls roar like lions somewhere far off in the distance.

"Harper, if he does manage to find a way back home, will you come with me?"

Drowsiness overtakes me, and I scrunch my eyebrows to make sure I registered that right. "Wha—"

"Will you come with—"

Neon floods my eyes, followed by a ringing in my ears. Weird. Did I fall asleep? I no longer feel the rumble of the train underneath the soles of my sandals.

Energy fills me seconds later, and I pry open my eyelids. We've plunged into darkness. Maybe the train stopped, experienced a power outage due to the lightning.

I appear to have fallen, because I feel something cool underneath my palm. I rub my hand back and forth on the smooth surface. Is this…marble? What a strange dream.

A flicker of firelight snags my attention near something gold and gleaming. Shakiness fills my legs as I rise to get a better look. I glimpse the head of this statue. Behind the throne upon which it sits, bloody shields decorate the back wall.

This twists knots in my intestines. I feel myself grow faint.

Do dreams feel this humid? I rub my knuckle against my upper lip and find Homer's silhouette gazing out into the distance. Rain splatters outside.

Shadows of figures dancing and chanting in the rows of torches on stands arrest my attention. Up at the front, through the misty haze, I spot a tub full of blood.

Man alive, I don't have the imagination to conjure this stuff up, not even in dreams.

My legs go wobbly again. "Homer?" I pinch my shoulder. Pain throbs in my arms and legs from when I must've landed on the stone.

He doesn't answer.

I stumble into a nearby column to keep my balance.

"Homer, what's happening?"

He gazes at me. Even in the darkness, I can spy his eyes soften, apologetic. "Looks like we have the answer to my question on the train."

A cold shock, like frozen lightning, jolts my veins. "What do you mean?"

"Harper." He exhales. "Welcome to Palikari."

Chapter Two
How the Foxes Find Their Dens

Yearbook Auditions, Two Years Ago

WE ALL GROAN ABOUT THE WHOLE idea of "yearbook auditions." In years past, students would sign up, and people would fit them wherever they could.

But ten photographers asked to join the class. They only have room for eight.

So a week before school starts, editor-in-chief Dakota Allen calls us in to show her photos we took over the summer to decide who took the best quality ones.

I clutch the pictures to my chest as I stride toward classroom 203. Then I pause right before I enter and flick through the photographs. Had to stop by Walmart an hour ago to get these printed—Dakota insists on physical photos.

Let's hope the money that could've *gone toward a meal with Homie is worth it.*

Images of Homer grimacing at a sour yogurt drink, of the swans in Hyde Park, of him in Paddington station looking off at a patisserie full of matcha treats pass through my fingertips.

You can do this, chica. You got this.

Warmth brimming in my chest, I draw in a deep breath and march into the room.

"You're early." Dakota peers up at me from her laptop screen. Red rims her eyes. She's served as editor-in-chief since the year prior and has been known to get an average of four to five hours of sleep a night.

I fan out the pictures on her desk. "Figure it never hurts to make a good first impression."

In truth, Mom has scored a job at school as the drama camp leader, and so she offered to drop me off. Saving me some gas and, with any luck, scoring me a longer conversation with Dakota about me joining yearbook.

Dakota stacks the photos and flickers through them like flashcards for a test. Her over-glossed lips sag.

She lifts a brow. "Did you take these on a phone?"

Her words puncture a hole into my chest. I feel my heart deflating on my ribcage. "Canon. It's a professional camera."

Her cheeks harshen to a shade darker, and she hands back my photos with a smile. "Sorry, girlie. I meant it as a compliment." She searches the water-stained ceiling, for more support, perhaps. "Phones take really high-quality photos these days. Sometimes you can't even tell them apart from the professional stuff."

My face scrunches until I stare at her through slits. I mimic her grin. Best not give away how I really feel inside. "Haha. For sure. Anyway, any chance you know when you'll announce who made it into the class?" I clap the photos onto my hip, face-down. "I know the guidance counselors are really strict about changing course schedules at the last minute."

She doesn't meet my gaze. Instead, her dark eyeliner highlights the whites of her eyes as she keeps her attention on the many tables full of Macs.

"Yep. I'll probably email the list in about an hour." She throws up a hand and waves, like wafting away a bad stench. "Thanks for stopping by."

I hunch into my shoulders like a tortoise and play on my phone for an hour outside of the theater. I tried helping Mom with another camp a year back, soccer camp. But turns out that eight-year-olds and I don't mesh well together. One juice box to the head later, I quit.

On the dot, the email appears in scathing bold at the top of my inbox. I draw in a long breath and click on the email.

"Hi, Ladies (and One Gentleman),

Thank you so much for coming today to show me your photos. List below on those who made it in the class."

My eyes scour the names up and down. The only H is Harley, the one gentleman. I spy the name Shyanne Wilson, and a jolt of surprise hits me. I've seen her photos on Instagram. Not terrible, but doctored with a million filters.

How did I lose to her?

I blink several times and force myself to finish the rest of the message.

"For those who didn't make it, better luck next year. The competition was really stiff. Keep trying and honing your craft."

I click out of the message and sigh.

You don't got this.

Palikari, The Present (or, really, 800 BCE)

Reality clicks like a gunshot and sends me to my knees onto the marble. My vision goes dark, and seconds later I realize why. I'm hyperventilating.

"Ho-mie. I ca-can't do this."

Mixed scents of wet air and incense burn my nostrils.

My skull collides with marble, and oxygen fills my lungs a second later. Homer hovers over me and offers an arm. Woozy, I take it, and he yanks me to my feet. Then he motions for me to totter after him beside the throne, where we'll be out of sight from those outside.

The chanting has stopped. They'll leave soon.

We collapse on the right side of the idol's throne, and the cool stone chills my neck. Blurry images of the fires on stands— no wait, Homer called them "tripods" on our calls—come into focus. I remembered that because we joked about how photographers use a different kind of tripod for photoshoots.

"Homer, I can't do this," I repeat when my lips stop trembling. I don't have this within me. I can't remember the Palikarian word for "eagle," let alone survive in an ancient country.

Did Homie feel this way when he landed in England, knowing not a single word of English? This panic that grips your chest so tight that it feels like it'll shatter your ribcage?

My heartbeat thrums so hard, I wonder if the Palikarians can hear it through the stone.

"Harper, I'm afraid we don't have a choice."

"I thought we couldn't travel *back* in time."

"Well apparently…" He makes jazz hands. In the firelight, the shadows look like spiders. "We can."

I hold back an eyeroll. Leave it to him to take on a joking tone at a time like this. "Why didn't the train car come with us?"

Or my phone for that matter? By instinct, I search my pocket-less dress for my device. Nothing. Man alive. Should've held onto my backpack.

Homer chews on a quivering lip. "When I got sent back, the blood disappeared from the laver, remember?"

Indeed I do. One minute, I snapped a picture of Homer emerging from a bloody tub in the British Museum. The next, all the red liquid drained into nothingness. Maybe magic had pulled us here after all and left the train behind in England.

This makes sense. The lighting, the metal container…

Another cold shock ripples through me. "Oh, Homer, the laver. They just did the sparrow ceremony. What are they going to do when they find you back here, when they thought you'd vanished?"

Hordes of footsteps echo against the stone flooring. I scrunch myself into the smallest ball I can muster. Homer's tongue pokes in and out.

"They may not recognize me. I grew a beard, and I'm a lot paler."

True. Two years ago, he sported a much darker skin tone and a clean-shaven face. Constant cloud cover in England lightened the former.

Besides, he worked as a slave in the temple. From my experience, people tend not to notice you when you don't have money. Maybe that's why Dakota ultimately went with Shyanne. The garage alone on that girl's mansion could swallow up my whole house.

I pinch myself again. No luck. We've gotten ourselves stuck in this nightmare forever.

"Okay, so what do we do now, Homie?"

His knees wobble. He places his hands on them to keep them still. "Lay low and find a way back home."

Fires burn in my stomach. First, we need to get food. Steal it, most likely. Thank goodness Palikari is a vegetarian nation too. At least, Homer refused meat the first time we offered it to him—so Uncle Laran drew this conclusion.

Strangely, when I asked my history teacher about vegetarian nations, he seemed to imply that was more of a modern thing…maybe Palikari was ahead of its time?

Footfalls continue to thunder within the trees of columns. I peer to the side of the statue and watch a family walk past a white-washed altar spattered in blood. My stomach twists. For a vegetarian nation, they sure do like to do a lot of animal sacrifice.

I turn back to Homer. "Okay, what's our first move?"

His mouth opens, but he clamps his lips closed seconds later. Whites expand in his eyes, and he stares at something right past me. I glance over my shoulder and freeze.

A woman in a billowing dress, sandals, and with beads laced in her hair stands before us. Three others, in less-stunning garments, flank her sides.

Shoot, so much for laying low.

She cocks her head to the side, and one of the pearl strings in her hair bobbles against her temples. Must've gotten loose somehow. "*Xeno*?"

I recognize that word from mine and Homer's calls.

Foreigner.

My nostrils wrinkle at the stench coming from her. An odd mixture of perfume and body odor, like she spritzed herself with Calvin Klein right after working out.

According to Uncle Laran, Greeks and Palikarians were obsessed with bathing, but without the modern invention of antiperspirant, scents would come in a mixed bag.

Homer clears his throat and switches to the Palikarian tongue. "We are friends of Palikari." Then he reaches out and grasps the woman's knees. Alarm shoots through me until I remember that Homer had explained this was the Palikarian way of begging for something. "We have made a long journey. Will you help us?"

The woman doesn't seem taken aback by the gesture. She doesn't flinch at all. She flicks her head to the left and whispers something to the male beside her. He darts away.

Great, did she call some government official to arrest us?

She stretches out a hand, then moves it over her shoulder, like she's throwing a ball to someone behind her. "Come."

Homer's elbow jabs into my side. I follow the woman, legs a-wobble. We weave our way past families going at slower paces. Homer tugs on my sleeve and motions for me to come closer.

I do so.

"Follow my lead," he says in English. "Only talk in Palikarian, and honestly, don't talk much. Women don't say much here."

Oh goodness, *that's* going to be tough.

Before I went to England two years ago, I'd say whatever came to my mind. Homer brought out my soft side, but if someone crosses me, I *will* filibuster until the cacti come home.

He reaches for my hand, squeezes it, and lets go. A female with a braid in her hair eyes us but says nothing. Instead, she quickens her pace and reaches the woman with pearls. Homer glances over his shoulder, and in the rain, he grows two shades paler. Water pelts my face and arms.

"What?" I ask in Palikarian.

"Do not look at the palisade."

"Why?"

"There are heads on it."

Icy arrows strike my chest. Oh boy, we ain't in Zona anymore.

"Spoils of war," he explains, and then pulls his gaze elsewhere. To the whitewashed barriers of the city, where guards stand on the walls with tripods of fire.

I keep my eyes on the sandals of the ladies in front of us and try my best to ignore the burning in my calves. Fiery thorns wrap around my lungs, minutes or hours later, I can't tell. We keep making our way upward through the dirt paths.

Doubled over, I raise a hand to call for a halt. My asthma's got the best of me today.

Once I regain my breath and the film flees from my eyes, we continue onward and upward. White-washed homes flank my periphery. I thought the suburbs had no imagination when it came to decoration.

The farther up we go, the larger the houses get. Then gates and fields border these near-palaces. I wouldn't call them castles—probably the size of a middle-class home in Arizona—but from what I can remember in my history classes, most people lived in one-room places in ancient cultures.

We reach a large gate, and a dog with matted fur springs to life. I jolt backward and raise my fists. Its jagged teeth disappear moments later when a man in rags throws a stone at it. The rock misses, but the dog whimpers and ducks away.

Sheep bleat in the distance.

The man leans on a walking stick and nods to the woman with the pearls. "Elin."

Elin, apparently, gestures at Homer with her chin. "We have guests."

Bowing, the man flourishes his arm and motions for us to step within the gates. We do so, and stone meets my sandals. Fiery pains jab into my ankles like needles. How long have we walked?

The white building sprawls before me, a stone courtyard in front of it. To the right, a pile of dung sits beside a pen for a farm animal. Judging by the scent, some creature that likes to roll in filth.

Servants bustle out of the double doors of the house, armed with chairs and tables.

"I am afraid we already partook of the evening meal." Elin stretches her arm toward the house. Her billowing fabric reminds me of a bird's wing. "But we will prepare what we can. You." She targets her chin at me. They must do this instead of using pointer fingers here. "My servants Brisei and Talith will attend to you."

Two women who stand beside her move to me. They must've been standing with her this whole time, I just didn't register them. Maybe call it shock.

The second one, the one in a veil rather than a braid, follows at a slower pace. Braid woman holds my arm and guides me toward the steps that lead into the house.

Warmth itches my cheeks when we step inside, like someone has left an oven open. I glance to my left and spot an unlit hearth. Tripods form weak light around it. Shields and armor coat the walls, just as they had back at the temple.

Braid lady ushers me up the steps. In the glow of the firelight that leads upstairs, I notice that no wrinkles mar her face. In fact, she looks about my age, maybe younger.

They lead me to a gleaming tub where an older woman pours water into steaming liquid. Oh…can I pass on this?

Before I can protest, veil lady fumbles around my dress to find a way to take it off. Shoot, they don't have zippers in the ancient world, right?

Worried about anachronisms or stepping on butterflies or whatever from what I've watched on *Doctor Who* episodes, I unclip my bra, then reach for the lacy fringe at the bottom of my dress and pull the fabric above my head.

I take off the rest and slip into the tub. Ten degrees too hot, the water sends an instant headache to my temples.

The three ladies don't say much. So I grip my elbows, hunch over, and try to stay conscious. Then the emotions hit me. Like when I try desperately hard not to cry in a sad movie, and then, in the theater parking lot, tears prick my eyes.

I'm not going back home again, am I?

Water spills down my cheeks and drips into the tub as a woman behind me pours something greasy onto my skin and hair. Like a perfumed olive oil, by the smell of it.

"My dear lady," the older woman says, "do not cry. It spoils the cheeks."

Great, we got a beauty guru in the house. I wipe them away with a fist and clench my gut. Do this hard enough, and I can keep the sadness away for a while. I'll allow myself to feel later when I go to bed.

The older woman disappears, and braid lady rubs the oil up and down my hands. Veil lady holds a clay jar off to the side.

"What is your name?" I ask her.

Braid lady pauses and then commences kneading again. "Brisei."

"The other one is Talith, then?" I jab my chin at veil lady, hoping I did the nonverbal communication right.

"She is from the land of Sidon, a Phoenician. We do not know her real name. She does not speak our language. She is—" Brisei halts and washes her hands in the tub water. "Talith has been here for two weeks."

Phoenician, eh? I'll bet Talith didn't come here for a summer job.

My eyes itch from the tears. How can I be crying now, when these girls probably got torn from their homes and forced to do this work?

Needle pains jab my stomach. Instinct takes over when I stare at these girls. If Homer and I get out of here, we need to take them with us.

At long last, Brisei lends me a hand to step out of the bath onto the slick marble. Brisei and Talith dry me by using some weird metal device. I guess it scrapes off the moisture. Would prefer a towel, but I suppose this works too.

They lead me to a perfumed room, the flowery scent so strong it almost knocks me over.

Makes sense. In a world without deodorant, you take what you can get.

A bed with furs and blankets sits against a window. I cover my chest and watch Brisei click open a trunk near a wall that depicts soldiers hoisting shields in battle. Another illustration shows a man with a sword lopping off one of the many heads of a reptilian creature. Ah yes, definitely what I would love to think about before drifting off to sleep.

Brisei pulls out a blue, perfumed garment and carries it over to me. "Lift your arms, my lady."

I do so and get drowned in the fabric. My head and arms find the holes in what I can best describe as a sheet of cerulean fabric, folded in half. Talith wraps a woven belt around my waist, giving some form to the dress.

Love the breeze around my ankles. Will *not* love the thigh chafing that is certain to ensue.

While Brisei twists a branch of leaves into a crown, I gaze out the window. A wooden ladder leads down from my bedroom to the courtyard.

I turn back to Brisei in time for her to place the leafy hat onto my head. Didn't just Olympic runners win these or something? Or did Homer forget to tell me about this Palikarian tradition? I suppose even in two years of FaceTime calls, we can only cover so much.

"This room used to belong to my mistress's daughter." Brisei fixes a leaf that has decided to poke me in the eyeball. She then reaches for the jar that Talith held in the bathroom.

"Where is she now?"

"Married." Her voice drops low along with her chin. She says the word like a death sentence. Then she oils my arms and legs until I glisten.

A knock on wood alerts me. Talith moves to unlatch the leather strap that keeps the door closed. Elin appears in the doorway.

"Your friend must bathe as well, while the food is preparing." She gestures down the steps with a fabric-covered arm. "Let me show you around the estate."

Chapter Three
How Blood Drips in the Garden

HOW YOU KNOW YOU'VE ENTERED AN ancient house—they have a room devoted to olive oil.

No joke, Elin leads me to a basement area full of trunks and amphorae. The trunks hold perfumed clothes, and judging by the weight of the jars, they got plenty of that olive juice in 'em.

We've made our way around the estate and past the beautiful garden. Man alive, I could've stayed back there forever. It would be the perfect place to snap a senior picture or engagement photo, vines weighed down by grapes wrapping around columns and wooden pergolas.

Every part of me itches for my sketchbook so I can commit this place to memory. Far as I can tell, they don't use papyrus or any writing tools here. Didn't see a book or scroll in sight anywhere in the house.

Then I remember that Homer mentioned writing didn't develop in the Greco world for another few decades. At least they don't have essay tests here, I suppose.

We ascend the steps to the storage area and Homer greets us with wet hair, bedecked in an olive branch crown and everything gleaming in oil.

Butterflies wriggle in my gut. Goodness, we need to have Homer wear oil more often, if we ever get back to England. I wonder what Uncle Laran will say when Homer gets his couches and carpets all greasy.

Needles drive into my chest. That is, if we ever get home.

Elin gestures for us to follow her out to the courtyard. There, servants drape animal furs onto gleaming wooden chairs.

I notice a chaise lounge sort of thing piled with what looks like deer skin. Two chairs are stationed a good distance away. In fact, the chaise has an entirely separate table before it.

Elin takes the seat at the head of the table the servants have just set up. They sponge down the surface. Then a woman holds a pitcher of water with a bowl. Elin places her hands above the bowl and receives a splash of water. I follow suit and park in the chair beside her.

Homer sprawls on the lounger.

Why do the men get to recline for the meals? My calves ache from the plane ride and my uphill journey here. Switch with me, Homie.

He doesn't acknowledge my eyebrow raise. Maybe men and women can't look at each other much here.

So instead, I watch Brisei place a footstool before me and the others. Then another woman replaces her and mixes water with some red paste in a bowl. Spirits fill my nostrils about two seconds later. Oh man, wine.

They don't have underage drinking rules in Greece, do they?

I wince. Well, the water probably isn't the best quality. Uncle Laran did say that I was eighteen and could drink under his supervision in England. Not to mention that I have sipped some wine in certain church services for communion.

The servant with a hunched back hands Elin the bowl. She lifts the wooden dish to the sky and pours out a portion of the liquid on the stone flooring.

"To the deathless gods," Elin says.

Fire ignites behind me. A male servant has lit a tripod. Goodness, how many people do they have working on this estate? On our tour, Elin mentioned plenty of pastures and pens that we didn't take a look at.

Elin hands the bowl back to the servant, who pours portions of it into clay cups.

Then the plates arrive.

Dish upon dish is set before us, from piles of fruit to bread in baskets. A collarbone juts out from one of the younger female servants, who can't be older than fourteen. How much do they feed them here? Would I get into enormous trouble if I sneak them some food?

"I do apologize for the last-minute preparations." Elin lifts her goblet to her lips and drains a mouthful. "When my husband, the shepherd of the people, returns from the warfront, I will guarantee you a proper feast."

I reach forward for a cluster of grapes, and then a fistful of bread. I hide it in the folds of my dress, hoping for a way to bring the food back to Brisei and Talith when I return to the house tonight.

A male servant with a crippled leg hobbles forward and brings Homer a plate of something steaming. My stomach twists at the scent of the fat.

Please don't tell me that's meat.

With a serrated knife, the servant saws off a portion of the thick animal. I guess it looks like ham, or maybe boar. Based on the farm animal noises that tickle my left ear, it's fresh.

Elin speaks. "Now, good sir, tell me about where you come from. What you are doing in Palikari, and how you made your journey here."

Ants crawl up and down my skin when the servant with the plate of meat approaches me. Can I shake my head to say no? Is that how they say no here?

I wince and lift up a hand, hoping it does the trick.

It does not. His eyes go wide, and Elin's cup about slips from her hand. She catches it, albeit spilling an ounce of liquid on the table. A girl materializes and sponges off the stain.

Craning my neck to the right, I plead with Homer with wide eyes. He gives me an ever-so-slight nod and then swallows the wad of meat in his mouth.

All these years, he ate animals. Why didn't he tell me?

"Certainly, my good lady," he says in response to Elin. "You may have noticed that we wore strange garments that seem foreign to Palikari–and that my lady has cut her hair quite short."

Huh, hadn't considered that. Now that I glance at the female servants who cluster around the table, everyone has their hair tied in a braid or forming waves down to their hips.

"That is because we are also from a tribe of Palikari. One that was attacked by the Greeks."

He doesn't use the word "Greek," per se. By this period of time, Greece was a group of ninety-plus tribes in the Mediterranean. Even the name they later united under, *Hellas*, doesn't show up for another few decades.

But the word he does use, *Hé*, refers to the surrounding country before you reach the "land beyond farms," the uncivilized peoples. Palikarians refer to themselves as *Palí*.

Palí and Hé, sworn enemies, like the Trojans and Greeks.

Wow, I *do* remember some of Homer's history lessons he gave me.

"We wished to disguise ourselves as foreigners to escape them as they ransacked our town. Fortunately, we escaped. Unfortunately for my lady, she lost her betrothed in the raids." He angles his head toward the meat plate. "She has decided to fast from good foods such as meat in her hour of grief."

Good call, Homie. But how long can I "grieve" the loss of my supposed fiancé?

Granted, we did read *The Iliad* and *The Odyssey* in my junior year English class, and Penelope got away with it for twenty years. Maybe I'll have similar luck.

Shadows fall over Brisei's face during the speech. She digs her nails into her arms and keeps her gaze pressed to the stone flooring.

"My deepest condolences, my dear." Elin clasps a hand onto my shoulder, squeezes. "There is not one soul here who has not been touched by the black hands of grief."

Wind rustles her hair, and she stares off into the inky night sky. Who has she lost?

She releases her grip and asks Homer more questions. I chew on sticky figs to prevent myself from having to add anything to the conversation. He, meanwhile, claims that he was a nobleman back at the palace. And that, when he helped me escape, he pretended to be my bodyguard. That my father, too, was shepherd of the people in my tribe until he was slaughtered in battle.

He also tells her our English names and claims we are part of a tribe of Palikari that has a slightly different dialect.

Palikari must have as many tribes as a land like Greece, because Elin doesn't feel compelled to fact-check names or any of these details.

We finish our meal, and the servants clear away the plates. I watch Brisei's legs wobble all the way back to the house. How much did that poor girl lose before being forced to work here?

I crane my neck back to Homer. He's risen from his seat and backs away from the servants who have begun sponging down his table.

"What a beautiful garden you have, my lady. I would love to see it sometime soon."

He doesn't stare at Elin. Instead, he lifts his eyebrows to me.

What he would do on video calls where he wanted to rant about Uncle Laran but couldn't say anything because Laran was in the other room.

Our secret language. I squint at him and then understand a moment later, so I nod.

Meet him in the garden. We'll discuss details later.

"What in the world, Homie? You eat meat?"

I hiss the words when I find Homer in the garden, at least an hour later. I had to wait for everyone to turn in for the night. Then I tried to escape my room but found Brisei and Talith sleeping outside my door in the hallway on mats. So I placed the bread I'd stolen on both of their stomachs and fled to the garden via the ladder route outside my window.

Thank goodness, by then, the guardsman and his dog had kept their heads on the path before them, and not behind.

Homer's lips twitch in the glint of the moonlight. He sits on a wooden bench, and an ivy leaf brushes his ear.

"What happened the first day you traveled to England? You refused the meat Uncle Laran gave you."

He shrugs. "People in my social class don't often eat meat. I was afraid he'd made a mistake and thought I was higher up." He rolls a grape in the palm of his hand, then closes his fist around it. "But after a while, I realized you didn't eat it by choice, so I figured it was a custom or something. By the time I figured out the truth, I was embarrassed to tell you any differently."

I groan and slump to the ground, aligning my spine with a column. Walls of trees hide us, shadow us. I reach out and clasp his hand. Warmth tingles in my fingertips.

"Homie, I'm assuming that being my pretend bodyguard

isn't the ancient equivalent of being my boyfriend?"

His nose scrunches. "Sorry, no."

"Why couldn't you say that you were my betrothed?"

Not gonna lie, I have a whole Pinterest board dedicated to that—a lifetime with him. But that would require me getting a job in the twenty-first century, since Homie doesn't have a birth certificate or anything "government official."

"Because that would make me a coward, which is far worse than being dead in this world. If we were really engaged, I should've stood my ground and fought them off, even if that meant my certain death. If I'm a coward, they could tell me to leave. Or worse, kill me. The only way I was allowed to run away in the story is if I helped you escape. It gives them grounds to let us stay here for a while and get our bearings."

"Yeah, more baths, hooray."

Homer sniggers and then pats the bench. I sidle beside him and lean into his shoulder.

"Be careful, Harper. Hospitality is dangerous."

"I mean, if the bath gets any hotter, they may boil me alive."

He shakes his head, bumping his chin into my cheek. "No, not that. They're being nice because they expect repayment. That's how it works in Palikari. We don't know who her husband or any of her other family members are. If they recognize me…"

My eyebrows pinch above my nose.

"But wait, we read *The Odyssey* in my class. Don't rich people feed beggars all the time?"

"Yes, because they believe that sometimes the gods disguise themselves as beggars and strangers to make sure mortals are behaving well. But if they discover that I'm the sparrow from the sparrow ceremony, that's another story. They're not going to think I'm a god at all. Remember what I said about cowards."

I think back to him mentioning the heads on the palisade wall, hours before. Feels like days by this point. Would they do that to Homer if they found out the truth?

"Okay." I breathe. "Before they have a chance to find out, how are we going to get out of here?"

"Thought about that. The soothsayer came up with the sparrow ceremony in the first place. He might have answers about how to replicate it and get us back to the present."

Soothsayer? Like the old guys who show up in Shakespeare plays that everyone gets annoyed at?

"Cool, cool, so let's go look for him tomorrow."

"There's no 'let's.' Women aren't to be seen with men unless they're married to them. Besides meeting in the garden, we can't be near each other."

Darkness fills my insides until gravity threatens to pull me off this bench. I dig my head into his shoulder harder.

"So *you* go find him? While I endure more baths, gotcha."

"He's probably one of the few who *will* recognize me, even with the beard. He did facilitate the sparrow ceremony, you know."

Oh, so it's up to me then.

Something throbs in my temples. Maybe doubt, or anxiety, or a lack of sleep these past two days. I wince. "You sure I can do this? I'm usually the last person to get picked for things, Homie."

Group projects, sports teams, even friends at school would send me invitations to events at the last minute.

"I chose you, didn't I?"

I let the words sink in. Then I smile. "Okay, what does this soothsayer look like?"

I bolt out of bed the second Brisei opens my door.

"Hello." I throw off the blankets and dab some of the sweat off my chest with my huge sheet dress. "I will be out today, but please send Elin my best wishes."

Brisei's eyes widen. "Out?"

"Need to meet with the soothsayer." You know how it be, girl. Gotta find a prophet so he can direct us to a wormhole. #JustTimeTravelThings

I throw the blankets back onto the bed in a haphazard fashion, much like I often do with my comforter and pillows back home. Then I beeline for the door, but she slides in front of it and slams it shut.

"My lady, you are not ready. Besides, an unmarried woman cannot be seen in public without a veil, and without being accompanied by servants. It is far too dangerous."

This slackens me. I take a few steps back.

After Homer had given me the lowdown on the soothsayer dude—apparently, he's the only one in town with one milky eye—he warned me to lay low. I have to play the part of the quiet woman.

"Very well. Brisei, would you like to accompany me?"

She scrunches her nose as if to say, *"Like and duty are two very different things."* Then she moves to the trunk near the bed and pulls out a comb. "Talith as well. At least let me fix your hair."

I sit on the bed. Sunlight glints on the handle of the brush. They've carved the wood into the shape of an—

"Eagle." The word trips out of my mouth, as it did on the call with Homer the other day.

Brisei freezes, stares at the comb, and then moves the bristles through my hair. Yikes, ow—how can anything so short get so many tangles? I flinch, and Brisei pulls the comb away.

"My lady." She pauses, draws in a breath. "You are not from Palikari, are you?"

Cold shock petrifies my chest, my face. I can't say anything. Part of me wishes I could break out into a fit of laughter at the preposterous nature of her statement.

Instead, I chew on my lip. "I am not from Palikari." Then I add, "But Homer is." Then, "How did you know?"

"I have had to learn the language of this land. I know when someone does not pronounce words in the right way, even if they come from a different tribe. And"—she smiles—"most Palikarians of high standing would not give someone like me a gift of food."

Should've known that eight hundred plus hours speaking with Homer in Palikarian wouldn't be enough. Even though I'd learned Spanish since elementary school, most native speakers could detect that English was my first language.

"Not to worry, my lady. I do not think others suspect you." She says this with an edge to her voice, scornful. Then her face softens. "Where are you from?"

How to explain this? "Somewhere far away from here. Only the soothsayer can get me back home."

Her pupils dart back and forth before drifting heavenward.

Homer's point about Palikarians sometimes viewing strangers and beggars as gods echoes in my skull.

"Who am I to refuse a stranger and her request?" She lifts herself from the bed and places the comb back into the chest.

"Where are you from, Brisei?"

She hesitates and twirls her finger around the end of her braid. "Greece."

At least, she says the word that closely resembles Greece, "Hé" as the idea of Greece doesn't quite fully exist yet.

I remember how her face darkened last night when Homer talked about raids and Greece. Palikari and Greece have been warring for decades, from what I can tell from Homer's history lessons. Did something like that happen to her hometown?

Brisei doesn't give me a second longer to ponder this. "We will search for the soothsayer this morning."

She grabs a veil from the chest and places it behind my head. She claims this will raise less suspicion. I guess women wear veils for modesty or for some reason. I can't quite catch what she mutters while arranging the headpiece.

"My lady." She holds up a "mirror." To be honest, this looking glass looks more like a baking sheet. The slight reflective surface shows a blur of my face. "Do you mind if I speak with you in Greek? My language sounds almost like Palikarian, and I have gone many months without practice."

A pang eats my stomach. Back at school, some of the Brazilian exchange students asked the same of me, and I would speak to them in Spanish. Turned out, I could understand Portuguese a lot more than I thought. Only every once in a while did we have to clarify words.

"Of course, Brisei."

She heads toward the door and pauses. "I am to assume that cosmetics are out of the question for today?"

Huh, so Greek does sound a lot like Palikarian. She taps her lips to indicate lipstick.

A grin slices my cheek. "We may understand each other far better than I thought."

Chapter Four
How the Vipers Brood

WHEN A SOOTHSAYER ISN'T, WELL, SOOTHSAYING, you can find him in one of three places, according to Brisei.

One: In a place where the nobles meet near Elin's house. A circular stone area where men sit on benches and discuss political matters. But considering half of those guys are gone fighting on the warfront in Greece, the soothsayer hasn't sat in on any meetings of late.

Two: The market.

Where Brisei and I stand now. Talith would have joined us, but Elin needed her to stay behind to grind extra grain. Soldiers will come home soon from the warfront for a brief leave, and she wants to be prepared.

A man with a walking stick bumps into me and advances toward a stall with hanging dry spices.

The stall reminds me of models of a Greek agora I've seen in the AP Euro classrooms. Except, instead of columned shops, wooden posts support the locals' stands. Most don't even have thatch or anything to shield them from the bright sunlight.

"Brisei, why would we find him in the market?"

I wrinkle my nose when we pass by a stall that has some strong-scented cheeses on plates. Flies buzz around one that wafts a peppery perfume.

"He often sells fish he catches."

"Why?" Does he not earn enough soothsaying?

Clusters of people ahead of me stop by posts and exchange animal pelts and baskets of fruit for other wares. Wait a second, why doesn't anyone pay with coins? Did those not get invented yet?

No wonder the soothsayer would need to pick up a side gig. He can't exactly barter his prophecies for a jar of honey.

We angle past a family. A small child tugs on the skirt of his mother. The mom hands a jar off to another servant and picks him up, hoisting him on her hip.

I adjust the band on my forehead that holds the veil in place. I feel like Mary the mother of Jesus with a sweatband.

My feet burn from the rubbing of my sandals. I halt near a station that sells woven shrouds and adjust the straps again. No doubt, the daughter who came before me, before she got married, had far skinnier feet.

"Is he in the market today?" I rise and grimace at the feeling of dirt getting caked on my toes and direct my nose away from the dung that lines the stalls to my right.

Brisei shakes her head. "We must go to the third location where we might find him."

Third: The ocean, where he catches his sea creatures.

Dust kicks up from a pair of young boys who dart in front of me. They toss a ball of some sort back and forth. I can't tell what it's made out of, a mixture of animal skins and something else I can't identify.

I halt and grip my sides, allowing more oxygen airflow. Asthma and dust motes don't make a lovely pair.

Pink burns onto my exposed shoulders, and I try to shimmy them farther into the fabric. Doesn't help that metallic straps keep the oodles of linen on me. Bright sunlight above has torched the bronze metal like it does the latch plate on a seatbelt in the dead heat of Arizona.

Sometimes we'd have to wear oven mitts when we got in

our cars, to prevent the seatbelts from cooking our fingers.

I duck into the shade of a large shop, if you could call it that.

A mixture of fire and clay fills my nostrils and transports me back to my 3-D art class when we created terracotta vases. On a gray mound, a girl, no older than twelve by the looks of her, stamps her feet on the huge silver lumps. The clay presses beneath her feet.

She pauses when she notices us, and a twinkle ignites her eyes. "Brisei." She steps down from the mound. A few paces away, a man moves his hands up and down on a potter's wheel. A long neck for a jar forms in his hands.

Brisei and the girl embrace in a long hug. They release and Brisei angles her shoulder to me.

"Cersei, this maiden is the lovely Harper. She has made a long journey here."

"A noblewoman?" Cersei eyes me up and down.

How can she tell? From the olive branch brooch on the bust of this dress? From the gold-patterned fabric that lines the seams of this outfit?

"Cersei trains under the local magician," Brisei explains. "He must be away, so she is helping her father."

Brisei's chin darts to where the father sat moments before on the potter's wheel. He has taken off. I spot him behind the shop in bright daylight near pools of gray water. Maybe he gets his clay from out there.

"Speaking of Father, he will want me to paint one of his newest creations." Cersei cocks her head at me, flyway red hairs fluttering near her ears like branches on a weeping willow. "Would you like to see?"

Something flits in my chest, a special sort of secret artists share when they allow another to peer into their world of creativity. "Yes."

A grin splits her clay-splotched cheeks. She leads me toward a wall where red faces, decorated with black shapes, line the dirt flooring. I pick up an amphora the size of my head and frown at the design.

Rudimentary triangles and half circles line the vessel's surface.

This looks nothing like any of the Ancient Greek vases at my local art museum. Did more complicated drawings get introduced later? Squinting, I try to recall if Homer and I ever talked about the history of art in Palikari.

"What do you think, my lady?"

I set the vase down and force a grin. "Are all the vases decorated in this way?"

Her shoulders slump, perhaps sensing my disappointment. "Yes."

I chew on my tongue, then remember what my art teacher would say when a student got stuck with artist's block. "Cersei, what is something you love?"

She considers the question for a moment, clenching her fist. Then she unrolls her fingers. "Animals." The idea sets the lights back into her eyes. "Pigs with tusks, goats with long horns, dolphins."

"Dolphins?"

"Yes, my lady. Like the beautiful ones that once graced Minos."

Minos, Minos, Minos… Does she mean that one place Uncle Laran described on a call I had with Homer back in March? A pre-Greek palace with red columns and mosaics full of… dolphins, now I remember.

They had thrived until a group of Myce—Myce-something—raided their island. Then they disappeared from the Mediterranean. Poof, gone.

Will the same happen to Palikari?

I shake my head to erase the question. Hopefully I won't have to find out if I locate that soothsayer. "Why not paint a dolphin onto one of those jars?"

Her eyebrows draw together. She sucks on her teeth and doesn't move for many seconds. Then she springs to life and picks up the jar her father just finished. It hasn't yet dried. Cersei picks up sharp metallic tools and carves a shape onto the shoulder of the vessel.

She dips a stick-like item into a jar of wet brown clay and holds it up. "Would you like to paint it, Harper?"

"Me?"

She grins. "Noblewomen are known to have skillful hands. I have carved out the shape, so you must simply fill it in."

Dread pools in my stomach. What if I screw this up? Like I did in 3-D art class, when the bear I painted turned into a pig when it exited the kiln. What if some archeologist finds this and dissolves into a fit of giggles?

Her eyelids scrunch, pleading.

"Very well." I pick up the brush from her hands and dip it into the brown paint mixture again. Then I do my best to fill in the lines, squinting the whole time. No wonder she only made triangle and circle shapes. The gray clay jar has turned brownish. You can scarce see the difference between the jar and the paint.

I finish and she sets the jar aside. "I shall show it to you when Father finishes it in the kiln."

Brisei hasn't spoken this whole time, but I felt her eyes on us. Now she opens her mouth. "My lady, we must away to the beach before we are missed back home." She turns to Cersei. "Did you see the soothsayer head to the waters?"

Cersei ascends the clay mountain once more. "I am not sure.

Perhaps. But soldiers are returning from the warfront any day now. Perhaps he is preparing for their arrival."

Brisei yanks the end of her dress away from the clay mound. Some gray has stamped itself into the fabric. Then she eyes me, eyebrows raised, in an expression that appears to say, *"We'll have to take our chances."*

My chin dips and I wave to Cersei. "Thank you."

We duck out of the shop and back into the blazing sunshine. The two of us pick up the pace and barrel down the dirt hill toward the rocky white cliffs that lead to the ocean.

"I believe he likes to sit on one of the cliff faces." Brisei pants and gathers her skirts into her fists. I follow, having almost tripped once or twice on our descent.

Sure enough, a man with a beard so thin it might as well be made out of smoke sits facing the cerulean ocean, with his back to us. His shaky arms cling to a rod, its string dipping all the way down to the sea.

Presumably sensing our footsteps, he turns, and I search both of his eyes. Disappointment slumps my shoulders when neither is milky.

"Perhaps he is in the wine-dark waters." Brisei advances down the slope of the cliffs that lead to the beach. I follow.

Hot white sand scorches my feet when we reach the bottom of the cliffs. Out on the sea perches a singular rowboat. Two young men pull up nets. Beside the boat, I watch a man emerge from the waves holding a mollusk in his hand. He tosses the shell into the boat and disappears back into the expanse.

"Brisei, he is not here."

She doesn't catch my words. Or maybe does, but she glides toward the ocean and sinks her soles into the sticky sand near the waters. Waves lap over her toes, and she inhales the air. I stand beside her and do the same. Memories carry me away to beach vacations when my dad still lived and would take me boogie boarding on the waves. How I loved the feeling of a wave looming over me, right before it crashed. There was something so powerful about the surge of the water rushing past your ankles. Where Dad would chase porpoises in the ocean and Mom would roll her eyes and stay on the beach with her towel, umbrella, and a book situated between her fingers.

The air tastes like nostalgia, longing.

Brisei gasps and then giggles. My eyes fling open, and I watch the triangular fin of a dolphin dip up and down, yards away from shore. Pure, unexplainable joy fills me at the sight of her laughing, the dolphin appearing and disappearing.

No wonder Cersei loves them so much.

"You were right to put that on the jar." Brisei hugs her elbows, keeping a several-foot distance from me.

I understand. I do that too, to avoid touch, avoid hurt. Two summers ago, Homer broke my barriers and initiated physical contact in little ways. But seldom do I let anyone else do that.

We follow the dolphin down the beach as best we can. I trip on snail shells and conches. Back home, whenever we'd go on vacation, I'd collect these in a mason jar.

The dolphin stops, reverses, and heads toward the horizon. A moment later, I realize why. Black ships cut through the waters, nearing shore. How did I not notice them until they were a breath away? Red paint decorates their bows and reminds me of scars.

All the light has died from Brisei's face.

Neither of us move, as if the white billowing sails and the endless oars coming from the sides of the boats have glued us to our spot. Until minutes later, the ships dock. Out steps a group of soldiers in glittering armor.

They must've returned from the warfront.

One of them, a man with large biceps, leans on another skinnier, tanner man. They hobble up the beach and then halt.

Bicep man cranes his neck at us, and revulsion wriggles like a worm in my gut. There's something about his stare that feels off. I can't put my finger on it, but it's something beyond a soldier doing a routine patrol. It's leering, predatory.

Then they totter toward us, bicep man a step in front of the other guy.

Man alive. I search the ground for some kind of weapon, driftwood or a sharp shell, to protect Brisei. Worst case, I can toss hot sand in his face.

They reach us, and the strong stench of sweat and seawater threatens to make me pass out.

"Who"—bicep man grins at me—"is this fair-cheeked maiden who is as lovely as a star, though she does not paint her face?"

Did he just say, "wow, you're pretty, even without makeup"? Because, boy—I roll my fists—we're about to have words.

In my periphery, Brisei shudders and takes a step back. Instinct kicks in and I plant a foot in front of her. *You go through me, dude, got it?* Two summers back, a similar protection mode overtook me when I found Homer in the British Museum.

The skinnier man appears to catch on to my stiffened spine and arched eyebrows. He pulls bicep man back. "Pandarus, we ought to go back to the village to get you treatment for your leg."

"A minute longer, Atro, with the fair maiden."

Beneath the circular shield Pandarus holds in his right arm, I notice a huge gash on the side of his calf. Did he get that on the warfront? Sunlight glints off the metal of his helmet. Two cheek plates on it remind me of metallic sideburns.

Atro glances at me, expression softening, like an apology for Pandarus's behavior.

Pandarus scrunches his face at the other guy, smiling. "Oh, Atro, you woman. Always the worrier. I will be fine speaking to these ladies a moment longer."

Did he just use "woman" as an insult? Heat bristles in my cheeks.

Atro presses his forehead to Pandarus's. Homer had mentioned that men in Palikari had more physical contact with one another. Many soldiers would press their foreheads with each other in a sign of bonding through all their struggles on the battlefield.

They break apart and Pandarus moves his shield up and down. "Pay no heed to Atro, master of the battle cry. He is all talk and no sting." He nods to a sword that gleams on Atro's belt. "Now, dear maiden, would you tell me your name? I already know hers." Pandarus waggles his eyebrows at Brisei. "Oh yes, I know hers very well."

Brisei flinches, and I shield her with my whole body.

"My name is none of your business."

With that, I link my arm with Brisei's and dart in the opposite direction of them. Ringing fills my ears, so I have no idea if Pandarus has decided to call after us or give up on the effort.

Memories of my junior year burn in my head as the sun beats down on us. When I found a girl scrunched up in the bathroom after prom, in a bubblegum pink dress with a huge tear in it. I can't blink away that face full of snot and tears and blotches all rolled into one. A boy had tried to make a very bad move on her on the dance floor, and I can't erase the girl's hiccupping sobs from my memory.

Brisei's arm goes limp. We stop and the ocean waters

smother us in coolness from the burning sand as the waves lap over our toes.

"You…" She swallows and blinks rapidly. "You should not have done that."

I don't ask her why. Just like I hadn't asked questions with the girl in the prom dress. Instead, I stand with her in silence, every part of me wishing I could wrap my arms around her shoulders.

Touch and I don't get along. But for a select few, they earn all my hugs in the world.

Wind caresses the loose hairs of Brisei's braid around her face. She stares at the ocean for either seconds or an eternity. The dolphin never returns.

She clears her throat. "Perhaps we could find the soothsayer another day?"

"Of course."

I try to bury the disappointment lodged like cotton in my throat. Let's hope Homer had some better leads, so I can get the two of us, and this poor girl, off this island.

We pull ourselves away from the water and make a steady trek uphill. I stop us every now and then to catch my breath. On one occasion, we halt near the pottery shop. It's vacant. In fact, most of the shops have cleared out.

Brisei explains that people take a break for the mid-morning meal. On cue, my stomach decides to imitate a whale call. I wonder if they have such creatures in their oceans here too. Now I have another animal suggestion for Cersei next time we bump into each other.

"What do you eat for the midday meal?" I ask.

She wets her lips, and I regret the question. I bet they give them leftovers. Last night, Homer indicated that those in lower classes didn't have access to meat.

"Because the soldiers have come home, I imagine they will make something lavish. At least, the evening meal tonight will be made of many good things."

It takes me a while to understand her sentence in Greek, so I ask her to translate it to Palikarian. Thank goodness I've only needed her to do this twice today so far. The two languages really do resemble each other.

"Good things, eh, Brisei? I will make sure you get some." Like I did last night with the bread.

Her eyes widen, and she fights a lip twitch. "Be careful."

We reach the gates of the house. The dog and the watchman have disappeared. Maybe they do the night shift only.

Be careful.

She warned me back at the beach too. "Brisei, how long are the soldiers staying?" That is, how long do we need to hide inside until Pandarus goes back to the battlefront?

Brisei doesn't answer me. Instead, she stills and sucks in a breath. I follow her line of sight, and my eyes go wide when they land on a figure in the courtyard.

A servant pats something onto the legs of a soldier. Maybe a salve?

Pandarus glances up at us, one side of his lips quirking. "You are called Harper, yes?"

I don't answer. Whatever glued me to the sand when the ships rolled in does so now in the stone courtyard.

A single laugh exits his throat. "Glad to know you will be staying at my father's estate."

The words take a moment to sink in.

This is Elin's son.

Chapter Five
How the King Feasts

BEING AN EIGHTEEN-YEAR-OLD, I do the adult thing in this situation.

I hole myself up in my room.

Hours have passed now, as far as I can judge by how the once yellow sunlight dips orange on the horizon outside my window. My finger caresses the cloth in which Brisei brought me some bread and cheese to tide me over for the afternoon meal. Talith, Brisei, and I split the food over my bed, until Talith got called out to grind more grain.

Bless Brisei for telling Elin that I felt faint from the sunlight and needed to rest a while.

However, we can't keep that excuse forever. One way or another, I'm going to have to face Pandarus again.

Speaking of Elin, I spot her in the mesh of people in the courtyard. So many have filled in over the past hour that I don't know how the servants will fit in enough chairs and tables to accommodate these guests. The men no longer wear their armor, but I can tell they're soldiers by how they clap each other on the back as I catch snatches of their war stories.

"—when the fleet-footed Temis shot an arrow through the stomach of that Greek soldier—"

"—you know not what you're talking about. Archers are nothing but looks—"

Elin breaks through a wall of men and cups the chin of her son. He glances down at her with scrunched brows and a smile, almost like he can't believe his luck that he gets to see her again.

One of my classmates had a father overseas. I imagine she'd look at him the same way when he returned, and him to her.

Acid eats away at my insides. I force my gaze away from the scene.

Mom, I really, really miss you.

Even though we haven't gotten along much in these past two years after Dad died, what I wouldn't give to argue with her over what show we'll watch on Netflix. Or to receive one more scolding from her when I try to sneak more Lucky Charms marshmallows into my cereal bowl when she isn't watching.

Tears blur my vision. I haven't had much of a chance to feel so far on this trip. But these past few hours have given me space to breathe, think…

A creak causes me to swing toward the door.

Brisei and Talith slip inside. Although they haven't put on any makeup, like some of the ladies I spied out in the courtyard, I can tell Brisei took a little extra time to tuck the flyaways into her braid and to scour out, best she could, any dirt splotches that got kicked up on the hem of her dress.

Dark circles have formed under Talith's eyes. She groans and rubs her knees.

I slide to the end of my bed, near the window, and pat the blankets. "Join me."

She throws me a grateful smile and sits, sighs, and rubs her knees again. "Sore." It takes my ears a moment to adjust. Her accent, a throaty garble, almost renders the word incomprehensible.

Brisei crinkles her eyelids in a grin. "She is learning." She gathers her skirts in her fists and moves to the window to watch the setup for the dinner banquet unfold. "Are you planning to attend tonight?"

I follow her gaze and snap my neck back to my hands when I spot Pandarus.

Brisei taps my shoulder with her hand. Releases. "What would a woman be without her bravery?"

"A man," I answer.

We break down into giggles. When our laughter dies, Brisei moves for the door. Despite uneasy tension in my chest, I rise, and Talith shadows me.

"Am I to assume we will do no cosmetics tonight?"

And give Pandarus more of a chance to keep his eyes on me? I think about some of the horrible guys at my high school who say that girls put on makeup just to tempt them to do something worse. As if lipstick could somehow get rid of all inhibitions. "No, thank you, Brisei."

She dips her chin and unlatches the door. I hitch my breath and begin the descent down the steps, to the left, and outside.

Cool night air does little to distract me from the body heat of the crowd. A servant outside the door wreaths my head, so all the nobles can wear matching olive leaf crowns. If these people wore short skirts or t-shirts, I could imagine we've walked right into a grad party.

Most people don't push the age of thirty here. Even Elin's husband, Ulix, only has a few flecks of gray in his dark curls. She introduced me to him before I fled inside.

I get stopped short by Atro, who almost bumps into me. Can't blame him with the number of bodies.

Everyone gleams with olive oil, including Atro.

"My apologies." Even though I haven't caught on to all the nuances of Palikarian, he does sound sincere.

"Do not fret. It seems this place is"—does Palikarian have a word for popular?—"well-loved."

He nods, and I swear at a grad party he'd be nursing a red solo cup right now. "The shepherd of the people is known to throw many feasts during war time. Although they appear to let anyone in." A twinkle ignites his eyes. He tilts his head at a loud man laughing about some spoils he'd gotten on the battlefield. "Like horse tamer Damas over there."

Horse tamer, swift-footed, fair-cheeked—does everyone get a title attached to them? Like a nickname? If you screw up, do you get a bad one?

A headache pounds my temples. I can only imagine what my nickname would be back home, a girl who joined no clubs, got Cs in most classes, and was generally unremarkable.

Damas waves his leather cap in the air. "Found this weasel-skinned hat on one of the Greek soldiers. He was dead, so he would not miss it."

Yikes, do they strip people who died? Does that explain all the armory and shields above the hearth?

Atro's voice pulls me back. "I must away, my lady. It would not do for me to speak to you when you may have won the hearts of other men."

He cricks his neck over his shoulder to gesture at someone. I don't want to follow the movement.

"What would men be without their jealousy?" He chuckles.

I bite back the comment, "women," and turn in the opposite direction of where he gestured. We will avoid Pandarus at all costs. I need to find Homer and hope he had better luck with leads.

Brisei and Talith continue to flank my sides, and I can't help but feel relief spill in my chest. What a treasure to have a band of ladies in a crowd of dangerous men.

We find our way to the edge of the courtyard wall. I stand on my tiptoes and scan the crowd for Homer. *There.* I spot him conversing with Ulix two yards away.

"What a beautiful garden you have on your estate." Homer catches my eyes and raises his eyebrows. "I could spend an eternity in it."

I nod. Understood, we'll convene there again tonight after the party.

I turn to the left and have to stifle a scream. Pandarus stands toe to toe with me. When did he make his way over here? How did he do it so sneakily with that leg injury? I retreat into the shadows of Talith and Brisei.

"Ah, it is the white-armed Harper. How do you like my father's banquet?"

"Ah, it is…you. Very nice."

Servants sponge down tables and one passes me by with a plate of something that smells and looks like chopped up olive relish. Weasel-cap Damas holds a double-handled cup full of pink liquid that has an onion as a garnish. I could be hearing wrong, but I think Damas says the goat cheese and wine within the drink taste fresh. Ugh, let's hope we don't all have to guzzle that tonight.

"We will sit for the evening meal soon," Pandarus tells me. "Greedy Damas decided to venture into the house and take his share before the proper hour."

"Silly, greedy Damas." My eyes dart over his shoulder for an escape route, and then to my side.

No luck. The crowd has formed a bubble near me to allow two acrobats to perform. Men in shorts walk on their hands. One hand-trots to a cauldron full of water and fishes out a spoon with his feet.

"Harper, I must say that you confound me."

Man alive, he's still going.

"Why a woman of your beauty would not grow out her hair or put rouge on her lips—"

The crowd hushes and then makes a rush for the tables, thank God. Brisei and Taith have disappeared, no doubt given a duty to hold the water bowl for the handwashing or to mix the wine paste with water.

I settle myself at the farthest end of the table possible. Elin spots me, rises from her chair at the opposite end, and tsks her tongue.

"My dear, do you not know that those of the highest standing sit at the head of the table?" She beckons me with a sweep of the arm. "Join me, my guest, beside me."

Past her shoulder, Pandarus parks at the end of the men's table, where the men lounge. Next to him sits Ulix, at the very head, and next to Ulix, Elin.

No, thank you, I would not like to be two seats away from your son, ma'am.

"Oh, you are kind." I flick my wrist in a wave of dismissal. "I imagine I will dine with you many nights. Perhaps another woman ought to take my place?"

"Dear Harper." She purses her lips in a catlike way. You can almost hear the purr. "Modesty is a beautiful virtue in women. That is why you deserve a high place at the table. Now, come."

Dread pools in my calves, but I march forward, slump into the seat, and lean as far to my left as possible.

After Ulix pours out the libation of wine onto the courtyard, the servants bring breadbaskets and plates full of food. One approaches me with a stack of steaming beef.

I put up my hand and shake my head. He moves on to the woman beside me, who sports a strong unibrow. In fact, now that I glance down the row of chairs at my table, all women have eyebrows that connect in the middle. Why didn't I notice this before? I guess some details become clearer later once you start to adjust to something.

Did I miss out on some fashion trend?

"Mother, why does Harper refuse the meat?"

My neck snaps to the men's table and instant regret fills me.

Pandarus shoves a fatty piece of something in his mouth, chews, and swallows. "Does she not know that we have slaughtered only the choicest of boars today for this meal?"

A man ambles by with a plate of tawny octopus tentacles. I swear they wriggle in my stomach now, even though I haven't eaten them.

"Beloved Pandarus, did you not know? Were you not informed?" Elin sweeps her gaze to me. Lines of sorrow dig into her forehead. She turns back to Pandarus. "Harper escaped from a raid on her village. She had to disguise herself as a man, so as not to be taken as a war captive, as so many women are known to do in wartime. How many people she must have lost."

Brisei holds a basket before the men's table. Homer reaches forward and breaks off a piece.

Even though Pandarus's lips are closed, I can see him clench his jaw through his thin cheek. "We have all lost many at the hands of the Greeks." He keeps his gaze pressed to the clay cup in his hands, but he doesn't sip from the vessel.

Much as I hate this guy, I can watch the ghosts dance in front of his eyes. Did he hear the screams of soldiers he lost on the battlefield every night?

Elin continues as though the interruption never happened. "Harper has lost her betrothed. She mourns now and will partake in no good foods such as meat."

Pandarus's dark eyes pierce mine. "How sad."

He doesn't sound or look it. In fact, in the fading light of the sun, a red glow highlights his lip slicing up his cheek.

Drunk, sleeping people litter the courtyard.

Not sure how they got that way. From what I can recall of what Uncle Laran said two summers back, when Homer inebriated himself on communion wine, the ancient stuff has far less alcohol content. Makes sense, since we don't drink much water here.

Brisei did, during lunch, offer me a curdled milk substance with figs. I guess they *do* have options other than wine.

But, boy, could those soldiers drink.

I descend the ladder with care and tiptoe over Damas. His weasel-skin cap placed over his nose muffles his snores.

I hobble barefoot toward the garden and sigh when my soles meet moss that lines the pathways. Man, when I get home, I will not miss these dirt roads.

Homer's silhouette waits on a bench with something bunched in his fist. My eyes adjust to the moonlight in time for him to hand me a makeshift bouquet of wildflowers. Poppies, lotus flowers, and some fuzzy, feathery plants greet me. I breathe in their perfume.

If I return to the village, I can get a vase from Cersei. Maybe she'll let me use the one with the dolphin on it.

Homer and I collapse into a hug. I put so much of my weight into him that we almost fly backward over the bench. We break apart and sit.

"Any leads?" The words stick in my throat. "I couldn't find the soothsayer." I recount for him my day of trying to find the old man at the village and at the ocean. When I tell him about our run-in with Pandarus on the beach, Homer stiffens.

"*What* did you say to him?"

"He was taunting Brisei, Homie. I have a feeling they have a history, and not one that Brisei had a say in. I couldn't just sit by. Besides, apparently it has no effect on him. He's come on even stronger."

"Strange. Usually, the men in Palikari prefer women not to be heard. Maybe he likes a challenge."

The thought almost sends vomit launching up my throat. I swallow and set the bouquet of flowers by my feet. "Any chance they're returning to the warfront soon?"

"The others, yes. Pandarus with that leg injury, no. I imagine he won't go back for many weeks. With you in the picture, he may feign the pain even longer to get to know you more. It's too bad you couldn't find the soothsayer today."

Guilt eats away at my chest. If I'd tried harder to find the soothsayer, maybe we'd have a ticket out of here. I let Homer down, just like I do with everyone else back at home. Why on earth would he trust me with such a monumental task?

Homer appears to sense my drooping neck. He slides his arm behind my back and pulls me close.

"I'm proud of you. For navigating a foreign city on the first day, and for standing up for Brisei. You have a knack for that."

My lips sag. "For what?"

"Loving the outcasts."

I lean on his shoulder and listen to the frogs and insects chirp. Starlight dances above us, and Homer points out the various constellations. Even though I can't make much of them, I try to imagine the Plow and Bear he motions to on the inky backdrop.

The fact that we exist under the same moon as the one back home comforts me. I stare at the bright orb in the sky for what feels like forever.

Suddenly, Homer sits up, and I lift my head from his shoulder. "Oh, I almost forgot. I did get a lead at the banquet."

A sharp breath shoots up my nostrils. "What?"

"The soothsayer will be at the assembly tomorrow."

"Assembly?" I blot out the images that first come to my mind. Of guys in tunics in the stands of my high school, with the cheerleaders begging them to get peppy. What a weird combination of images. This must be what happens to your brain when you time travel—you get all mixed up.

"It's a gathering of all the leaders in Palikari. Because a lot of them were at the warfront and are back on temporary leave, they're going to meet tomorrow. Ulix says so."

Strange. With all this shepherd-of-the-people business, I'd assumed Ulix leads his people like a king. Did they have a sort of democracy before it made it big in Greece? Speaking of Ulix…

"Did he recognize you? Did *anyone* recognize you?"

Homer squints at blades of rustling grass that stick out of the tiles of the pathway. "I don't think so. Pandarus is one of the only ones who said I had a familiar face. This was after Elin told him the story of how I was your bodyguard and helped you escape the city."

My palm claps my forehead.

Great, not only does Pandarus flirt with me, but he might suspect my boyfriend of pretending to be noble class.

"Okay, so I just need to go to that assembly thing tomorrow and confront the soothsayer and get us out of here."

Homer shakes his head. "Women aren't allowed."

Of course not, how silly of me. "Do *you* want to, then?"

"Again, can't take too many risks. What I may do, though, is try to get word about cities of refuge we can flee to, in case everything goes to—" He grins. "I didn't teach you the Palikarian curse words, so it wouldn't be fair of me to use the ones in English."

Cities of refuge? A vague memory floats in my brain of a pastor or priest talking about this. Didn't murderers go to those places to hide from the angry families of those they murdered? "Unless you're planning on killing Pandarus, isn't that extreme?"

"Not really. Considering sometime in the next few months, maybe even weeks, Greece will invade Palikari."

All the breath leaves my lungs.

How could I forget about that? Uncle Laran talked about how Greece took over Palikari, and that it took archeologists more than a century to even realize Palikari was a separate country.

But months, weeks? Why did the time travel machine decide to spit us out here?

My words find my tongue. "While you scout for an apocalypse bunker, how am I supposed to get to the soothsayer if I'm not allowed at that meeting?"

"You'll think of something." He winks and plants a kiss on my cheek.

The ghost of the touch tingles long after I head back up the ladder to my room.

Chapter Six
How the Sand Speaks Life

How do I convince Brisei that I do not want a unibrow today?

I find Brisei and Talith downstairs. Apparently rich people in Palikari sleep in most days, and eating breakfast is considered a lower-class thing to do. The servants gather around the columns near the courtyard and chew on bread they've dipped into wine.

Not exactly Lucky Charms, but you do what you gotta do.

There I notice Talith scraping something black between her eyebrows. Moments later, I recognize the charcoal that forms a messy line between her brows.

Brisei spots me, shoves the rest of her bread wad into her mouth, and interrogates me as to why I've gotten up right as the "rosy-fingered dawn appeared."

In truth, Homer mentioned last night that he sneaks to the garden in the mornings to watch the sunrise. Something he enjoyed doing at the temple before he'd have to do the difficult tasks of the day.

I really want to give him a piece of my mind after my nightmare from last night.

Last night I dreamt I found myself in a pit of snakes in the courtyard. When I spotted Homer standing nearby, I looked at him with pleading eyes. His knees wobbled, and he fled in the opposite direction.

I awoke, sweat glistening off my neck. I patted myself dry and realized, moments later, that one of the vipers had taken on the face of Pandarus.

Don't get me wrong, I have a few family members and

friends back home who I struggle to confront. It is far harder to stand up to those you know than to fight with strangers. But for Homer, I'd go toe-to-toe with even my mom. In fact, I have. Several times.

For someone who speaks so much about cowardice and how his culture frowns upon it, Homer sure does like to stay in the shadows.

Which leaves me to find the soothsayer. I *get* it. Homer could get recognized. Considering, though, how women could get murdered for doing literally anything in this culture, let alone sneaking into a no-women-allowed assembly…

Brisei's eyes dart back and forth between me and Talith's charcoal unibrow. Then a grin wriggles up her cheek. "Harper." Her voice is almost taunting.

"No. Absolutely not." *You will not give me a unibrow, missy.*

Nevertheless, she grabs the charcoal stone out of Talith's fist and chases me up the stairs with it. I retreat to my room, but not in enough time to slam the door. Talith and Brisei burst in, stifling their giggles.

Brisei finds her breath and sets the charcoal stone on my wooden bed post. "My lady, the connected brow represents intelligence and beauty."

Neither of which I've been known to have. "Thank you, but no thank you."

She slaps her thighs and lets out a groan—maybe a Greek way of expressing frustration. "You must at least let me apply some cosmetics. You draw more attention to yourself when you do not wear them."

My jaw sinks, shuts.

True, last night Pandarus had made a big deal about the fact that I hadn't worn any makeup. I did catch quite a few stares from the ladies after dinner, most of their eyes drawn to the bridge between my eyebrows.

I look out the window. Geese honk outside and peck at grain tossed into troughs. One woman grabs a scooped wooden paddle and winnows grain up and down. I notice she, too, has drawn a black smear between her brows.

My shoulders slump. "Very well."

I flop onto my bed and try to ignore the squeals of delight from Brisei and Talith as they probe the trunk in the room for makeup. They hold up clay containers that remind me of mini pots you'd bring to a picnic or potluck.

Brisei inspects a white powder with one eye and then sets the pallet back into the chest. "You do not need the lightening powder. You are far paler than any woman in Palikari."

Lightening? My stomach drops a few floors. Does that thing have lead in it?

Memories from our Shakespearean unit in English class flood my mind. Our teacher discussed how the ladies would put white powder on their faces to make their complexion appear paler. But the lead inside the makeup poisoned them and led to a shorter lifespan.

Did that sort of thing date back further into ancient times?

Talith uncorks an amphora and slathers some olive oil on her fingertips. She rubs the liquid all over my cheeks like a moisturizer. A honeyed scent drifts from the mouth of the bottle.

"Now, my lady." Brisei holds up a stick she just dipped in a dark liquid, probably charcoal. "Are we off to see the soothsayer once more today?"

"We are." I lift a brow. How did she know? Did she somehow listen in on our garden conversation?

I shut my eyelids. The stick scrapes against my skin, and I

do my best not to wince as she applies the eyeliner. "We have a problem. He is speaking at the assembly this morning."

"They are calling the assembly this morning?" Her voice flutters.

"Yes?" Did I get my info wrong from Homer?

The stick releases from my skin and my eyes flutter open.

She stares at her dust-caked sandals. "I wish to go." Brisei brushes the stick in my eyebrows to fill them out more. What a sight this'll be, a blonde girl with black brows. She draws on the space between my brows, and I lift up a praise that I can't see well in the mirrors they have here. No one likes a Harper with a unibrow.

"Most ladies use goat's hair," Brisei explains. She sets her brush down. "They glue it on with sap. Now, about going to the assembly."

"Women are not allowed, Brisei."

"That has never stopped me." Her nose wrinkles and blush crawls into her cheeks.

Has she gone before? Do we—have a sneaky sneakster on our hands? I stare up at her and hope my expression gives away more admiration than shock.

Talith approaches me with a powder and taps the red dust onto my cheeks.

"Why do you go, Brisei?"

"I hide in the bushes." She shields her face with the lid of the trunk. "There is something so beautiful about the idea of hearing from all before making an important decision."

Like democracy, yes.

"Perhaps one day, my lady, they will allow *all* men to sit in the circle to discuss matters of the state."

Part of me wonders how long the idea takes to catch fire in Greece.

Talith dabs something scarlet and waxy onto my lips while Brisei places the veil and band onto my head. When they finish, I rise and nod at the window behind me. "Off to the assembly, then?"

Time for a game of ancient hide-and-seek.

We arrive before the men do and squat behind a tamarisk shrub. My knees ache by the time men start filling the benches in the circular stone area. I can only imagine how much pain Talith feels in her joints from all of her household chores.

Her neck curves like Homer's did when I first met him in England, the result of hunching over and doing hard manual labor each day.

Straighten her spine and put her in a hoodie with earbuds, and she could've sat in the back of homeroom unnoticed. A pang drills a hole into my stomach. How many girls here had to grow up far too fast?

Unaware of my stare, Talith draws markings into a pile of sand beside her. I squint at it and make out a familiar shape.

Funny, turn that letter sideways and it reminds me of an A.

I turn my gaze back to the men in the circle and try my best to avoid swiping at a fly—or moth, based on the size of it—that buzzes near my ear. Goodness, they grow those little bugs big here.

A man with a smoky beard sits in view of my eyehole in the tamarisk bush. Tangerine sunlight bounces off his milky eye. Got it, we have our soothsayer.

An even older man with graying skin lifts himself up on a stick. Conversation dies down around the circle. He hobbles to the center of the floor and speaks. I wince to listen in better, since his Palikarian comes out muffled and shaky.

"Members of the assembly, men-at-arms, as the eldest among you, I must begin this gathering by discussing matters of the warfront. Our great leader, Ulix, has brought me word that the gods have chosen to favor the Greeks in this hour."

Mutterings break out between the men.

The old man taps his stick against the stony floor, and they fall silent once more.

"Our soothsayer has performed a sparrow ceremony to appease the gods, as the burnt offerings appear not to reach the heavens. But I know not if we have succeeded in swaying their minds."

A hand squeezes around my gut. Did they make Homer go through all that pain and suffering, facing possible death, just to get some nonexistent beings in the sky to help them on the battlefield?

No wonder he wanted to hide.

Guilt gnaws at my skin, and I hunch into my belly more to make my knees stop aching. Why did I even *think* about confronting him this morning? Even if he was hiding—and he isn't because he's trying to find us a place of safety—who can blame him?

"Soothsayer, speak," the old man says.

He hands the stick to the soothsayer, who approaches the center of the floor. They must use that staff as a speaking stick of sorts.

The soothsayer sways the rod back and forth and paces around the circle. Right as he opens his mouth to speak, a screech in the skies interrupts his words. I glance up and watch a golden eagle swoop down above the crowd.

It circles above the stone benches, carrying something in its yellow claws. A snake, with orange stripes on its back, writhes and twists in the clutches of the bird.

Then the reptile curves its neck and chomps down on the eagle's ankle. The bird cries, releases, and the snake plummets to land next to the speaker's staff, somehow unscathed. The creature slithers in our direction and forms curved shapes.

It takes everything within me not to scream when the snake wriggles past us.

My heartbeat slams against my chest, and my hearing returns seconds later. Long enough for the gasps of the crowd to hush.

Ulix gestures at the soothsayer with a grand sweep of his cloaked arm. "Soothsayer, you are aware of the signs of the gods that come in the form of omens. Birds are especially revered in Palikari. What say you about this sign sent to us?"

Omens? I know that some people interpret bird droppings as signs of the future. Did bird-y prophecy originate here?

Ulix's deep, reassuring voice reminds me of my father's.

Like my father, did he drink to forget? Lash out at Elin and Pandarus?

How much responsibility falls on his shoulders? I can't say. Maybe he's like Odysseus in *The Odyssey*, where everything in Ithaca falls to ruin until he returns home and claims his rightful place as ruler.

Granted, that involved dozens of deaths, so let's hope Ulix doesn't take after our homeboy.

The soothsayer considers his sandals for a moment. Then he lifts his chin to Ulix. "The eagle represents Greece." He gestures to the sky with a shaky arm. "They have us in their grip at present. But, like the snake, we shall strike back."

Cheers arise from the crowd. They stomp their feet against the floor until the stones echo. The soothsayer returns to his seat and passes the stick to Ulix beside him.

Ulix rises and white-knuckles the rod. He plants himself dead center, doesn't pace.

"The soothsayer has spoken. We will return to the war in a few days' time to revive our other troops on the battlefield. Knowing that we will claim the victory."

Except they won't. Within months, Greece will take over. As the men continue to cheer, the same heavy stones fill my ribcage. They sink me lower and lower into the ground until, at last, I breathe in the dust.

The perk of stalking an old man in Greece—he leaves the assembly last.

Can't blame him.

During Grandparents' Day at my school, they allowed an extra seven minutes between changing classes. That way, the old folks wouldn't get trampled by us rowdy youth in the halls. Believe me, in those bottleneck areas, more than one person with a cane went down for the count.

Cicadas scream at us in the trees as we follow behind him, keeping a safe distance so he doesn't turn around.

Don't want to arouse any suspicion that we watched the assembly to get to him. Who knows what would happen to me— to Brisei and Talith?

In *The Odyssey*, Odysseus killed servants over almost nothing. Do they do the same thing to people here if they exercise the slightest disobedience?

We pass by a sheepfold on a hill. A shepherd hunches over

an ewe and squeezes liquid out of her udders into a pail. Flies buzz around the metal container and the sheep's black fur.

My gown trails in the dust, and I can imagine the ire of whoever has to clean this on laundry day. Maybe when they do that, I can go with them and help.

No wonder women don't venture out of the house much. Most of the females I spot in the proto-agora are either selling their wares or bustling up the hill toward their houses. I hear one passing by me complain about how the sun has darkened her skin.

In Zona, classmates have poked fun at my paleness, and have, on more than one occasion, called me "vampire girl." Dakota has gifted me self-tanner wipes on more than one occasion.

It seems that no one, in history, can accept themselves for all their beautiful kaleidoscope of pigments.

We follow the soothsayer into the marketplace. A man with a topknot attempts to sell us something that reeks in a metal tray. Eels, or at least some sort of watery snake. I keep my eyes pressed forward until the soothsayer ducks into his stall.

Before I shadow him, I halt and peer into Cersei's pottery palace.

Nowhere can I spot her or her father, so maybe we've gotten here too early. Half the shops don't even have a merchant or items set up. But I do notice she's added several more vases of varying sizes to the wall. The ones closest to my feet sport an octopus and a whale. Our girl has gotten more creative.

This sends a sunbeam to burn bright in my chest. I step out of the pottery barn and into the soothsayer's stall in time for him to almost clash into my nose with a silvery fish. Its dead yellow eyes peer into mine.

Dust flies when I spring back. Talith catches and steadies me.

White spreads in the soothsayer's one good eye. He cocks his head and lifts a brow, as if to say, *"What's a noblewoman like you doing in a shop like mine?"*

"Sir." I clear my throat. "I wondered if I might ask you a question."

Great, I hate how the garbled words trip over my tongue, like I've had too much wine. I practiced what I would say all night, after that nightmare about the snakes, all for naught.

"Ask." He busies himself with a metal vessel that sloshes with liquid. The container sends a rank stink throughout the wooden walls of this place.

"The sparrow ceremony." I chew on my lip. "Can you do it again?"

This question took me forever to formulate in the late hours of night. In the soothsayer's eyes, they sent Homer to the underworld, to the mercy of the gods. So in no way could I ask anything about time travel or wormholes.

"To ensure victory against the Greeks," I clarify. I wince and glance back at Brisei. Sorry, girl. Promise I don't mean any of this. "So many have lost the ones they love."

If my query affects her, she doesn't let on. Instead, she observes Talith, who has crouched to draw more markings in the dirt. I angle back toward the soothsayer.

Softness has filled the wrinkles around his eyes and chin. "I fear we cannot. Once the gods have accepted a sparrow, they will not accept another."

I open my mouth to protest. Then a memory stings me. Homer had told me a story of when they tried the sparrow ceremony out on another slave at the temple. They held him under the blood for so long, he drowned.

Lightning never struck that time.

Even if I could convince this guy to whip up a bathtub of bird blood for me and my boyfriend, what if he holds us under for too long?

The soothsayer swings around his shop with a fishing rod and bucket in his grip. He heads for the beach without so much as a goodbye to us. Makes sense. Men in this culture don't like it when a woman speaks, so he wouldn't think he owes us anything else.

Perfect, another dead end. Let's hope Homer's got a plan B.

I turn on my heel and watch Talith finish the line on one of her drawings, another letter.

This one reminds me of a T.

Brisei lifts her chin at me. "Do you recognize these? She often draws."

"Perhaps a…" I don't know the Palikarian word for letter, so I say it in English. This causes Brisei to cock her head.

"Let-ter," she repeats the word.

"Some languages use these to make words, writing. Like mine."

She purses her lips. "Writing. Some song-stitchers mention places such as Minos that used such things. What do you do with the words?"

"Tell stories." An oversimplification, yes, but I don't feel like getting into how people can also use words to get into comment battles over controversial posts on social media. "Make those stories last forever."

Talith rises and brushes the dust off her fingertips. Brisei won't keep her eyes off the letter.

"Will you tell mine? Ours. When you get home?" Moisture brims in Brisei's waterline.

The question hitches my breath. Homer had asked me the same two summers ago. Because the tales of the poor, the prisoners of war, the powerless never seemed to make the pages of history books.

"Of course. Every story is worth telling."

Chapter Seven
How the Calf Lies with the Lion

Homeroom, Junior Year
The First Week of School

Juliana, an exchange student from Brazil, enters the room clutching a bundle of pamphlets to her chest. They bumped back the schedule at school today so each homeroom class could spend fifteen minutes at the school's club fair.

I stay in my seat. Since I didn't make the yearbook team, my decision is made for me. I'll go home every day and learn Palikarian with Homer—no clubs needed.

When I first told Mom the news, a certain snaky vein in her neck surfaced. "What do you mean you aren't going out for any of the school activities?"

"I mean that I'm awful at sports, and I can take classes for anything that interests me. No extracurriculars are needed."

"Art?"

"Classes."

"Photography?"

"I don't know, Mom. They have contests for that sort of thing and art showcases. Unless you're on yearbook, you don't take photos for things for a club."

She'd pinched the bridge of her nose between her thumb and empty ring finger. "Sweetie, you don't have the grades to get a scholarship at a college. Don't you want to improve your chances somewhere else?"

Maybe they'd be impressed that I learned a dead language,

or Uncle Laran could pull some strings to help me get a secretarial job at his university in England.

But since no historians could agree on what Palikarian sounded like, who would believe that some teen figured it out? As far as positions went, even retail jobs had started to ask for a bachelor's degree from their workers.

Juliana spreads the fliers from the various clubs out onto her desk.

Today she sports a t-shirt from her favorite Brazilian soccer team, the Corinthians. She got into a heated Snapchat debate with her brother back home during lunch our first day in school. He supports Cruzeiro.

"Hey, Ju." Another girl slides into a desk beside her. Still haven't caught her name. She pops a purple sucker in and out of her mouth. The wrapper on her desk indicates she got the candy from the chess team's table. "Which club do you think you're going to go for?"

"So hard to choose." Juliana rests her chin on her fist and glances at a burn-your-eyes-out neon orange paper. "I like theater, and tennis, and film club, and—"

"Slow down, Ju. I said which *one*?"

Juliana's glossed lips wilt. "I can only choose one? Plenty of movies about America show students doing more than one activity."

"Movies get it wrong." Sucker girl slumps into her chair and jabs an acrylic nail at another girl who hobbles on crutches to the end of the room. "Her, for instance. She's been playing softball since she could lift a bat. At ten, she was doing the sport year-round. She barely has enough time to do her schoolwork, and him—"

A student in a *Hamilton* t-shirt with AirPods in slides into a seat nearest to the bookshelf in the back of homeroom. He pulls out a bright yellow folder with the words "Sheet Music" written in purple marker.

"He's been doing show choir since middle school. They place first in every competition and the director has them rehearsing six days a week. You better believe he can't do anything else."

She pulls out her sucker and places the sticky candy onto the wrapper. Then she leans back and adjusts the velvety scrunchy she has hoisting her hair up into a high ponytail. "Me? I've done competitive cheer since I was six. I don't even have time to do our school's cheer squad, because mine calls me out to competitions across the country all the time."

Juliana's shoulders slump, and she collects the flyers and stuffs them into her small backpack. "How do you know which one to pick, if you can only pick one?"

Sucker girl uncorks her water bottle and drains a long sip. She sets it on the desk with a clank. "Whatever you're the best at." She caps the mouthpiece. "With the way most high schools work, there are JV teams for JV teams, and you better be the absolute best at something or"—she eyes me, looks away— "you'll wind up being nothing."

Palikari, 800 BCE

Outside of the loom room, I try my best not to think about how I couldn't get any leads from the soothsayer. One can only imagine the disappointment that will be etched on Homer's face when I tell him I failed again.

Speaking of, where has he gone off to? Brisei mentioned that the boys were going out for a hunt, so maybe he joined them.

In that case, I'll have to find a time to speak with him tonight and form a new plan.

Since we returned around the time the servants have begun their daily tasks, Brisei got a start on hers. Even though Elin has instructed her and Talith to accompany me whenever I leave my room, since women don't get out much, Elin seems to also want them to stick with their work around the estate.

For Brisei, that means helping to weave the burial shroud for a distant relative Elin lost to the war. Greeks invaded his village two months ago. Elin received word two weeks later.

"Elin comes from a different tribe."

Brisei explains this as she heads to the loom. Rocks hang from strings and clank against one another. The servants have set up the loom near the blackened hearth. Part of me wishes they hadn't. With the fires running in the kitchen oven, the whole bottom floor of the house is sweltering.

"Elin and Ulix met at a hecatomb."

Hecatomb? Homer never taught me that word. Does it involve a tomb somehow?

Brisei appears to read the question in my eyes. "A tradition that takes place once a year, during a new moon. They sacrifice one hundred oxen—"

Sourness fills my stomach. Bad enough that they slaughter animals at the estate on the daily, but that sounds awful.

Brisei grabs an oval-shaped wooden paddle and moves it in between the rows of white strings. This causes a scarlet piece of wool to move to the top of the tapestry. She hasn't made much progress on it, maybe a few inches. "I do not know why my mistress has given me this task. I am not nearly as accomplished on the loom as graceful-handed Elin."

Graceful-handed, another epithet. Does Palikari work like

my high school? Where people ranked you based on whether you made JV or varsity, or what chair you played in the orchestra?

Here, did you also have to be the best of the best?

"What are you good at, Brisei?"

Her cheeks darken, but she continues to form more crimson lines on the shroud. "Back in Greece, my husband called me silver-tongued. We enjoyed debating with one another about philosophy, the gods, politics."

Gravity sinks my chest. Brisei never mentioned a husband before this.

Much less one who wanted to hear a woman's opinions and discuss them at length.

Echoes of video calls with Homer flit across my vision. He and I would love to spend hours talking about free will and the injustices that fell upon the working class. Brisei had lost her Homer. I can see it in the way her eyes crinkle in a wince.

She halts and sets the oval paddle down. Her arms wrap around her stomach. Inhale, exhale, something snaps her spine straight, and she returns to the loom. Red lines form in our silence.

Then she hands me the paddle. "You must be very skilled at the loom, my lady."

I try my best not to conjure up the images of the scarf I attempted to knit for my relatives up north. An entire hand could fit through one of the holes I made in the pattern. "Oh? Why do you say that?"

She grips my wrist and shows off my hand to another nearby servant, who scrubs the floor with a sponge. "Does she not have such large hands? What beauties."

Strange, they revere large hands in Palikari? Twenty-first century, please take notes.

"Everyone knows that a woman who has large hands must

excel at the household tasks." Brisei releases her grip and sighs at her bony wrists. "Those of higher standing are known to be very good at many things."

Wait, do they think that if you're rich you're suddenly amazing at everything? Because, girl, I'd love to show you a classmate of mine, whose dad has a net worth of millions, who can't do basic addition without a calculator.

I grab the paddle from her and attempt to replicate her movements.

Disaster strikes within my first passage of the paddle through the strings. Don't know how I manage to accomplish this, but I've tangled the red wire so much that it takes us a few minutes to unweave the damage.

Brisei cocks her head and taps one of the weight stones with her foot. "Perhaps I was wrong. But most women who lead the household affairs do excel in one manner or another. Do you excel in all matters culinary?"

In the kitchen? Burnt cheese fills my nostrils from the memory of my attempt to make Mom's famous five-layered mac and cheese.

"How about the managing of finances for the household?"

I think I remember a history teacher mentioning the men let women do that in Ancient Greece.

Funny, because they trusted them with little else.

Considering I have to scrounge the laundry room for quarters just to pay for the vending machine snacks in my school's cafeteria, we'll have to say no to this one as well.

When Brisei receives no answer from me, she returns to the shroud. She hums a tune, and the servant behind her joins in. I get lost in the sorrow of the song's notes. When she finishes, she taps the red string up to fit with the rest.

"My lady, what *do* you excel at then?"

I chew on the skin inside my cheek until I taste blood. *Good question.*

Occasions when you expect to dance: proms, flash mobs, and weddings where your Aunt Cheryl gets drunk and tells you embarrassing stories about your mom.

Occasions when you do *not* expect to dance: before an animal sacrifice.

Although the soothsayer guaranteed victory against the Greeks from the eagle omen this morning, the people decided to throw in a little heifer slaughter, as a good luck charm.

The same fare from last night's party has returned as salmon-colored clouds trace lines in the sky. I don't know who carried an altar to the far-left end of the courtyard, but it must have happened while I ate lunch, because when I returned to the loom with Brisei, I spotted the stone slab.

Before we can get to that, a man at the gates croons a sad, but somehow upbeat song.

Someone grabs my wrist right as a woman trills on a reed instrument.

Atro takes hold of my other arm, and we whirl in circles. He laughs, and when the dizziness overtakes me, I do too.

Shave his beard and give him a mullet, and he could resemble one of my friends back home who does theater. Unlike what sucker girl said, that boy, when he failed to get parts in the school plays, would audition for local theater.

Never once did he get a part with less than one hundred lines at the community theater stage.

"It's simple, really. I don't want to be the best, Harper. Too

many people get burned out that way. So I went somewhere where I could be myself."

Burned out, indeed. The girl who hobbled on crutches during homeroom had quit softball by October of that year. She went to class every day with red-rimmed eyes. Hollow, like someone had taken away her very soul.

But by November, a bounce had filled her steps again. She didn't have to be the best, and that made all the difference.

As far as the community theater plays went, many of the actors couldn't land the right notes. People often forgot a line, and the actors would stare at each other in silence until someone else remembered and said the words for them.

Yet, my friend glowed with the same effervescence of softball girl.

Colorful sashes of the girls in the circle arrest my eye and pull me back to the dance. Ahead, I watch servants stack wood into a large pile on the altar.

The music stuns to a halt after one final flourish of the reed instrument.

We cheer and pant. I grip my sides. I didn't realize how much they inflamed until now. Someone gasps beside me. To catch their breath, I assume, until whites show in the eyes of everyone around the circle.

I crane my neck to the left and watch a boy exchange an apple with a girl, who sports a goat-hair unibrow. She clutches the fruit to her chest and giggles into a bubble of females that surround her. The boy smirks and retreats to a cluster of men. An army of arms pat him on the back and swallows him whole.

Okey dokey, then, I guess we'll figure out what in the world just happened later.

Clumps of people break apart, and we form rows to watch

the animal sacrifice. I make sure to secure a place in the back where a tall man blocks my view of the altar. Whatever I can do to prevent myself from seeing this go down.

Talith and Brisei find me and station themselves by my sides. Anxiety pricks my chest, and my gaze roams the crowd for Pandarus.

Praise, he stands several rows in front of me, supporting himself on Atro's shoulder due to his leg. He must not have joined in the dance because of the injury. Pandarus didn't make an appearance at lunch today. Someone brought his food up to his room, two doors away from mine.

A servant leads a brown cow through the gate.

Something glitters on her horns in the firelight. Gold or some other metal, I assume. They guide the animal to the front, where a woman carrying a bowl of water and flowers sprinkles the liquid mixture over the cow.

Smoky incense fills my nostrils. I notice someone off to the side of the altar lighting something herbal in a tripod.

Meanwhile, a man pulls out a knife, shaves some bristles from the cow, and casts the hairs into the fire. Another woman tosses some grains into the pyre as well.

Then the man with the knife sets the weapon down and dips his hands into the water bowl. Droplets form rivers down his arms that he lifts to the heavens.

"Oh, deathless gods, hear our prayers, accept our offering to you, and grant us victory over our enemies."

A man slides under the cow and holds up a large bowl. Someone taps my shoulder and whispers, in English, "You may want to close your eyes for this part."

I do so and shove my fingers into my ears as well.

Nothing but ringing and the quick thrum of my heart fill my senses. I don't know how much later, but I receive another tap on my shoulder. Homer grins and slides a few inches to the left, before someone notices.

Well, besides Brisei, who lifts her brows at me, but says nothing.

"Homer, we need to talk about the soothsayer," I tell him in English, averting my gaze from the altar.

Men approach the stone slab with five-pronged forks. This reminds me of some bonfires my classmates held after their graduation parties. We would skewer marshmallows on sticks we found in the woods, since most of them didn't have enough roasting forks.

"What about the soothsayer, Harper?"

"It's a dead end. He didn't have any answers."

I glimpse his gaze and fully expect all of his features to sag. Instead, nothing changes.

He bobbles back and forth on his ankles. "We knew that was a possibility. After all, we couldn't replicate the ceremony completely back in England."

True, when lightning struck the cast-iron tub, it didn't transport the dead archeologist found inside. I shudder and keep my gaze planted on my toes. "Do we give up? Do we start looking into cities of refuge?"

"No, we still have one more option."

My "what?" gets cut off by a woman with a tray full of barley praying. She lifts the grains to the skies and lets out guttural cries. I regret looking in her direction in an instant. A large animal figure burns in the fire.

I shut my eyes and whisper, again, "What?"

"Uncle Laran had always suggested the possibility of the use of magic playing a role in the ceremony, the one thing we didn't have back home."

With a mother like mine who hissed about the very idea of the *Harry Potter* movies, of course we'd had no luck convincing her to do anything other than read the text about the sparrow ceremony historians had gotten from Herodotus.

"Didn't Uncle Laran still say some incantations?"

"For a magic spell to work, you need someone who works with magic regularly. At least, that's why people in Palikari don't visit a swordsman to get magic amulets. Because the swordsman doesn't practice witchcraft or sorcery. The amulets would be no good for warding off evil spirits."

Hmm, that does make sense.

Although the idea of sorcery twists my gut, we don't have many options.

A memory kicks in, and I deflate. "Cersei says that the local magician is out. She doesn't know when he'll return."

This time, Homer does sag. He spots me eyeing him and stiffens his spine. Good ol' Homie, never the complainer. Even if he experiences disappointment, he never wants me to see it.

"Cersei?" he asks.

Maybe I didn't mention her to Homie in the garden. We spent so many hours reminiscing about home that she never came up. "She's training under him, I think. At least, she mentioned that when she was showing us how to make pottery."

"She's training under the magician?"

"Yeah, but I personally think she has a knack for clay. I swear I've seen some of her stuff in museums back home."

Homer shakes his head. Then nods. "Harper, tomorrow, ask

her what she knows. About the sparrow ceremony, what magic it takes to transport someone."

A man jabs his fork into the charred figure in the fire.

I clench my teeth, my fists. "You think she's learned enough to help us?"

"I think"—Homer sucks his teeth—"she's our last chance at getting home."

Chapter Eight
How the Jealous Make Fierce Graves

WHIMPERING FROM PANDARUS'S ROOM AT NIGHT brings me to the courtyard early in the morning.

Much as I hate the guy, the sound can't help but draw out painful memories from me like a bucket in a well, covered in spikes. Ever since that archeologist tried to kill us, and Homer drowned him, we each fight flashbacks every night.

We made it a point never to put our phones on Do Not Disturb. That way, if either of us needed to call the other at three a.m. our time, we could oblige the other.

One night in particular, when thunder crackled outside Homer's video call screen, tears streamed down his face.

"Will it ever go aw-away, Harper?"

Itchiness filled my eyes. "No, but I will be here to hold you in my wings. Until you can fly again."

Who did Pandarus have to hold him? Would Greek machismo even allow him to collapse into his mother's arms?

I have to exit the gate to get to the stables and walk up a hundred meters on the road before we reach the large structure on a plot of grassy land. This morning, I passed by Talith and Brisei unnoticed as they ate their wine-dipped bread. *Without shoes, without makeup?* I know they would say. I'm taking a great deal of risk venturing out here.

But I need time to myself, even with such lovelies as them.

I watch my steps as my soles hit the stable flooring covered in hay.

"Harper?"

A jolt causes me to stumble back when a male voice claps against my ear. I glance up and find Atro running a comb through the dark brown mane of a horse. He holds an amphora in his other palm. A sheen glimmers on the horse's hairs.

Why do they feel the need to put oil on everything here?

"Morning, Atro."

"My lady, what are you doing awake so early? Without servants by your side?" The question doesn't come out unkind, more curious. I swear with smooth skin like his on his forehead, he couldn't be older than a senior in high school.

They must call the boys to war early in Palikari.

"Dreams." I don't explain that they were Pandarus's rather than mine. When I passed his door, I heard snippets about soldiers getting crushed by chariots and a sword catching in someone's neck. I didn't stick around to catch the rest. "Needed to be alone."

Atro nods, features sagging.

He stares off into the other stalls, perhaps lost in a memory. Atro shakes his head in a violent motion and returns to me. "They plague of all those who remain living." He sets the comb at his feet and uncorks the bottle. Then he slathers on the oil into any spots he must deem missing a shine. "The gods seem to plague Pandarus the most. We share a tent on the battlefield."

Hips sore from all the walking we've done these past few days, I lean against a wooden post. I hope Pandarus can return to the battlefield with Atro. They get along so much better.

"Do you wish he would come with you back to the warfront?"

After all, Atro put his horse in Pandarus's family stables. That had to mean something, right? They must be really good friends. All the soldiers will ship off to the beach by this afternoon, and so I'd think Atro would want to spend time with his family instead of waiting for his war companion to wake up.

Unless, does Atro still have a family?

Dark shadows fall over Atro's face. "I do not wish that for him."

I cock my head. "Because you want to see him safe and without injury?"

Atro hunches his head. "No, there is no honor in staying home. But I find myself glad that he will not join me at arms today." He plugs the cork into the bottle and lays the jar down sideways. With the tipped bottom, no one could set it on the ground vertically. "Alone is a beautiful word."

His words take a while to make sense. Then, they click all at once.

He doesn't like Pandarus any more than I do. Like me, he found himself forced into small living quarters with him.

"Then why do you share a tent with him?" If he was annoyed with his roommate, couldn't he trade with another one of the soldiers?

One side of Atro's lips quirks in a you-wouldn't-understand way. "Soldiers are not given the luxury of choices. I am from a different tribe in Palikari and was a scared boy when I was first taken into the army. Had I joined now—" He breaks off and smooths out oily patches on the horse with his fingertips. "It does not do well to dwell on what could have been."

No wonder he didn't go home to his family but stayed the night at Pandarus's house. He comes from another tribe. When we studied *The Iliad,* our teacher explained that many Greek tribes banded together to defeat Troy.

"Women also have fewer choices, Harper." He raises his eyebrows at me. "Best return to the house before someone misses you."

True, I've stirred up too much suspicion already. Thank goodness Atro alone spotted me. I dip my chin and flee out of the stables, down the dirt road, and back into the courtyard.

Brisei, clutching my sandals in her right hand, juts her shoulders up two inches when she spots me. Talith, beside her, carries my veil, band, and girdle.

"My lady, where have you been?"

I pick off hay that's gotten stuck between my toes. "I will not do it again, promise."

She sighs and dips to her knees, putting on my footwear Cinderella-style. Talith shadows me and clamps on the veil and belt. While they do this, I explain how I need to go to the pottery shop in town to find a possible way home.

What I don't tell them is that Homer has agreed to meet me there. We can't walk together. But while men jabbed forks into the sacrifice, I begged him to join me.

"Homie, I'm screwing up everything. It would comfort me a lot more if you came."

Maybe if he joins me, we can finally get a yes. Because knowing my track record, that ain't happening with just me.

He agreed, but he'll come from the opposite direction. Said he wanted to watch the sunrise on the beach this morning, before the soldiers crowded the area with their ships.

"Very well." Brisei rises and dusts her hands on her dress. "But my mistress has asked me to deliver a gift to her husband on the beach." She un-fists her hand, and a golden brooch featuring a gorgon's head glitters in the sunlight. "It symbolizes luck."

"Why is she having you deliver it?"

Doesn't she want to say goodbye to her husband? Or, like Atro, perhaps she's been forced into close proximity with him, without any say in the matter.

"She has received word that her daughter, in the nearest town, has fallen ill during childbirth. She wishes to visit in case…"

Brisei doesn't finish her sentence. We stare at a billowing tamarisk bush in silence.

"My mistress will make sure to say goodbye to her husband before she leaves."

Okay, to the pottery shop and to the beach. We have our agenda set.

I do my best to ignore the burn in my thighs on the way to Cersei's shop. What I wouldn't give for a pair of Spanx, or for toilet paper for that matter.

Pottery shards make a poor substitute for the latter. At least they have *sort-of* toilets here.

The pungent scent of body odor punches me in the nose, and I realize it's coming from me. I think over the past few days I've adjusted to the odd mixture of sweat and perfume that every human carries here. Including myself now.

Talith casts a wistful stare at a stall full of metallic figurines. Mythical creatures from centaurs to chimeras decorate the table. Maybe back in Phoenicia she knew someone who worked in metallurgy, or they remind her of a different memory.

Brisei, on the other hand, peers at tunics that hang on hooks. One of them has the same triangular pattern as the one Homer wears now.

"My lady, may I ask a question?"

"I think you just did."

Her lips twitch. "The way you spoke to Homer last night. How you looked in his eyes." She spreadeagles her arms, and a chill seizes me. Then she drops them. "Never mind. It is not my business."

"I…" Should I tell her the truth? What will she do? Will anyone actually believe her?

At the sacrifice last night, I overheard a woman wearing triple-berry style earrings mention how one of her servants had stolen one of her expensive perfumes. "You simply cannot place your trust in anyone of inferior birth," she said. "The deathless gods choose whom they give fortune to wisely."

I dug into my ears to make sure no wax had changed up the words. But sure enough, she continued to go on and on about how the gods chose the rich because they're talented, beautiful, and trustworthy.

So even if Brisei told…

"Homer and I love each other," I whisper. "No one else knows."

Brisei clutches her fists to her chest and sighs. She squeezes her eyes shut and grins. "Thank you."

Something bounces in her voice, hope or something happy. We reach the pottery place and dip into the shadows.

Cersei beams at us when we enter the shop, and Homer holds up a tiny amphora. "I made this for you," he says in English.

My eyes go wide. "Homie."

He throws a wave of dismissal at me. "Cersei and I go way back. We use a lot of oil at the temple, so they sent me to get a lot of pottery from her." He elbows her, and she giggles. She plays with a centaur figurine on the floor. "She recognized me instantly when I visited yesterday. I explained our dilemma and need to get home."

I take the jar from his hands and stare at the black figure etched on the surface—a bird. At least, I think so. Homer created the painting out of a lot of jagged lines.

I squint at it a little longer until my eyes trace the shape of an eagle in the design.

Brisei cocks her head. "What language are you speaking in?"

"The one of my land," I tell her in Palikarian, then lift one brow at Homer. "We should speak in Palikarian until we get back there."

He sniggers and pats the ground beside him. Realization overtakes him, and he freezes.

"I told them." I park beside him and nestle my head into his shoulder.

Talith and Brisei settle themselves near the clay mound. They stare at us with stars glittering in their eyes, smiles playing upon their lips. Everything in here wafts a sweet scent of smoke and wet clay.

"We were just talking," Homer whispers in my ear, in English, "about the sparrow ceremony and if this magician's assistant can help us with it." He taps his head against mine and turns to Cersei. His language switches to Palikarian. "What did you just tell me about the magic involved in the ceremony?"

"Right."

She sets down a large jar near us. I notice she's painted a war scene onto the face of the red clay. Something tells me the soldiers stopped by, and she used their battlefield stories as subjects of her paintings.

Cersei folds her knees underneath her. Her neck droops.

"Magic was used in the ceremony. Although the soothsayer created the ceremony, he could not, on his own power, do much without the help of the gods." She lifts her hands heavenward. "Therefore, he needed my master, the magician."

This confirms why we couldn't do anything in England. Maybe at the same time the magic sent Homer to England, it took us back to Palikari. We did land in this country right when his past self left, after all.

I place Homer's eagle jar on my lap and lace my fingers with his. Fire crackles between our fingertips. "Can you replicate it?"

She tilts her head backward. "No. Unfortunately. He has not yet returned. He never takes this long in the other village. I fear the worst."

Terrible possibilities from bandits to a sudden sickness flit across my mind. I shake my skull like a Magic 8 Ball and sink back into Homer. I crane my chin up at him. "What now?"

He bites his lower lip. Then in English, "We have to look into cities of refuge."

Gravity sinks me into the floor. Some part of me knew this would be the answer. But I'd hoped.

"We're giving up on home, then?" I whisper.

At least this time we can say we *both* screwed up, and I don't have to take the blame for another failure.

"Maybe not entirely, but I'm certainly losing a lot of hope." Homer sighs. "Aren't you?"

We reach the beach before the soldiers do.

We head to the shore, and I go into autopilot mode. Back in the Outer Banks, I would create turtles out of sand and watch the ocean wash them away, until the waters only left behind the seashells I'd found for the turtles' "shells."

Brisei and Talith watch until I finish the turtle's mound before asking what I'm doing.

I explain the process, and they get started on animals of their own. Brisei creates a squiggly snake that wriggles around my turtle. Perhaps she reaped inspiration from when we sneaked into the assembly yesterday.

She hands the broach for Ulix off to Homer so she can

continue to form stripes on the creature's back. Homer closes the shiny object in his fist and watches the black ships docked at shore. Soon the soldiers will fill the many benches and paddle off.

Sea salt air tingles my nose, and the wind whips my hair.

Instead of working on a creature, Talith has decided to write a series of Phoenician letters. I recognize the A shape of one of them. She dips her thumb into the ocean, what she used to draw the word, and beams at me.

"Name." She thumps her chest with her palm.

Oh, *her* name. I squint at the letters and wish I could make out all of them. We know that she has an A in it. Indigo, foamy waves lick up the name moments later. When they recede, nothing remains behind.

My turtle and Brisei's snake have dissolved too.

I glance up the beach. Sun flares blind me. I lower my lids and catch a glimpse of the soldiers making their way up the beach with Ulix in the lead. Purple horsehair forms a crest on his helmet. Beams of light bounce off the guards' armor. He holds a spear in his grip. Scarlet and blue helmets follow behind, a rainbow of different armor. I wonder if the different colors represent different tribes.

We rise and brush the sand off our fabric. The ocean has soaked the bottom half and made the linen stick to our legs.

We waddle up the beach to greet them. Sand kicks in and out of my sandals.

I spot Atro with a scarlet horsehair plume in the line of soldiers, and frosty fingers squeeze my gut. Leaning on his shoulder, Pandarus hobbles. Hope flickers in my chest. Atro mentioned that a soldier would dishonor himself if he stayed home, even with an injury.

Ulix halts when Brisei approaches him. She dips her chin

and presents the broach to him. She must have retrieved it from Homer when we spied the soldiers.

He pinches it out of her palm, kisses it—weird, considering it's a gorgon's head—and clamps the item in his fist. No way can he try to shove that pin through the leather armor he's got on.

Ulix then heads for the ships, with the soldiers following behind. Pandarus yanks Atro to the side and pats his chin in what I can assume is a friendly Palikarian soldier gesture. Atro flinches.

How cruel of me to want Pandarus to go back to the warfront.

Pandarus then claps Atro's face, the space not covered by a cheek plate, and hobbles up the beach. His steps slow and he lumbers around. He appears to have spotted something, maybe a pretty shell.

He totters forward, toward Homer.

Yikes on all the trikes, this can't end well. I march toward Homer as well. He first spots Pandarus, then me, and then lifts a palm toward me. I halt.

Why is he making me stop?

Instead, I watch the line of soldiers snake their way to the black ships. The red scar on the bow of the boat before me sends a shudder down my spine. Does it remind the soldiers of the many injuries Pandarus muttered about in his sleep? Of split skulls and gashed midsections?

Pandarus's deep rumble speaks first. I do my best to listen in. The soldiers don't talk much. Instead, they continue their somber march. Blackness shows beneath their eyelids. They must not have gotten much sleep either.

"You are called Homer?" Pandarus asks.

"Yes?"

"Silver-footed Homer? Spear-wielding Homer? What do they call you back home?"

What's Pandarus getting at here?

In our garden talks, Homer mentioned that everyone of the upper class had a nice epithet attached to their name. Maybe Pandarus is trying to sniff him out and prove Homer doesn't come from the nobility.

Cersei recognized him. Others might follow.

Homer doesn't answer at first, and my breath hitches. "Pandarus, I have a great respect for you, as you are my host and as a son to a great leader of this tribe. If you wish to say something, I bid you speak it."

"No matter what rank you were among your peoples, you were never the shepherd of the people. Do I speak true?"

"You do." An edge in Homer's voice threatens to cut me open.

"Therefore, I outrank you and have a rightful claim to whatever my heart pleases."

Ugh, he means me. Eels wriggle inside me.

"You…" Homer's voice falters. He does this when he wants to choose his words with care. "You do outrank me."

"If that be the case, I wish for you to cease all interactions with her."

Pandarus doesn't specify the "her." But I can feel the burn of his gesture land on me, even with my back turned to him.

"After all, I am your host." He lowers his voice to a hiss. "If you are even to lay eyes on her once again, you will taste the sting of my blade. Have I made myself clear?"

Again? That must mean he spotted us last night at the sacrifice.

I want to kick myself for not waiting until Homer and I could sneak away to the garden. Because of me, I put his life in danger. I also shouldn't have made him go to the pottery shop. Who knows what Pandarus could have done if he spotted us there? Soldiers did stop by, given the subjects of Cersei's paintings.

An eagle makes lazy circles in the sky above the boats. This time, it clasps no snake. I have no idea what that means.

"Of course, Lord Pandarus."

My teeth clamp down hard on my lower lip, until I tear skin away. We need to find a city refuge, and fast.

Part Two – Love

"…There is the heat of Love, the pulsing rush of Longing, the lover's whisper, irresistible—magic to make the sanest man go mad."

—Homer, *The Iliad*

Chapter Nine
How the Nations Gather in Uproar

THE RULES OF PALIKARIAN HOSPITALITY, ACCORDING to Brisei when I ask her, when we get back home:

Rule one—if your host gives you a gift, they expect one in return. This could mean you give them gold or a donkey when you depart from their land. Or if they ever happen to come to where you live, you need to host them for however long they need. People stay literal months, even years, with their gracious hosts.

Rule two—you cannot refuse a gift given to you. Even if you don't like the milk all curdled in fig juice, if Elin offers you a cup, you sip away. Although you can get away with avoiding meat for a while if you say you're in mourning.

Rule three—you cannot fight with your host in a duel. It does not matter if they've come from a foreign country with whom you're at war. If someone hosts you, you cannot hurt, maim, or kill them in any way.

In other words, Homer can't fight back. If Pandarus wants to make a move, we'll have to hope we find a city to flee to quick.

A Video Call on March 15, My Junior Year

"Pop quiz, Harper. What happened in Palikari in 800 BCE?"

"Uncle Laran, can you please stop bursting into Homer's room and asking me random questions?"

He stands before the computer, nursing a cup of tea on a

plate in his hands. I can tell it's still warm from the wisps coming from the red mug. On the dish sit two large cookies, one of their halves dipped in chocolate.

During my time in England, we split many a teatime biscuit with one another. He filled his dishwasher constantly with mugs.

"I have a test I'm administering tomorrow, and I want to make sure that I'm asking the right questions."

I squeeze my backpack to my stomach. I pulled into my garage not two minutes ago and immediately flipped open my laptop to call Homer for our hour of Palikarian.

"Laran, it's eleven at night there. Couldn't you have chosen literally any other time to do this?"

"With some of the information Homer has been giving me, I've had to make adjustments to my lectures and the test." He taps his large nose with an index finger. "This won't take but five minutes."

There crept in that fake British accent.

Even though Uncle Laran has lived in England for several years, he originated from America. Try as he might to muster the rhyming cockney slang and say words like "queue" and "very well, thank you," he could never stamp the 'merican out of himself.

I toss my arms heavenward. "Fine. But please tell me these are multiple choice. Because I don't know squat about history."

Laran sets his mug on a table and frowns as he crunches into one of the digestive cookies. "You and Homer never talked about his history before?"

"Here and there." I lift my backpack, biceps shaking from the weight of my books. "But with the amount of homework I have to do after these calls, I don't remember everything."

"Very well. Most of these are multiple choice. Barring a few essay questions at the end. First question." He pulls a packet of papers from off screen and shields his face with them. "What innovation of the Palikarians and Greeks brought Greece out of the Dark Ages and into the Archaic Age? Is the answer…

"A, writing, using the Phoenician alphabet as a guide to form the Greek alphabet,

"B, democracy, using the model of group assemblies to allow for all free men to contribute and cast their votes on decisions,

"C, the Olympics, where funeral games were transformed into events, where city-states competed against one another for prizes and for honor,

"D, advancements in art, especially in pottery, bringing the Greeks out of the proto-geometric phase into the geometric phase, or "E, all of the above?"

I rub the bridge of my nose between my index finger and thumb. "Laran, I don't even *know* history, and the answer is obviously E."

A rare feather flits in my chest. Perhaps if I could escape high school and get into a college, maybe my classes wouldn't be so hard.

Teachers threatened constantly that we had it easier in our classes at high school.

"In college, they won't stand for a late paper. You turn it in a day late, you get an auto-F."

"At college, they expect you to be fully involved in extracurriculars. It's not enough to have a 4.0 GPA anymore. They care just as much about what you do after school as in school."

"Universities expect top-tier papers. You throw in a being verb, you lose an entire letter grade on that assignment."

Funny how they considered college the only worthwhile option. A girl who sat next to me hoped to pursue cosmetology. One day, she burst into tears at her locker. I overheard her asking her locker-mate, "Am I making the biggest mistake of my life?"

Uncle Laran shrugs and sips from his mug. "You certainly don't know some of the students who sit in the back of my lectures. I have no idea how they got into university in the first place. All right." He taps the packet of paper. "Next question. Which of the following is a factor that led to the Palikarian collapse?

A, the death of chieftains, or shepherds of the people, leaving tribes in Palikari vulnerable to Greek attack.

B, colonization of the Grecian World, more popular later in the 700s when the Greeks invaded more lands to expand their reach.

C, siege warfare, similar to how the Babylonians operated, where they'd cloister the enemy within a city and starve them out.

D, misinterpreting omens, believing that the gods had favored them in the battle, giving them false confidence, or

E, all of the above?"

I guffaw, almost choking on some pieces of my granola bar I'd fished out of my backpack during the barrage of answers. "Uncle Laran, are *all* the answers to the multiple-choice questions 'all of the above'?"

He squints at the pages in the weak lighting of the room. Homer has disappeared from his seat. A toilet flush follows Laran's silence. *Good call, buddy.*

"Hmm, let's skip to the essay question."

"Uncle Laran! I don't know anything about their history."

"Apparently you do. All right, here's the question. Why Did Palikari and Greece go to war in the first place?"

This stumps me. I chew on my lip and glance out my window. A yellow bus rolls up to the end of my neighborhood and sets loose elementary students. Their backpacks flail from left to right as they dart into their houses.

"I don't know. We just finished *The Iliad* and *The Odyssey* in our English class. In *The Iliad*, they fought over a woman, I think. I actually SparkNoted most of it. Seriously, like three hundred of the pages were just details of how people died. Somehow it was still boring."

Raisins hit my teeth when I bite into the granola bar again. A sweet cinnamon kick grazes my tongue. "They didn't happen to fight over a woman, did they, Uncle Laran?"

Laran grins, and his chin sways from side to side. "It's a trick question. We actually don't know why they went to war in the first place. We don't have enough historical documentation to back up a singular cause. Could've been because the Greeks got greedy and wanted more land. Could've been that it was a dog-eat-dog world, and if you didn't take prisoners of war, you'd became one." He sips from his mug again. "We only know how the war ends."

"Where Palikiari loses to Greece," I say as Homer appears on the screen with a cup in his hands.

"And gets Hellenized by Greece and nearly lost to history forever. Yes."

Palikari (800 BCE)
T-minus Months, Maybe Weeks until the Greeks Invade

Brisei, Talith, and I giggle as we chew on laurel leaves spread on the fur blankets on my bed. A minty, somewhat alcoholic taste explodes in my mouth. This beats the other toothbrushing method we've been using these past few weeks of chewing sticks covered in charcoal. We've also wrapped cloth around our fingers and rubbed it against our teeth. I wonder what my dentist would think of me now.

We pull out the wadded leaves and place them in a basket beside the bed that holds the apple cores. I stole the fruit from dinner and brought them up for us to share.

A memory stirs up of the boy giving the girl an apple at the dance. Did that mean something? A way to flirt with her, I guess, based on the way she giggled.

Over two weeks have passed since the soldiers went off to war. Homer and I haven't made contact since. Can't really blame him, since Pandarus spends his days pacing the courtyard. He says he does it to help strengthen his leg. But considering how much he eyes my window, I have a feeling he wants to catch me escaping with Homer somewhere in town.

Speaking of his leg, we've spotted improvements. Even in just a little more than a week's time, he doesn't hobble so much. Something tells me he overreacted about the wound in battle.

Why? Not sure.

From some of the stories he shares with Elin at the table, I can understand why someone would want a few more days, or weeks, from leave to stretch and relax.

Elin announced a week ago that her daughter delivered a beautiful baby boy and recovered. I want to ask her what happened to the magician, who'd gone to the same town as her daughter.

But that could arouse unnecessary suspicion. Why would an out-of-towner such as myself care about such matters? No less a woman who shouldn't leave her room except to go to the hearth and weave burial shrouds.

We have to wait until Pandarus leaves before we can figure out our next move.

Speaking of the hearth, I have made some improvements. Brisei and I alternate spots on the loom when the other's arm gets tired. We pass the time by singing. She's taught me and Talith the "Song of Linus," a popular tune from her home.

Although Talith doesn't know all that much Greek, she sings a word here or there, so she doesn't feel left out.

I couldn't join them in the singing last week owing to a special time of month. Let's say we didn't leave our room, and I decided that I missed painkillers most from home.

Talith plucks the wad of leaves out of her mouth and tosses them into the basket. "Sweet."

She's picked up on a lot of Palikarian words.

Every once in a while, during down time, she'll trace the Phoenician letters in the sand. Brisei has asked her to sound out each one. Elin broke this up right away. She slapped her thighs and told them to get back to work.

Although I haven't seen many interactions between Elin and the other servants on the estate since I spent most of the first few weeks either in pain in my room or out in the town, I've seen plenty of scars on their legs, and on their backs where the dresses and tunics don't cover their shoulders.

I can't decide who I hate more in her family—Elin or Pandarus. Sad that Ulix has won my heart by default because we never see him.

The minty aftertaste of the leaves reminds me of a mint tea I made Uncle Laran try back in England. He insisted on English breakfast tea and *only* English breakfast tea. The thought pulls up the memory of him and his pop quiz.

"Brisei." My tongue probes my front teeth for any leftover plant pulp. "What caused the war between the Greeks and Palikarians in the first place?"

Light disappears from her cheeks. She grips the bristles of one of the fur blankets in her fists.

"It has been happening for so many years I—" Her fingertips grip and release. Grip and release. "I do not think even the men know why they fight."

That would explain the somber expressions on the beach.

Those men, as they developed blisters and calluses from holding leather straps on the oars, must've asked one another why they continued to row. Why they couldn't stop, jump overboard, and swim home?

I wish I could tell you that the Greeks win. That could give her hope, or some sense of vindication.

Instead, I ask, "Do you hope that the Greeks win?"

Her bare foot grazes the floor as her leg swings back and forth. "I—I hope the gods do what is just. That is all one can hope for." She draws in a breath, exhales. "In war, my lady, there are no winners. Only the grateful dead, and those who must live with the consequences."

In the morning, I race to the courtyard. Pandarus hasn't gotten up yet, so I can at last escape this room I've spent the greater part of a week in aside from dinner last night. My legs ache from lack of use, so I stretch far as I can heavenward.

Warm air tickles my cheeks. Because I've spent so long indoors, any sunburn has gone back down to a pale shade. Harper comes in two colors—lobster and mayonnaise.

Cool stone soothes my soles.

Talith and Brisei sit behind me, on the steps that lead up to the house. They chew their breakfasts. I've told them that I won't stray far, so they don't have to shadow my every movement. Even though we've talked many nights together, I have difficulty getting a sense of their individual personalities.

Laran had mentioned, on one of our video calls, that the Palikarians live in a collectivist culture. Meaning, they would think more in "our" terms than "I."

But I do manage to jot some mental notes about the two.

Brisei loves politics and debate and philosophy—does philosophy exist yet? She has an unquenchable curiosity and will risk even her life to learn new information, like we did at the assembly.

Talith loves words and yearns for children of her own. When Elin came home and brought news of her daughter, Talith hugged her stomach and grinned.

Both of them are kind, full of laughter, and deserving of so much love.

A farmer to my left dumps acorns into a feeding trough. Tusked pigs filter around his legs like water droplets to get to them.

On the dirt road, a group of teens toss a ball back and forth to each other in a circle. They punch the animal-skin-covered thing with one hand, reminding me of volleyball. Whenever the ball hits the ground, whoever it landed nearest to must exit the game. The match continues back and forth between two sweaty guys.

Not a cloud dots the indigo sky. I squint up at the sun and scan the sky for any eagles.

None have made an appearance since the soldiers left the beach.

Instead, a group of gulls squawk overhead and flap in the direction of the ocean.

"A beautiful morning."

I bristle when I hear Pandarus's voice behind me.

I turn on my heel and force a smile. "Indeed."

"Did you watch Dawn appear? She was robed in saffron this morning."

"I did not."

Even if certain abdominal pains hadn't taken me down for the count last week, I wouldn't dare venture into the courtyard in the mornings. Pandarus got out there before the sun rose and stayed out there until it set.

But we'd hoped for better this morning, since he disappeared inside…

"Perhaps we can watch Dawn appear another morning, fair-cheeked Harper?"

Tension pounds in my temples. *No, thank you, no, thank you, no, thank you.*

Footsteps clap behind me, gracing me with an out to avoid giving Pandarus an answer. My shoulders tense when I watch Homer emerge from the house and swivel to his right toward the garden.

As he does this, a rush of movement pounds behind me. The teens have driven themselves into the courtyard. I can tell by the way they slathered themselves in oil and by the primness of their tunics and cloaks that they come from richer families.

"Would you like to join us?" One of them with rare blond curls directs the question at Pandarus.

Pandarus lets out a one-note laugh. "I would love to. But I must rest my leg." He hobbles on his injured leg in a more exaggerated fashion than he has these past two weeks. Then he squinches his eyes at me, all puppy-dog like, as if begging,

"Please hold me. I hurt. Kiss it and make it better."

My lips form a thin line. *No, thanks. We save these bad boys for a greater purpose.*

"Greater Purpose" gets surrounded by the teens after Pandarus tells them no.

"Will you join us?" one of them begs Homer. "Atro always joins us. He is excellent at this game."

Atro does sports? He would have to be in excellent shape to keep up with an army, but I wonder why I never heard about this.

Homer glances over his shoulder at the garden. "I—um."

"You are of noble birth, are you not?" one of the teens, who holds the ball, challenges.

"I—am."

"Then you ought to excel at the game. Join us over there."

Ah, the idea that all rich people are good at sports arises again. Granted, Homer explained he didn't have much downtime at the temple. When he did, he spent his time telling stories rather than throwing a ball around.

Man alive, I miss those stories he would tell me on video calls. I used to be the one to read him portions of *The Iliad* and *The Odyssey*, but after a while, he started to tell me tales. I listened, absorbed, drowned in them.

Without giving him a moment to answer, the teens barrel back toward the street. Homer glances at Pandarus, who smirks.

"Come now, Homer. Surely you are not afraid of a simple challenge from the youths? Many of them have not even grown a beard yet." Pandarus claws at his own bristles.

I clench my fists until nails dig into my palms. Pandarus is challenging Homer's nobility and his honor.

"Surely not," Homer says through gritted teeth. He follows the teens out onto the street.

Every part of me wishes I could tear my eyes away. Because the minute the ball flies up, Homer misses and it claps near his feet. Many rounds go like this, Homer getting knocked out first. He's eliminated third in one of the later rounds because they didn't toss the ball to him until two others got out.

"He plays like a feeble woman," Pandarus says when Homer faceplants in the dirt on the tenth or eleventh round. I've lost count.

I don't respond. Instead, I watch Pandarus squint at Homer in a way that causes my heart to pound. My mouth dries, and words get stuck in my parched throat. That look from him makes me nervous.

I've witnessed this squint from so many of my classmates.

When they try to figure out where they've seen someone before.

Chapter Ten
How the Heart Pours Living Water

LAUNDRY DAY BACK HOME TENDS TO consist of my mom and me piling up clothes in the laundry room in baskets until the stacks of socks plummet to the floor. Once the first item smacks the concrete, we have to throw the items in the washer and spend an entire day folding.

I made good use of my video calls with Homer by putting many a garment into drawers.

Apparently, laundry day in Palikari also occurs once a month. But it includes taking the clothes of everyone in the household—dozens, including the workers—and carrying everything to the river.

When Elin got word that I wanted to join the other ladies on the way to the water, she quirked a brow. Even asked, "Why?"

The truth? *This will get me out of your house and away from your creepy son.*

The lie? "It helps me to relax. I feel *nosto* when I do laundry." Nosto, the word for longing for home. No doubt, she feels it too when her husband and son disappear for war.

Anyone can tell you from the Tide PODS fiasco of last December—I will never speak of what happened on that day to a soul—that laundry days do anything but un-knot the tangles in my shoulders. But a day at the river sounds glorious compared to watching Pandarus pace the courtyard from my window. Plus, in this heat, we could use a cool dip.

Elin relented and told me to bunch my hair up into a headwrap like the rest of the laundry girls have. She says she would hate to see the river spoil my golden hairs. I vow, in my head, to dunk myself headfirst in the waters, just to spite her.

In a rush, Elin calls for the men in the stables to bring a donkey and cart to carry the baskets of laundry and me to the river.

Brisei hoists a woven basket full of soiled linens on her hip. Her lips sag at the sight of the makeshift carriage. "Elin never uses this for when we wash the linens."

I can see why. Because Talith uses a hand to lift me onto the board. When the ladies pile their baskets into the wagon, I realize that only three can ride on the way to the river.

The rest of the twelve have to walk.

I lean over the wooden railing and hiss at Brisei, "I can walk. We should let someone else who needs rest stand on here."

Brisei bites on her lower lip and throws a hurried glance over her shoulder at Elin. She glances back at me, and I nod. "We will make a change once we are out of her view."

The donkey surges forward, and I have to grip the wooden railing for dear life not to fly out the back. Thank goodness the cart travels at walking speed, so the others can keep up. I watch over my shoulder as the white house disappears into the distance. When Elin ambles up the driveway, and after we've passed the stables, I ask Brisei to stop the cart.

She does so with the click of her tongue.

I hop off and motion to Talith to get on. Talith protests in Phoenician, sprinkling in some Palikarian words like "no" and "walk."

"Her knees could use the rest," I tell Brisei over my shoulder.

Brisei approaches Talith and offers a hand. After they

exchange some growls and no's, Talith relents and allows Brisei to lift her up onto the platform.

"Two more can fit on the cart." I scan the crowd and land on a woman with a leathery face and bone-thin arms, the same one who told me not to cry in the tub on the first night in Palikari. She has to be pushing fifty or sixty. Although on our calls, Homer mentioned most didn't make it past their thirties. "You. You could use some rest."

She swats the air and says she'll be fine. But her knees wobble as she carries a small basket of laundry that wouldn't fit into the cart. I take the clothes from her, and two girls coax her onto the platform.

Another woman, swelling with an eight-month pregnancy, is chosen to take the last spot. She scrunches herself into a ball and rests her neck against a pile of dresses. Sweat glistens on her upper lip and forehead, even though the sun hasn't escaped from the low cloud cover on the horizon. Nevertheless, the air does feel sticky.

Anger bubbles in my stomach.

Elin should let her rest. She looks ready to pop at any moment. Will the hard labor she does on a daily basis hurt the baby?

I hoist the small basket on my hip, and we plod on.

Several houses later, asthma burns my lungs. Brisei takes notice of my heavy breathing and grabs the basket from me.

"Thank you." I grip my sides. "I can take it from you when I can breathe again."

"Absolutely not. You have already given up your place on the chariot. I will not let you do all the work." She grins and wipes the sweat on her lip on one of the dirty pieces of cloth on her pile.

"Is it a long way to the river?" Thorns wrap around my calves. We haven't gone walking much these past two weeks.

"Yes. But we love to tell stories on the way. Would you like to hear my favorite one?"

Sure beats the sound of my ragged breaths. I nod. So she begins.

She tells the story of how she met her husband. He found her listening in on an assembly. Her father, the shepherd of the people, led the meeting after the eldest person in the circle started. Instead of reporting her to the authorities, Brisei's future husband told her to meet him at the beach to discuss her punishment for breaking the law of her land.

She went. But instead, she found him at the beach sitting on a circle he'd drawn in the sand. He handed her a large stick and said she had the floor. Her punishment was she'd have to discuss matters of the city and how they should proceed.

Brisei did so. Let's just say, she appears to have knocked his socks off, if socks existed during this time.

Every day from then on, they would meet and discuss at the beach. Until one day, he decided they would veer the conversation to marriage proposals and the importance they had on the welfare of their city.

"Lovely Brisei, would you not say that marriage proposals promote the growth of the population and therefore, are beneficial to all tribes?"

"I would say so."

"Would you say it is your duty as a citizen of a tribe to participate in all matters that help to increase that population's growth?"

She grinned. "Indeed."

"Would it convince you to participate in this if I had, say, given your father several racehorses, ten goats, and talents of gold...and received his blessing already?"

Well, it certainly beats my cousin's story of getting proposed to in an Applebee's parking lot.

The way Brisei tells it spills warmth into my chest. Frost overtakes me, moments later, when I realize that the Palikarians killed the same man who married her.

Brisei clears her throat and pants. Having regained oxygen again, I take the basket from her, and we dip into the shadows of poplar trees on the downward hill toward the river. Muddy paths threaten to glue my sandals in place.

Thorny olive trees slash my calves on our descent. A mixed scent of wet and green from the leaves helps to cancel out the overwhelming stink of the laundry.

"Now is your turn to tell a story, my lady. Would you like to speak of how you and Homer met?"

Flush crawls up her neck and cheeks. Like she's asked me to spill my greatest secret.

Oh boy, how can I share the story of how we met without committing some serious anachronisms?

"I found him in a—" They don't have a word for museum. "Marketplace. Evil men were chasing after him." After all, the museum did try to sell some ridiculous merchandise in their stores. That counted as a marketplace, right?

Brisei's eyes widen. Two ladies in conversation beside her hush to listen. "How exciting! Do go on."

I do. I try my best to convey taking him back to my uncle's apartment and keeping him away from the archeologist. Details get changed, of course. My uncle is the shepherd of the people in this story, and the archeologist transforms into an enemy solider.

Silence has fallen over all the ladies. The pregnant woman in the cart presses her ear to the holes in the wood slats to hear.

When I finish, Brisei gasps. "Harper, you tell stories as

eloquently as story-stitchers." Murmurs of agreement thrum throughout the group. "Sadly, I know not one female story-stitcher."

Makes sense. Brisei and I spoke about some jobs that men do in Palikari and Greece on a particularly bad day of my blood week. These ranged from wool workers to pilots of ships to doctors. In all of the jobs we listed, Brisei didn't know a single female who worked them.

I smile and then grimace at a muddy rock that's gotten caught in my sandals. "You should hear Homer. He tells stories far better than I do."

A mosquito lets out a high shrill shriek in my ear. I bat the bug away. On my left, a small deer gallops away into the forest. Birdsong surrounds us in the canopies of trees.

"We have yet to hear Homer tell one," another woman toward the back of the crowd pipes up. "He is so quiet. You would think he is mute."

He acted the same way when he arrived in England. After we spent months together, he would keep me up late at night with how much he talked. "Not with me. With me, he could tell stories for hours."

"You coax the brave out of him." Brisei grins at Talith. "You do that with all of us."

I do? No one has ever told me that before. With how much my mom harps on me for being an energy drain for her, I figured I was anti-motivation for most people.

We reach the riverside and unload the laundry. As one of the girls unhitches the donkey from his yoke, I notice how much sweat moistens his back. He plows for the water and takes in greedy gulps.

I'm tempted to do the same. Images from my biology class

of slides full of dangerous bacteria in rivers keep me from cupping my hands and shoveling water into my mouth.

Plus, we've packed cheese and bread wrapped in cloth. And goatskins full of wine. After we finish the laundry, we can help ourselves.

Brisei approaches the water first with a garment full of brown blotches. She places the cloth near a running stream and grinds it back and forth on a rock. She slaps the clothing against the stone and piles handfuls of water onto it.

The rest of us follow. Chilled waters cool my feet and ankles. On this muggy day, this place has gone down ten degrees.

Can we stay here forever? Away from Pandarus and the imminent invasion of the Greeks? Something about forests pauses time. Slap some tennis shoes on us, and we could've been a handful of girls going on a hike somewhere in the mountains.

I almost slip and fall on a mossy rock as I find a place to scour handfuls of dresses. Talith leads us in a Phoenician song. We hum along, not knowing the words. Hours or minutes pass, and I feel faint from the sunlight beating down on us from above the trees. Elin made a good call with the headwrap, because my hair sticks to my forehead like someone has glued the locks down.

We finish and lay the clothes out to dry on the sandy beach.

I collapse onto the shore with a thud. Brisei hands me a chunk of cheese and the wineskin. I down the first one and wash the meal down with several gulps of wine. Woowee, dizziness fills my skull.

To distract myself from the urge to vomit, my fingers trace constellations out of the bug bites on my calves.

Earth takes a few minutes to stop spinning so fast.

When it does, I spot Talith with her skirts hitched up to her thighs. She plunges headfirst into the river and lets out a squeal of delight when she surfaces.

With joyful shrieks, we follow and shove each other under the rapids. I let out a gasp when I throw all of myself in. My body floats up and the dress bubbles around my legs and arms. Neat, I come with a mini raft.

My footing gets lost and found again when my soles crash into a jagged rock. Without a doubt, I'll find a gash when I exit to the shore.

I spot Talith nearby and splash her. She returns the gesture, and soon, everyone claps each other with this algae-scented liquid. Brisei sloshes to shore—where the old woman and pregnant lady watch us and dip their toes—and digs something out of a tattered animal-skin bag.

It reminds me of the ball the boys played with yesterday. Except someone has covered the surface in tar and yarn and anything else to hold the contents together.

"We have a little cheese left." She holds up the ball. "Whoever wins will eat the food before we return home."

She splashes into the water and lobs the ball toward a girl who has a large birthmark on her forehead. Birthmark girl smacks the ball at me. I dive and smash into the water, nicking my chin on a sharp rock.

Declared out, I swim to the other side of shore and find myself near a gray clay deposit. I wonder if Cersei gets the materiel of her pots from here. As I watch the various girls slip on mossy rocks and miss the ball, I sculpt a dolphin. By the time Talith wins, I've formed the curve on the dorsal fin.

They had to pause the game once because a water snake slithered past their ankles. I wonder how many dangers await us in the river. Then again, I do hail from Zona, where we have venomous snakes and spiders.

The girls call me back into the river as Talith races to the shore to get her cheesy prize.

We continue to play for the next few rounds. I notice the ladies don't toss me the ball until a few others get out. Probably out of pity.

In the fourth round, Brisei spikes the ball at me. My foot catches on something slippery, and I flail backward. Thankfully, my head doesn't hit any rocks on my landing. Brisei stifles a snigger under her nose.

"My lady, I fear you are somehow worse at this game than even Homer."

I giggle and accept her arm that she offers to lift me up. Something hisses on shore, and I worry the water snake has returned. But then the old woman clicks her tongue to indicate the noise came from her.

"For shame, speaking to her in this way. Do you want her to report back to the household with rumors of what insults you heap upon her?"

Did she just say I might go back and tattle because I couldn't take a joke?

Images from Homer's game yesterday flash before my eyes. Pandarus had gotten suspicious that Homer had no athletic ability whatsoever. It made him, and the boys, question Homer's nobility. Maybe this old woman thinks Brisei is doing the same here.

"She is different." Tiny fish swim past Brisei's wobbling ankles. Is she thinking about what would happen if I *did* tell Elin?

The old woman on shore harrumphs. She mutters something under her breath and shields her belly with her arms.

I return to my clay deposit dolphin to get to work on the snout.

While I carve the nose between my fingertips, I feel something brush against my leg. In my periphery, something large floats past and gets stuck in the clay deposit beside me. I bend down into the water to wash off my grayed fingertips and make out the shape of the floater.

Ice constricts my throat and chokes out the scream.

Still, I must make enough noise because the girls in the water take notice and latch their eyes onto the ashen body floating downriver.

An arrow juts out of his back.

I draw my knees up to my chest and force my gaze onto Brisei's face to fight the flashbacks from two summers back. Her cheeks have lost all color.

"The feathers on that arrow." Her arm wobbles as she gestures at the body. "Those come from Greece. My brother was an archer."

"The man wears no armor," a girl beside Brisei cries.

"Yes, he has either been stripped of it, or is not a soldier," someone else says. Hard to distinguish which voice belongs to who at this distance, and with my ears full of ringing. "Perhaps they have pillaged a town. The man looks quite well along in years. He could not be young enough to fight in an army."

My eyes dart in the opposite direction. Do Greeks hide in the thorny bushes, and in the large trees? Will we find ourselves in a barrage of arrows soon?

"He has been dead for some time." Brisei's voice calls me back. Although she lays a hand on the shoulder of a shaking girl as a gesture of comfort, she can't keep the quiver out of her voice. "This river travels through many Palikarian tribes."

"But it means the Greeks are getting nearer?" The girl with the birthmark stares upriver, just as I did moments ago.

"Yes." Brisei bites her lip. "It would appear so."

Chapter Eleven
How the Men Flee to Caves

NEVER EXPECTED MY FIRST SLEEPOVER TO take place in 800 BCE.

Back home, when sleepovers were a thing, I never got invited to them. Because I left homecoming and prom early to FaceTime Homer in the morning, I didn't bother going to any sort of after party. Back in middle school, the idea of anything girly from nail polish to sharing crushes sent red ants running up and down my veins.

Now, I sit on Talith's mat next to my bed and pull her hair into pigtail braids. I vow to undo them before morning, unsure when pigtail braids actually come into existence in the world.

If we don't find that magician, or worse, if he's passed on, I'll have to figure out from Homer what anachronisms to avoid committing.

Brisei parks on her mat, which rests next to the trunk. Only two of us could fit on that twin-sized bed, and she and Talith would hear nothing of me sleeping on the floor tonight.

Guilt gnaws at my gut. Knowing how I woke up in sweats after the archeologist incident, I can only imagine what will happen tonight after seeing the dead body floating in the river.

We each grabbed a part of that corpse and floated it to shore. It took the effort of nearly a dozen girls to lift the body onto the cart. All of us walked on the way home, including the pregnant woman. When we arrived at the town square, one of the elders identified the colors on the man's outfit from a specific Palikarian tribe.

"The soothsayer looked worried," I say through a piece of

leather string stuck between my teeth. When I finish this braid, I'll tie Talith's hair with it.

Although, he told everyone that the Greeks were ages away and that the city's fortifications would hold them back.

Brisei clenches and unclenches the bedding on her mat with her fists. Her jaw hinges, unhinges so much, I can hear the click of her teeth.

"Are you all right, Brisei?"

Her nostrils flare and she shuts her eyelids. "They said the same for my city, before the Palikarians attacked. That we had plenty of time before they would invade. That very night they came." A shudder ripples down her spine. "They came like thieves in the night. We could not so much as blink before they set fire to everything."

My heartbeat throbs in my eardrums. My fingers shake as I tie the end of Talith's braid with the leather cord. "That being the case, how much time would you say we have left before the Greeks overtake this city?"

She sucks her teeth and traces indiscernible shapes onto her mat. Shrill cries of mosquitoes hum in my ear, and I swat the insects away with my free hand.

"It is difficult to say. But if you are planning to flee this city to return home, I would do so quickly."

I glance over my shoulder at the salmon pink skies. Pandarus's guffaw echoes off the stone courtyard. He stayed out there long after dinner to play ball with the teens across the street.

Leg injury, yeah right.

"With Pandarus keeping an eye on Homer, it is impossible to do what you ask, Brisei. We have not had a chance to meet in over two weeks."

Brisei's hands still.

She stares at me, the window, and then back at me. She draws in a sharp breath and rises.

"I will not be gone long."

She flicks her braid over her shoulder and vanishes out the door. I drop Talith's finished braid and scurry up to my bed.

Brisei appears outside moments later and approaches the circle of boys. When they spot her coming, they whistle and whoop at her.

Fire broils in my cheeks. Lord help me if I don't climb down this ladder and nail one of them in the jaw with my fist.

Brisei motions for Pandarus to speak with her a yard away from the circle. I can catch no words, but she gestures at my window. Pandarus's dark eyes connect with mine.

Nope, nope, nope, we don't like that. I muffle a shriek and plunge my head into my pillow. Feathers jab at my nostrils, but I refuse to move until I hear my door creak behind me. Brisei enters, rather pale.

"What did you say to him?"

Her knees crack when she returns to her spot on the mat. "He will join a group of men on a hunt tomorrow morning. This should give you and Homer time to talk about how you will return home. I will lead you to a place."

"A hunt?" How in the world did she convince him to do that instead of watch my window all day?

"Yes, I have promised that you will eat whatever he catches, so he is quite determined."

My chest freezes. Oh no. I knew I might have to eat meat at some point if we overstayed our welcome in Palikari. But I didn't expect to have to do it less than a month in.

She appears to read my expression.

"Fret not. We are to prepare you a lentil stew in a separate bowl before we add the meat to the broth. He will not be able to tell the difference when you take a bite."

I deflate a little, relief spilling into me. But what if they give me the wrong bowl? What if he notices that there aren't any meat chunks floating in it and makes me try his?

My knees bounce against the bedding. I steal one more glance at the courtyard and whip my chin away when I spot his eyes still on me. I sink into my pillow again and sigh.

For Homie, I'd eat a ribeye steak.

"Very well, Brisei." I clench my fists and notice my palms have gone all sweaty, so I wipe them against my dress. "Tell me about this secret place you are taking us to tomorrow."

Sure enough, in the morning, I awaken to the sound of barking.

Squinting, I raise myself just enough to peer out the window. Dogs weave around the legs of men covered in pelts, ready for a hunt. I bet by the time we hit afternoon, they're gonna drown in sweat.

I dip back into my pillow and watch Brisei's eyelids flutter.

Neither of us moves until the conversation and barking disappear in the distance. Then she throws herself off the bed into a standing position. She must've stood too fast because she grips the wall for support for several seconds. I kick off my covers and mirror her, slower so I don't get a black film over my eyes.

Last night, we agreed to leave Talith behind. Whenever I went out, Elin would work the girls late into the evening to make up for the hours they missed when they took me around town. Brisei says that she enjoys weaving when she can't sleep, so she doesn't mind the work when she returns.

Guilt burrowed a hole into me when she told me that.

Wish I could just go off alone, so you don't risk her getting mad at you. But if I ventured off by myself, I would draw attention.

Speaking of, Brisei plans to have me and Homer meet at a cave in the mountainside. She told Homer last night after she spoke with Pandarus to come to us from the opposite direction.

"The pottery shop is too dangerous. The people in this town love rumors, and if they see you two together, they will spread stories like fire."

She'd said this right before drifting off to sleep. But her words kept me wide awake for another several hours.

Even if Pandarus hadn't spotted Homer and I talking the night of the sacrifice, he could've gotten word from other sources. Again, until Pandarus goes back to the warfront…

As I exit my room, I grip a basket with two apples and some cheese I stole from dinner last night. Brisei wouldn't stop for breakfast this morning, in case the men return from the hunt before evening. I brought these along for a roadside snack.

I hand her a piece of fruit and bite into my own. Tart juice explodes in my mouth.

We pass a field where a man gives a horse water. Another man soaks the horse with a cauldron of water.

Elin made sure the servants scrubbed the heck out of me in the bath yesterday after my dip in the river. Even though I bathe once a day, she wanted to make sure I got the algae stench off me.

Brisei and I finish our apples and deposit the cores on the roadside. For the rest of the journey, we exchange stories, but she asks me to tell more of them.

The path turns rocky, and even through my leather sandals, stones jab into my soles. I can only imagine the pain Brisei feels with the various holes in her shoes. When I spy the mouth of the cave, the air surrounding us cools by ten degrees. A small creek runs through the cave mouth and toward the silhouette of Homer.

Ignoring the pains in my calves, I rush to him and bury myself into his chest.

He laughs and squeezes me tight. "Careful," he says in English. "Pandarus might be hunting a mountain lion near here."

We spring apart and I search the cave above me for the supposed lion. Instead, tree roots crawl through the holes, where sunlight pokes through. Above me, clusters of small bats sleep in packs. I duck to make sure I don't bump my head against them.

"How did you find this place, Bri—"

My words stop short in my throat when something at the far end of the cave catches my attention. I walk over to the wooden structure and make out a makeshift loom. Brisei must've constructed this thing out of twigs and rocks she found in the forest.

She hasn't made much headway on the pattern, if you can even call it that. It looks like she's stolen any spare bits of string she can find, so mishmashes of yellow, white, and blue twine form the first few rows of a blanket.

"When my mistress sends me into town, I steal away into here and work an hour at the loom."

"What are you making?"

"A shroud for my late husband. I can only hope he received a proper burial when I was taken."

Gravity pulls at my chest. How awful that she doesn't know what happened to him, and if he even got his own burial mound, or whatever they do here.

Homer speaks to me in English again, his voice echoing off the cave walls. "We have to hope that he did. Palikarians and Greeks both believe that if you aren't properly buried, you don't make it into the afterlife."

A vague memory of Uncle Laran telling me the same thing

flits across my skull. That explained why Homer, when he saw a Palikarin corpse in the British Museum, mourned. Because someone had dug up the body and taken them away from heaven, or whatever the Palikarians believed in.

"Time is not on our side." An edge to Brisei's voice pulls me away from the loom and back to them.

Homer kneels on the ground and grabs handfuls of rocks from the stream. A spider scurries past his hand to dodge around him and the water.

"This." He holds up a rock. "Represents our tribe." Homer places the rock in front of his knees. "These." Two stones, each gray. "Are the two tribes to the left and right of us." So they go on the ground. "These are our best options for finding a city of refuge, until the Greeks invade. Then we will need to find a new place."

I frown. "Only these two? Nowhere much farther away?"

Because as soon as the Greeks attack our village, they'll go for the two surrounding ones. I would think we'd want to go for the ones farthest away to save time.

Homer shakes his head. Water drips on his curls from the tree roots above. "These past two weeks, I have been collecting whatever information I can. From safe people." He eyes me.

Got it, people who don't recognize him.

"It seems that all the surrounding tribes have been either overtaken or are on the brink of being overtaken. If we want to stay safe for a little longer, we need to go to one of these two." He taps the stones.

That won't buy us much time. When the Greeks invade, then what? Do we flee to some place that doesn't belong to Greece or Palikari?

"Plus," he says in English, "the magician is supposedly in

one of the towns. If we get to him, maybe we can get him to help us go home."

I pick off some loose skin on my fingernail and feel a twinge of pain. Blood fills my cuticle. We don't have a guarantee that the magician hasn't died yet. Two weeks ago, Cersei mentioned he didn't usually venture off for longer than a day.

But like Homer said, we don't have many options.

"So when do we go?" I leap to my feet and almost forget about the bats. Thankfully, they rest a few inches away from my head.

"That depends"—he smacks his thigh and wipes off a bug carcass—"on when Pandarus leaves for war."

"Right." I rub the blood on my fingertip until crimson covers the entire side of my finger.

Guess I really need to enjoy the soup tonight.

We return less than an hour before Pandarus's hunting pack does. So I flee to the loom with Brisei. Before she continues her work on Elin's shroud, she informs the kitchen staff about the plan with the soup. They agree to make me a plain lentil broth before they add in the meat for the others.

Heavy footsteps thunder behind me soon after. I glance up and worms writhe in my gut as I watch Pandarus carry a fawn, slung over his shoulders, into the kitchen. An arrow still sticks out of its neck.

He reappears moments after to grin at me and tell me, "You shall eat well tonight, fair-cheeked Harper."

Sourness pools in my stomach. I doubt I could even force down goat cheese.

To distract me from how much my tight chest hurts, Brisei and I pass the time by exchanging more stories. She tells me of a time her brother chased her around with a snake. He'd severed the head and used the skull as a finger puppet.

Funny, my neighbors did that once. I tell her about it, and we dissolve into giggles.

I wish I could bottle laughter and drink it on days like this.

Dinner arrives and Brisei freshens up my oil and makeup. Realization that I have to eat Pandarus's soup hits me when Brisei stencils in the eyebrows. I have to remind myself that my bowl won't include meat inside it.

But if we stay here forever, it will have to eventually, right?

My art teacher, also a vegetarian, told us about a trip she took to Russia back in high school. "They gave us meat, so I ate it. Because it would've been rude not to. They gave us so much vodka that I had to pretend to be drunk and throw it over my shoulder." Her cheeks had grown dark. "Let's just say my teacher who led the trip didn't catch onto that trick. He laughed a lot that night."

If she ate meat, maybe I'll have to at one point.

The train of my gown drags behind me. Brisei made me change into something new. Those in the house only switch outfits every once in a while. The slaves, almost never.

"Pandarus insisted. He wanted to see you in something bright and colorful."

Eyesore indeed. This yellow dress with scarlet swirls on the hem could give anyone a headache. It sounds just like something Pandarus would pick out for a woman to wear.

We heave the ridiculous thing outside, where the frogs and insects chirp. I wash my hands and wait for Elin to pour out the libation onto the stone threshold. Liquid flows toward my dress, so I let the scarlet wine soak the bottom of my fabric. Maybe they'll let me change out of it once they see it got stained.

After we take our seats, servants bring out bowls of stew for us. I can feel Pandarus's eyes on me as I poke the contents with my spoon.

Whew, nothing meat-like floats to the top.

"What an excellent catch today, my son." Elin slurps from her wooden spoon. "Do you not think so, Harper?"

I dig out a pile of brown beans and shove them into my mouth. A smoky flavor grazes my tongue, and I swallow. Oof, they let this thing go cold. Can't really fault them, though. They did have to make me a separate soup before adding in the deer.

"Excellent." I wipe off some liquid that dribbles down my chin and pray that my review can convince Elin to tell her son to go back to the war. After all, if he could catch a deer, why not catch a few Greeks as well?

Instead, she digs into her bowl and procures a fatty piece of meat. "Harper, it is a delight to see you in such cheerful garments and with rouge on your face. I am happy to see my estate has pulled you out of your sorrow."

What? No, lady, tell your son to go back to war since his leg injury is apparently healed enough to go on a hunting trip. Let's not make the dinner topic about why we put Harper in a highlighter-yellow dress.

"It is good to see that you are out of mourning, fair-cheeked Harper." Pandarus licks his lips. "Perhaps you will be open to far more than soup in the coming days."

What the—what?

Realization of his words smacks me so hard, I almost topple backward in my chair. I steady myself and hope that the earth will stop spinning.

Great, Pandarus thinks I'm back on the market. Knowing him, he won't waste much time making the next move.

Chapter Twelve
How the King Dances without Shame

I PRAY THIS CHOKER CAN SUFFOCATE me before I have to go to the party tonight.

My fingers graze the snake pattern that wraps around my neck. Muffled conversation sounds from my window. In the dim light of the sunset, I watch the men gather in the courtyard and guffaw.

Two days after I ate Pandarus's stupid soup, the soldiers have returned from war.

Brisei tucks some of my flyaway hairs into my veil. She pats them down with some oil greased on her fingertips.

Through my open doorway I hear Pandarus and another soldier talk about the battlefront.

"Pandarus, we need you. You have slain dozens of Greeks in a single battle. Will you join us when our ships leave tomorrow?"

"Perhaps so. Perhaps not."

Something about the way Pandarus's voice hitches in his throat causes me to dig my fingernails into my palm. What more does he want? He already thinks I've somehow "gotten over" my dead fiancé within the span of three weeks. Elin has informed me, over lunch today, that women usually stop mourning right after funerals, which I guess take place over the span of several days here.

"Tis better to find a worthy man than to wait for all the good ones to be snatched up," she said right before biting into a fig.

Glad to know that they get over deaths here faster than most people at my school rebounded from relationships.

"Brisei." I untuck one of the locks of hair she buried into my headband. Something about the rebellious hair hanging down makes tonight more bearable. "The soldiers seem to go on leave a lot. Is this common?"

From what I could tell from my classmates who had parents and siblings overseas, people went months, even years, without coming back home.

She firms her jaw, reaches for my hair that has gone loose, thinks better of it, and drops her arm. "No. They have come back to retrieve the injured to help fight off the Greeks."

Yeesh, they must be getting desperate. Even one of the soldiers who sustained an arrow to his shoulder told Damas in the courtyard that he would return to the ships in the morning. Said it was "dishonorable" not to join arms with them.

I wonder how much time we have left. If they're recruiting the wounded, not much.

Sticky night air clings to my arms and legs. I fan myself with my palm and try not to stare down at the eyesore dress. Yesterday I attempted to slip back into the muted-colored one, and Elin threw a fit.

"Why do you return to the garments of mourning? Rejoice, dear one. For a greater future awaits those who no longer dwell in the past."

Funny, my teachers told me something similar when I got my report cards back from my final semesters in high school. I only applied to two colleges, but they sent rejections so fast, you would think my applications had burned their fingers and they wanted them back in the mailbox faster than you could say, "We regret to inform you."

Part of me wishes I could stay in Palikari.

To start fresh, sans the grades, sans gen-eds, and sans

community colleges telling me that if I do a couple semesters with them that maybe a state school will take pity on me.

"My lady, shall we descend to the courtyard?" Brisei asks.

I sigh and grip my dress in my fists. "Let us do so."

She grins and trails behind me. I amble down the steps and into the wall of noise in the courtyard. Once I spot Pandarus far enough away, I weave myself into a bubble that surrounds Damas, anything I can do to avoid Elin's son tonight.

"—and then I held my shield like so." Damas raises a dish he must have stolen from one of the kitchen staff. "And thrust the spear at my opponent." With his other hand, he jabs a stick toward one of the girls in the circle. She shrieks and hides herself behind one of her friends.

Where have I seen that stick before? My eyes rove to the gates, where the guardsman with his dogs sits without his walking stick.

"Why did no one attack you as you fought off the man with your spear?" One of the ladies, who applied so much blush to her cheeks tonight that she looks sunburned, inches toward Damas.

"Why, no one may attack a man when he has engaged in a duel of spears."

He proceeds to explain the rules of spear-offs.

"The first rule is you have to defend your honor."

Of course, because honor is everything in the ancient world.

"Second rule, you must fight with weapons of equal value. Sword against sword, for instance."

Okay?

"Rule number three, if you reach a draw, you must give each other a gift. Finally, rule number four, the fight continues until someone draws or dies."

Damas flashes a cheetah pelt on his shoulders. "I stripped

this off the man who challenged me to a duel on the battlefield." He leans toward the girl who has shuffled her way over to him. She giggles and pets the fur. "I wished to behead him and feed him to the dogs, but alas, his brethren surrounded him and would not let me tamper with the body any further."

Great, that was the strangest version of show-and-tell that I've ever had to witness.

I back out of the circle and bump into someone behind me. My skirts trip my legs when I whirl around, and I almost collapse into Pandarus's chest.

"Good evening, my bright star."

Good evening, thorn in my side. "Hello." I back away a few inches.

"I fear that not all the guests have arrived to celebrate with us tonight."

With a quick scan of the crowd, I pick out a few missing soldiers. "Atro? Ulix?"

People fill only half of the courtyard, unlike the army's first leave here. They must've only sent a select few to retrieve and recruit who they could.

The scent of some woman's strong flowery perfume sends my skull floating on water. Most people have doused themselves in fragrant oils tonight, but we'll take that over the body odor that follows everyone here.

"No, the story-stitcher. He is to regale us with stories of heroes and monsters as we dine."

Story-stitcher. The ladies had mentioned this word on the way to the river. Homer would make a great one, if he told tales to these people with the same vigor that he did to me on video calls. I spot him talking with a soldier near the pigsty.

"A shame. Perhaps he will join us later." I step to the side and angle my way toward musicians, who tune their instruments.

Something grips my arm and yanks me back.

"Perhaps, but we shall entertain ourselves until he arrives."

Pandarus, I swear, touch me again, and I sink a spear into your intestines. Before I can issue the threat, stringed music pricks my ears. A rush of footsteps surrounds me as the men and women form a circle and grip each other's wrists.

"Come, Harper, let us dance."

He drags me to the loop, and someone beside me with very sweaty palms grips my right wrist. Pandarus clings for dear life to the other, so much that my pulse throbs in my forearm. Someone yanks me to the right, and we spin back and forth.

Stones scrape my toes as we switch directions during changes in the music. I still haven't figured out the pattern yet.

My sandals keep catching, and I pray I'll twist my ankle so I can sit the next number out.

Pandarus releases his grip when the tune gets faster to reach for something behind him.

When the music ceases with a flute flourish, he shoves something into my belly. I grip the item and catch myself before I fall backward onto my butt. I glance down at the cold thing in my fingertips—an apple.

My eyebrows scrunch, and I glance up at him. He races over to a huddle of men who clap him on the back.

Girls bubble around me and giggle. One, with a golden ring on her middle finger, grazes the green fruit with her fingertips.

What. Just. Happened?

Possibilities whirl around in my brain. Something similar happened the last time our group danced in the courtyard.

Did he... Horror freezes my chest. *Did he just propose?*

That could explain why he wouldn't say whether or not he

would go back to war. Because he wanted an answer to *that* question first.

By taking the apple, did I accept his offer? Not that he gave me much of a choice *shoving the thing into my abdomen.*

The cluster around me breaks apart, and the temperature cools five degrees. I race to Brisei, who balances a place of fruit on her palm. My gaze arrows to the green apples. He had to have stolen one from this platter. "Brisei." I choke on my words, swallow them. "Please tell me I did not just agree to marry him."

Her bottom lip quivers. "He did not propose. But—"

"But?" Breath gets trapped in my lungs until they burn.

"If you are planning to return home, you must do it soon. Otherwise…"

A clap pricks my ears. I whirl around, and Elin spreads her arms out like a Greek goddess statue, gesturing toward the tables. "Come. Eat."

After the handwashing and libation-pouring, we settle into our seats. A servant places a chunk of meat onto my plate. Oh right, they think I eat this now, since the soup incident. I feel someone's shadow loom behind me.

"My lady, hand it to me when no one watches."

Bless you, Brisei. When I don't feel the burn of anyone's eyes, I pass her the fatty slice. She disappears, and I pray she gets a good meal tonight.

"Pandarus." Food flies off Damas's lips. A man lounging near him receives the wad to his cheek. "Did you not promise us a story-stitcher tonight? Where is he?"

"Late." A growl lodges in his throat when groans sound from every end of every table.

Man, they take their stories seriously here. Homer had told me, in England two years ago, that they passed most of the time at the temple telling tales. Aside from tossing around an animal-skin ball, they don't have much in terms of entertainment in these parts.

"Perhaps someone else can entertain us until he arrives?" Damas wipes his lips on his sleeve. "Is there a story-stitcher among us?"

My eyes lock, in an instant, on Homer's. He slinks into his shoulders like a turtle.

I squinch my eyelids. Come on, Homie. They already questioned your nobility when you failed at sports. Maybe if you show off your storytelling skills, they'll think you're talented and received a grand rich-boy education and yada, yada, yada.

After all, everyone here who is anybody has to be the best at something.

He firms his jaw, nods at me, and lifts himself from his lounging couch. "I have a few stories."

Cheers follow him up to the front of the courtyard. He hunches over and makes what I like to call dinosaur claw arms, inviting us to lean in and listen. A man with a lyre sidles up beside him and plucks the string.

Then Homer begins his story about two men named Achilles and Hector, who have met on the battlefield for a duel.

"Achilles, I am not going to run from you anymore. I have already been chased by you three times round."

I recognize the speech from Hector. My teacher made me stand to say it in front of the class. Homer must've memorized the passage when I read him the book on our video calls for my homework assignment. Palikari is, after all, an oral culture. They could memorize entire four-hundred-page stories if they wanted to.

He imitates the voices of the soldiers very well and pretends to lift his shield and spear as his characters start their duel. I glimpse the crowd. Everyone but Pandarus has leaned forward, clinging to his every word.

Right as "Achilles" jabs his spear down at Hector, a man with a graying beard stumbles through the gates to the courtyard.

Homer halts his story. Everyone withdraws to their seats, blinking rapidly, as if recovering from a magic spell.

"Are you the story-stitcher?" Homer asks this in time for the man to stagger into him.

"S-speaking." The story-stitcher trips and regains his balance. Spirits from the wine bowl before me dizzy my senses. Did this guy get too much to drink before he came here? That would explain why he arrived so late.

"I will allow you to take the floor." Homer returns to his seat but flashes me a grin. I mimic the gesture. *Well done, babe.*

Brisei's words from the river echo in my skull, in the space between my ears. *"You coax the brave out of him."* Did I help convince him to tell the stories tonight?

"Less-see." The story-stitcher slurs his words and motions. With the waggle of his eyebrows, he indicates for the lyre-ist to pluck his strings once more.

Then he begins his story. About a cowardly boy who refused to go to war after he sustained an arm injury. Instead, the boy, in his foolish young age, pursued many lovers in town, who spurned his advances.

Strange, I thought story-stitchers made up characters, instead of using people from the audience.

My high school had an improv troupe who would often poke fun at popular students, teachers, and administrators. Whether or not the story-stitchers do that too, this guy doesn't seem to care. He chuckles at all his jokes.

Pandarus, meanwhile, slams his fist against the table and storms into the house.

During the story-stitcher's bit about how the faint-hearted man dresses himself as a woman to spy on the ladies as they do laundry, Pandarus rushes back onto the courtyard and thrusts a spear at the feet of the story-stitcher. The metal clatters against the stone.

"I will not allow my honor to be insulted. Pick it up."

The story-stitcher lifts a brow, chuckles, and a strange sobriety overtakes him and hardens his face. "A youth wishes to challenge his elder, who has served in many great wars before him. Very well." He leans down and picks up the weapon.

No wonder he made Pandarus out to be a spineless guy in the story. He didn't appreciate how he stayed home while all the other injured soldiers continued to fight.

A servant emerges from the household with a soot-covered spear and shield. He must've grabbed them from the hearth. The story-stitcher takes these from him, and a bubble forms around the two duelers.

I locate Brisei toward the outer ring and race to her, squeezing her hand in mine. "They cannot fight. The story-stitcher is drunk."

Brisei's fingers slacken. "Once a man's anger is ignited, my lady, only bloodshed can quench it."

Trembling overtakes me, and I turn back to watch the story-stitcher lift his shield up to his chin. Pandarus parrots the move and hunches down, reminding me of a snake about to launch at some unsuspecting ankle.

Pandarus makes the first move and jabs his spear at the story-sticher's left side. The other man parries the move in time, but staggers to the left. Hisses and whoops pass throughout the crowd. I can't distinguish who they root for and against.

With a growl, Pandarus lunges again, this time aiming for the story-stitchers's ankles. My own wobble as the old man hobbles back and forth on his sandals like someone has placed hot coals beneath him.

Again, again, Pandarus lunges toward the man's feet, until, at last, the story-stitcher lowers his shield to protect his shins.

A glint fills Pandarus's eyes, and he wastes no time to lunge his spear at the man's exposed belly.

He strikes true.

A gurgle sounds from the story-stitcher's throat when he slumps to the ground. Blood spills out of his mouth.

Hot vomit launches up my throat, and I spin around in time to puke on the stones behind me. Based on the shrieks I hear above me, I may have hit someone's feet. Blackness coats my vision, and it takes me a few seconds to realize that I'm hyperventilating again.

Someone pats my shoulders and helps me to uncurl myself from my hunched over position.

The mysterious hands spin me back toward the corpse that Pandarus stands over. He grips the spear shaft and yanks the weapon out of the body. Bile rises to my throat again. Dizziness overtakes me, and two people in my periphery steady me until the earth stops shaking.

Pandarus lifts the spear. Firelight gleams off the metal. Dark liquid spatters the sharpened tip.

"Does anyone else wish to challenge my honor?" Pandarus glares at Homer, who sinks so far into his shoulders, I swear he'll concave in on himself like a black hole in space.

No one answers him. Screeches of bats in the trees fill the silence.

"Good." Pandarus tosses his spear onto the ground. The metal clatters with a dull ding, but it sends my ears ringing again. "No more stories for tonight." He storms inside the house and shuts the double doors behind him with a bang.

Chapter Thirteen
How the Eagle Cries Woe

Fall Semester, Senior Year
Extra Credit Field Trip to an Art Museum

"AN ARTIST HELPS US TO SEE the world as it was, as it is, and as it can be."

The leader of the extra credit trip, Ms. Ramos, has gathered us in the atrium of the art museum. High-lofted white ceilings make the room feel gigantic. Huddles of children in neon-green vests and women carrying notepads filter past us toward the hallways that lead to the various exhibits.

I can't help but drown in the memories of the British Museum, where I first found Homer. He understood that I needed to forfeit the video call today to make a long trip here. Anything for a little grade boost.

Placed near the back of the cluster, I whip out of my phone and scroll through the email I got last night, the one that solidified me messaging Ms. Ramos on Instagram, asking if she had any spots left on the bus that would leave at seven a.m. this Saturday morning. Then I find another message.

For the first time ever, someone from a college had sent me something other than a form rejection.

Dear Harper,

Finding your application in my inbox, I cannot help but remember a version of myself who roamed the high school hallways (I wish I could say it was several years ago, but let's be honest, I'd rather not count how many years it's actually been).

I love your passion, your drive, and your heart for the humanities.

There's a lot of grit and determination found in your voice, and I can tell, based on your essay, that you've had to climb a long way to get here.

Unfortunately, the average GPA of our incoming freshmen is 3.5. Seeing that your transcript and SAT scores aren't where we'd need them to be, I'm afraid this may not be the email you were hoping to find in your inbox. I will not be able to offer you an acceptance to Rodos State University at this time.

However, seeing that you'd mentioned you are currently living in a single-parent household, and that your household income is well below that of many of our incoming students, I would love to offer you the opportunity to re-apply in the next open period in January.

If you manage to pull your GPA up for the rest of the fall semester and get involved in at least one extracurricular activity or major school event (especially one that relates to the field you want to go into), I may be able to pull some strings on my end. I'll go ahead and wave the application fee. Go ahead and hit reply to this message if you do wish to apply again, and I'll send along a code to bypass the fee.

Thank you once again for applying to Rodos, and I look forward to hearing from you soon!

Regards,

Bella Demos, Director of Admissions

Ms. Ramos had offered the field trip as an opportunity to take a look at an exhibit that featured some paintings by an alum from our high school. Anyone who attended could get ten bonus points for the class of their choice. Those ten bad boys would go right toward my D in Calc.

We rode a bus that stunk of mildew all the way to the museum. Juliana, being the only person I knew on the vehicle, shared a seat with me. We got off the bus and huddled together in the atrium of the museum, to listen to Ramos's instructions for the field trip.

"For your extra credit assignment." Ramos lifts her brows at me, pulling me back to the present. My pulse quickens, and I shove the phone into my jeans pocket. "I would like you to find one painting that speaks to you. Take a picture and write a five-hundred-word essay on why this artist shows you the world as we know it now, and the world as it could be. And please." Her burning gaze swivels to another boy who tries to hide his phone behind a friend's backpack. "Visit Nita Adams's gallery on the second floor. Not many schools can say they have alumni who have their works in a state art museum."

Before Ramos can even finish her sentence, the crowd has dissolved.

The boy with the phone heads toward a sculpture garden near the lobby of the museum. Mom and I have visited this place so many summers, I could list all the permanent exhibits by memory. Although I could fudge the assignment and simply snap a selfie by an East Asian statue, like I see one girl doing now, something tells me I should check out the Nita Adams paintings.

Maybe those could get a spark igniting in my chest.

I haven't touched my sketchbook in months. Every time I pick up my charcoal pencil, I get another rejection email from a college, or another C on an art assignment, and all the inspiration drains out of me.

Perhaps seeing the work of a girl who walked the same hallways as me can help me rekindle that.

We ride an escalator to the second floor. I watch my classmates duck into a gift shop and promise myself to buy Mom one of those handmade bowls stationed behind glass windows. She always gazes at them so wistfully whenever we visit here.

Juliana charges into a room with a sign out front marked, "Temporary Exhibition: Then and Now." A security guard paces the hallways with his walkie-talkie garbling something I can't catch.

I follow Juliana into the room and stop short when I spot the first painting. In it, King Henry VIII wears a hoodie and sweatpants. A falcon sits on his forearm. In his other hand, he grips a tennis racket, and a sweatband clamps onto his forehead.

Wait, did I get that right? Or does his face just look like the same painting I saw in England all those years ago of the infamous monarch?

A laminated placard on a stand beneath the painting reads,

COPPERNOSE, Nita Adams, 2018
Oil on Canvas, 20" X 24"

Based on portraits of King Henry VIII, Adams has reimagined what the monarch would look like in the 21st century. Henry VIII was known for a variety of hobbies from falconry to playing tennis (and, of course, marrying, killing, and divorcing women).

Six rings adorn his ring finger on his falconry glove.

Huh, sure enough. My gaze roams the room and I spot famous leaders from George Washington to Cleopatra in leggings and Nikes.

I backtrack to the entrance and read the description, explaining the exhibition.

THEN AND NOW

These portraits of famous leaders, created in the years 2016-2018, take famous paintings of leaders and reimagine what they would look like as their modern counterparts. The artist, Nita Adams, hopes that people will be able to see how no matter how many years divide us, we really aren't all that different from those who came before us.

Now Ramos's assignment makes more sense. She hoped we'd come here and learn about how art's language transcended cultures and time itself. *"An artist helps us to see the world as it was, as it is, and as it can be."*

Juliana's wedges stomp in front of a portrait of a woman with dark hair and beautiful chestnut skin in a crop top. Similar to the one Juliana wears now.

An ember ignites in my chest. By instinct, I pull out my camera and raise the viewfinder to my eye and zoom in on her glancing at the painting like she's stationed herself in front of a mirror.

My finger clicks the shutter.

The flash makes her flinch. She clasps her necklace and furrows her brows at me.

"Sorry." I lower the camera and click on the image review button. "Had to take the picture. You look just like her."

She sidles beside me and glances down at the photo. A gasp fills her. "Harper. It's beautiful."

"Really?" Doubt pools into my gut. "Because the lighting in here is awful. See those shadows by your ankles? I'm not sure if there's a glare on the portrait."

Juliana shakes her head again and rubs her thumb against the pendant that hangs from her neck. "You made me see"—she searches the tall ceilings for the word—"differently. Therefore, it's art."

For the first time in a long time, I am an artist again.

Palikari, 800 BCE

I awake, panting and clutching my blankets to my chest.

Itchiness fills my throat, and I realize moments later I must've screamed, because Talith and Brisei both sit on my bed. They clasp my shoulders with one hand and rub their eyes with the other.

"Bad dream?" Talith asks.

Words don't trip out of my mouth at first. Then, all at once, "I cannot do this." Tears prick my eyelids as I blink away flashes of what took place in the courtyard hours ago. I. Watched a man. Die.

Although I did, yes, witness Homer drowning Henry two years ago, I never had to see him gasping for breath or see the life vanish from his eyes when his body went slack. Never had to prod the corpse in the tub after Laran confirmed he'd died. I never *saw*.

Until tonight.

"Do what, my lady?"

"This." I gesture at nothing, causing Talith and Brisei to lift their touch from me. "All of this."

Gods or demons or magic or whatever divine intervention that opened up a wormhole sent the wrong girl. If I slip up or Homer does, will Pandarus drive a spear into us? Or worse, will I let him make more advances to prevent either of our deaths from happening?

Something claws at my hair. I realize that Talith has reached forward to massage my scalp. "Brave."

"Indeed." Brisei nods and lifts herself from the bed. She almost bumps the apple on the windowsill with her elbow. "Brave."

I didn't know what to do with the apple, so I just left it there. Brisei still hasn't had a chance to explain to me what it means. At least we can cling to the hope that he didn't propose to me.

"No." My eyelids squeeze shut to stop the tears from escaping. "I am not brave. Someone chose the wrong girl for the wrong place. I am not…" Shoot, what's the Palikarian word? "I am not *equipped* for any of this."

They didn't exactly run us through how to survive ancient civilizations in school when we learned about the mitochondria and its function in the cell.

Neither of them speaks for a while. Brisei's thin hand returns to my shoulder.

"Perhaps, my lady, you should consider that the gods chose the right woman for the right time, such as this." Her tongue clicks. "After all, what is a hero without his doubts? Certainly not someone worth telling stories about."

Minutes pass before they return to the mats. I draw my blankets up to my nose and let Brisei's words run in my mind over and over again, until everything fades to black.

"Fair-cheeked Harper, you will walk with me."

Glad to see Pandarus is giving me a choice when I stumble into him in the courtyard this morning.

He motions to the dirt road behind him. "To the beach. The ships for the army leave within the hour. My family awaits me there to wish me farewell."

Oh, thank you, God, he's going back to the battlefront.

I rub the heel of my hand against my eyes. Not a clue how long I slept in, but well enough into the morning that the sun doesn't glow orange like it usually does when I wake. Instead, the bright yellow bulb sits in a cloudless sky.

"Very well." Because what else can I say to a man I saw murder a drunk guy last night? Talith and Brisei shadow behind me, and I envision them as eagles, guarding me in their wings.

We head off on the road, kicking up dust in our sandals. I keep my eyes pressed to the path in front of me.

His voice pricks my ears a few steps into the journey. "It is a shame that your family has perished at the hands of the Greeks. For when I return for leave again, I should have liked to have given them many gifts of livestock and racehorses and talents of fine metal."

Wow, way to be all like, "Man, girl, your family is dead. So no Christmas gifts for them this year."

A forced grin shoves up my cheeks. "Your family has already been so hospitable. I would not dream of it."

One note of a laugh bounces off his throat, in a, "haha-you're-hilarious," sort of way. Did he think I joked about something? Or did he mean something else by, "hey girl, I wanna give you some pigs"?

I switch the subject and ask him to tell me stories about the warfront. He obliges and I tune out every other word except "spear" and "stab" and "many spoils."

Roars from the waves capture my ears while we're knee-deep in a story about a duel against a Greek with a plumed helmet Pandarus really wanted to steal. Something about the clap of water against the shore soothes me.

Sand burns my toes as we approach the beach. A cluster of soldiers and their families wait by the black ships docked at shore.

Homer stands near Elin, keeping a healthy few yards between them.

In my periphery, I spot a rowboat bob up and down. I turn my gaze to the left and see the soothsayer tug at some nets he has hanging off the side of his boat.

Shrieks pierce the air. I clap my hands to my ears and trace the noise to the sky. Two golden eagles wrestle in mid-air. They tangle their claws together and plunge headfirst into the ocean.

Another clap of water follows. A soothsayer has fallen out of his boat. He breaks the surface and wipes the water out of his eyes. His arm shakes when he motions to where the birds flew moments before, drenched beard trembling.

"What does that mean?" I ask no one in particular.

Ants crawl up my skin when I remember that Pandarus stands next to me. His skin has gone pale. But he faces me and forces a smile. I can tell it's not genuine. His lips don't stretch as wide as they often do.

"It is not right for a woman to be fearful on such matters. The eagles mean nothing."

Got it. It means something terrible, then.

He clasps one of my hands in both of his. "Now, fair-cheeked Harper, I must take my leave." I glance behind me and wriggle my fingers out of his grip. Sure enough, men in armor trudge up to the large ships. Could be my imagination, but I swear one of them has lost the red paint on the bow. Scorch marks from what looks like fire have turned it black.

"Promise you will not forget me, dear Harper."

My nose wrinkles. *I promise to purge you as best I can from my memory.* "Of course." To my vow, not his.

He jerks his chin toward the ships and bounds off toward them. After his mother pulls him into a tight embrace, he joins the queue of soldiers. I amble my way toward the group and keep enough space between myself and Homer.

All of us watch the ships fade into the horizon. The farther they disappear into the indigo waters, the more my chest fills with helium. I may float away if someone doesn't attach weights to my ankles soon.

People filter off the beach, but I don't move from my spot. In my periphery, Homer does the same. A grin slices up my cheek. Great minds.

So while people leave, I watch the place where the eagles dive-bombed. Did either one make it out? I'd gotten distracted by the soothsayer, so I have no idea what happened.

At last, I feel Elin's shadow that hovers behind me flee.

Salty sea air fills my nostrils in the largest inhale I've taken since we've arrived in Palikari. All tension releases from my insides. I whirl around to check and make sure that everyone but me, Homie, Brisei, and Talith have disappeared from the beach.

Indeed, Brisei and Talith draw letters in the sand. First Talith goes, then Brisei copies with a similar form, but looking more like the alphabet I know.

Homer and I lock gazes and light explodes within me.

He races to me and wraps his arms around me. We whirl around in circles until I want to drop into the sand from dizziness. I break apart first and check over my shoulder again, remembering what Brisei said about rumors.

Meanwhile, Homer tosses up sand like confetti. Grains take flight on the wind and disappear down the stretch of beach.

"I thought he'd never leave." I grip my sides and steady myself. Electricity fills me.

Homer's features harden. He drops his next handful of sand and wipes off his palms on his tunic. "Well, we're not safe yet. He may come back soon."

"Why? Don't they need more soldiers at the front?"

He points at the sky where the eagles fought. "In Palikarian culture, that's a bad omen. It means that the fight's coming to us soon. You saw how the soothsayer fell into the water when he spotted the birds."

Do omens have any weight here? At the assembly, when the eagle gripped the snake, they said it meant the complete opposite, that Palikari would take over more Greek territory.

But these people don't have the benefit of a history lesson like we received from Uncle Laran.

The dead man floating in the river indicated the Greeks will come soon. When they do, Palikari will vanish without so much as a shriek.

"So what do we do?"

Homer examines the grains left on his palm and flicks them off with his index finger. "We make sure we're not here when he gets back."

When I get back to the house, I drop Pandarus's apple from my window. It lands on the stone courtyard with a satisfying crack.

Chapter Fourteen
How the Heart-Seal Wards away Death

"Kill me like you mean it."

Thunder claps outside the cave as Brisei jabs her stick at Homer's ankles. He jumps back and shields his calves with the makeshift shield he created out of a large chunk of bark he found in the forest outside.

Rain spits on Talith and me as we watch the fake fight between the two.

Brisei growls and aims her "spear" at Homer's belly. He averts the stab in time but slams himself against the back wall of the cave.

"Good, sir." Brisei thrusts her weapon down and slaps her thighs. She lets out a groan in case anyone questioned her exasperation. "Your fighting strategy cannot be running away every time someone throws a weapon at you."

"But I am very good at running." Homer winks at me.

During one of our calls, he described how he and his fellow slaves would practice sprinting loops around the temple in their down time. They'd give away extra slices of bread to the winners of races. Homer said those were the only days he didn't operate on an empty stomach, as he passed the "finish line" far before the others did.

"Running yourself into corners, yes." Brisei kicks her stick and slumps to the ground, panting. "What would have happened if Pandarus backed you into the courtyard walls and aimed one more thrust at your belly?"

The smile slips from Homer's face. He hunches his neck.

With a grunt, Brisei rises and grabs her fake spear. "Again."

She lunges first, this time at his side. Homer barely has enough time to pick up his shield and jerk away. Her spear grazes his ribcage.

Now he takes a turn smacking his legs. It must be an ancient body language gesture. He throws down his stick and seeks shelter near Talith and me. Brisei gets the hint that he wants to take a break and sets her spear against the cave wall.

"What I do not understand"—he shields his side with his palm—"is why Pandarus would fight someone he is hosting. Sure, he has threatened me. But it goes against Palikarian hospitality. Guests do not fight their hosts, and likewise, neither do the hosts kill their guests."

Raindrops thrum against the cave wall. The storm hasn't awoken the sleeping bats.

Brisei growls. "Pandarus cares not for the ways of his people. If he desires something, he will have it."

I see the jaw clench through her cheek and wonder what pain lies behind those misty eyes.

She never mentioned how her husband died, exactly. But she has described to me what took place in her tribe in Greece before Palikari ransacked all the buildings. The army had gotten cloistered in the city, driven back from the battlefield.

She watched her husband die.

Because Pandarus took her as a war prize, does that mean she witnessed him spearing her husband? He made a big deal bragging about all his war prizes at meals before he left for the battlefront again.

If so, no wonder Brisei wanted Homer to get ready in case Pandarus challenges him to a duel. She doesn't want to watch someone else die at his hands.

"Let us hope we have left this village before he returns, then." Homer's knees crack when he sits beside me and Talith. His fingers, warm from wood-burns from the stick, grip mine.

I shiver because of the rain and lean into him. Coldness sticks to our clothing, and I miss the dry Arizona heat and sun.

"Speaking of leaving." My head hits his shoulder, and I relax. "When are we going to head to the town where the magician is?"

"Tomorrow."

Everyone springs up when Homer says this, even Talith.

He shrugs. "I would have chosen today, but there is a wedding in town. Because families are coming in from various tribes, they have increased the number of guards in the city."

Weddings, from what I understand from Brisei describing them, take place over the course of a few days in Palikari and Greece. But the actual wedding only happened on the last one, meaning, today. Everything else beforehand mimicked a bachelorette party—girls hanging out, eating food, and getting ready for that special honeymoon time.

"Not to mention," Homer whispers to me in English, "it's probably good to allow one more day, without arousing Elin's suspicion. She has been overworking the girls."

Elin, apparently annoyed I had stayed at the beach far too long yesterday with Talith and Brisei—and Homer—made Brisei spend the whole night cleaning dishes she claimed the other servants hadn't scrubbed hard enough after the party.

For good measure, she made Brisei scour the oven with yellow sponges until she turned several black.

By the time Brisei got her mat outside my room, she collapsed. Her head never even reached her straw pillow.

Even now she rubs the dark circles underneath her eyes. It

concerns me that she managed to stab Homer multiple times in their practice fights. If a girl with heavy exhaustion could get him, what could stop a battle-hardened man from spearing Homer in the gut as soon as their duel started?

I shudder and brush away the images of the story-stitcher from the night of the party.

"Homie. I think it may be good to keep practicing. What if he follows us into the next town over?"

He cocks his head. He switches to English. "Into a city of refuge? People can't do that. Even if I killed Pandarus's father before him, by accident, if we flee into a city of refuge, he can't touch us there."

My jaw sinks to protest that Brisei *just* mentioned how Pandarus doesn't care about laws, but Brisei's voice interrupts mine.

"Palikarian, please."

Heat crawls into my cheeks. Homer and I *have* been talking in English a lot.

"Sorry," we both mutter in Palikarian.

Brisei draws her knees up to her chin when she sits. Talith beside her hums a tune. We listen to the sorrowful notes echo off the cave wall. When she finishes, she unfolds a cloth of foods I stole from last night's meal—cheese and some bread covered in barley seeds.

Nutty flavor fills my tongue when I bite into the bread. I swallow. "Talith and Brisei, we would like for you to come with us when we leave tomorrow, if that is all right with you."

Maybe Pandarus will freak when he gets back and finds out we left. But Elin? Something tells me she won't pursue us into a city of refuge, even if I take some of her girls.

When Homer appeared in the British Museum, we didn't

give him much of a choice. Security guards had chased after him, and with the language barrier, I couldn't explain why I dragged him back to my uncle's apartment.

Although he later said he wanted to go anywhere I went, guilt gnaws at me anytime those memories appear. Did I truly give Homer an option that day when I brought him to Uncle Laran?

Elin and Pandarus dragged these girls from their homes. If they were to move again, I want to make sure they choose that path.

I study Brisei's face to watch her reaction. She keeps her gaze pressed to the cave floor, where a spider scuttles past. No doubt the insect got annoyed that the rainstorm destroyed her web she wove at the front.

Brisei's shoulders lower and mist appears in her waterline. "I would gladly travel all the way onto the battlefield for you."

When the rain settles, we decide to make our way back to the house before Elin misses us too much and gives Brisei more side projects. Giddiness fills Talith's and Brisei's steps, and Talith sings the whole way down the hill.

Brisei attempts to explain to her about how we will depart. Her eyes light up after the third or fourth description.

"Yes. Yes, yes, yes, yes, yes." She claps her hands.

All righty, I guess she understands.

Talith and Brisei clasp their hands against their shoulders as they dodge around puddles left behind on the dirt path. I can only imagine their thoughts now. Probably fantasizing about what life will look like when they can sleep in, not have to watch people eat lavish meals in front of them while their stomachs burn within them, and finally get a day off work.

Water droplets drip on me from above from a scented cypress. Everything smells like fresh rain and greenery. Mist clouds the sides of the path. A creek bubbles over rocks beneath the cliffs. I can allow myself to drown in the sound of the water rushing until my thoughts float to the top of my head.

A horrible realization overtakes me when we reach the bottom of the hill that leads to the cave. "Homer, where are we going to stay?"

"Cities of refuge are built to house people coming in from other tribes. If we act like we have fled a warzone, someone will provide. Whether it be their own house or a house marked for refugees."

I clutch the amber beads strung around my neck and force myself to relax.

If a woman like Elin can provide her home to you, someone else might too.

"Besides." Homer grins. "I hear Elin's daughter lives in the village. Maybe we can get her to let us stay in her house for a little while."

I snigger. Yeah right, like Elin will let that happen. Besides, I think that daughter gave birth recently. I ain't the love-to-listen-to-screaming-infants type.

We pass by the downtown shops, and I don't spot Cersei at the potter's wheel. Strange, we haven't even reached the time when people take their mid-afternoon meal. Maybe she took hers early.

Something about the black paint etched on the red clay jars fills me with longing. Could we take Cersei with us too? Maybe she'd want to see the magician.

I shake my head. Best keep our numbers low. Who knows what we'll encounter on our journey out of here?

After I take a breather from the uphill climb near a field full of corn, we trek toward the houses. Mid-way, I spy the silhouette of Cersei at her gate. When we get close enough, she bobs up and down and waves us inside the gates.

No guardsman sits outside. Not that a house of this size would allow for that. It's single level with maybe three rooms.

We step into the courtyard and Cersei jerks her chin at the door to the house. "My sister is inside."

"Oh?" Nice? "We would love to meet her."

"She is taking a bath."

"Oh." Maybe later, then.

Cersei giggles and grabs my hand. She drags me toward some footstools someone has set up outside. We park on them. "She is taking the bath of purity. Today is her wedding day."

My eyebrows furrow and recede when the realization hits me. Cersei's sister is the one having the wedding. Cersei describes to me the events of the past two days and how her sister, Ecu, presented her girdle and many offerings to the goddess of love. They had to trek to another village to do so, since this one has the house of the god of death.

Not exactly the guy you'd want to ring up for prenuptials.

Relatives and friends of the sister—at least, I assume—crowd the courtyard. Many share Cersei's sharp jawline. I give up my seat to an older woman who wobbles on a wooden cane.

"After the bath, you will see her in her beautiful gown." Stars sparkle in Cersei's pupils.

"You must be very excited for her."

"She ought to be," the old woman interjects, her voice quivering as much as her legs. "Her wedding will take place in three years or so." She gestures at Cersei.

Cersei, now standing because another elderly relative took

her footstool, hunches into herself. She reminds me of when Mom sprays a bug in our house with insect killer. Curling into their shells, gasping for breath.

All the light has died from her eyes.

I motion with my chin for her to follow me where we can get a bubble of space away from earshot.

"You look sad, Cersei."

Her barefoot toes trace a Phoenician A into the sand. So she *did* pay attention to Talith's drawings outside her shop. Speaking of, Talith and the others stand at the other end of the courtyard, engaged in conversation with a rotund, balding man. He uses large arm gestures and laughs a lot.

"I do not like to think about what will take place in three years."

"You are not excited to get married." It's not a question. The girl can't push twelve years old. At her age, I couldn't even get the word bouquet right on a spelling test. Insane how someone so young would have to dive into something so big.

She doesn't answer. Instead, she races into the house. Did I scare her away?

If I did, no wonder. I remember when I shot my cousin's wedding last summer. Homer asked if my mom could film the whole thing on her phone. He watched the live stream and talked with me about how much the couple looked like they loved each other when they said their vows.

"Well, of course they love each other." I'd wrinkled my nose. "Well, at least her husband loves her. She seems to be really interested in the number of zeros in his paycheck." I frowned. "Do people in Palikari not love each other when they get married?"

"It's…" He sighed. "Rare. Not unheard of, but very, very rare. Most girls are fifteen or sixteen when they get married. Their husbands, thirty."

Cersei emerges from the front door a few seconds later with a jar in her hands. She shoves it into my arms and beams at me.

"I meant to give you this the other day."

My fingers trace the dolphin.

"Grandmother." She jerks her chin at the old woman on the stool. "She says that some of my paintings are 'too busy.' I may have gotten carried away after I heard some of the soldier's stories. But many of the traders were interested in my jars."

"Traders?"

"As long as they are not from Greece, we sell to them."

A lot of different ships do dock at the beach. Although Uncle Laran told me the trade routes between countries had closed off during the Greek Dark Ages, maybe they'd opened again by 800 BCE.

"Cersei, you are very talented. What if you made art for the rest of your life?"

She bounces up and down at the idea. Then she slows to a halt, slumps again. "That does sound like a lovely dream from which you would never want to wake up."

"Perhaps when the magician returns, you could spend more years learning from him. Maybe postpone the wedding for a while?" Until, I don't know, you reach the legal age or something crazy like that.

"Perhaps. If he is ever to return."

I make a mental note to track down the magician the minute we get to Elin's daughter's town.

The front door to the house creaks open again. A woman in a silvery dress emerges, and the crowd gasps. Cersei's sister. The gown doesn't fit her right. Fabric sags in the chest area, and her skinny arms drown in the sleeves.

Something tells me she borrowed this dress from a family member.

A metal crown in the shape of laurel leaves gleams on her head. Only a little rust tarnishes some of the edges. Women surround her and place colorful flowers around the circlet. I can't tell if she seems happy, nervous, or what. Her expression gives no indication of an emotion. Really, she looks like Brisei when Elin has given her yet another chore to do.

Cersei bounces and muffles a squeal. "She looks like a goddess." She reaches for my hand and squeezes. "I have not seen her this happy since her betrothed handed her an apple."

Huh, so she must have a permanent stoic expression. Maybe this will be one of the rare times where the bride loves her husband in Palikari.

Wait a second…

"Apple?" I thought Brisei said that an apple doesn't mean that a guy proposed. "Cersei, what does it mean when a man gives an apple to a woman?"

She doesn't hear or answer. Instead, she watches a woman with a silver streak in her hair lift a tripod. The woman lifts a prayer to the skies, and once she finishes, she ventures into the house.

"That is my mother." Cersei brushes a mosquito off her shoulder. "She is lighting the tripod with the fire of our hearth. Then the procession must begin."

Cersei's mom returns to the courtyard.

We all follow her to the dirt streets. A wagon, like the one that towed our laundry, awaits the bride. She steps onto the platform, and the donkey sallies forth. The rest of us walk up the road until we reach a house that has cornices that run along the wall.

The farther up the hill we go, the richer people must get.

A woman in a bright-colored garment with golden stitching approaches Cersei's mother. Beside her stands a man who wears a golden circlet. The soon-to-be husband, I assume, based on how his cheeks light on fire when he spots the bride.

"That is the mother-in-law," Cersei whispers to me. "She will take the fire from our hearth and give it to her son to light the hearth in their home."

The mother-in-law dips her unlit tripod onto the other one. It ignites. She hands the torch off to her son while women help the bride off the wagon. Ecu approaches the man. He snatches her wrist.

Eager much? No one else in the crowd flinches at the aggressive gesture. Must be a Palikarian tradition.

I try to think of some American wedding traditions that might turn a Palikarian head. The tossing of the garter, the smashing of wedding cake into each other's faces. Yeah…I could see quite a few of our own wedding practices quirking a brow.

We follow the bride and groom into the house. At least, those of us who can. The crowd blocks the door and spills into the courtyard as the bride and groom walk a few circles in the hearth room before they tip the tripod onto the hearth. Firelight explodes around the room in warm beams.

Sweat brims on my lip. Cersei bends down to grab a handful of something red in a basket by her legs. The rest of the crowd follows and pelts the little bullets at the couple.

What in the—

Cersei shows me her palm. "Pomegranate seeds." She aims her arm back, softball-pitching style, and wallops the groom in the soldier. Seeds explode everywhere like fireworks.

Before I can process what in the world is happening, the crowd rushes back outside and creates a bubble for the bride and groom. A baby's cry pierces the air. In my periphery, at the courtyard gate, I watch a body slump to its knees.

I turn on my heel. A hush has fallen over the crowd as we witness a woman with a child pressed to her chest unhinge her jaw. She looks like she's screaming, but no noise comes out.

"Elin's daughter," someone behind me says, and rushes forward to help the girl to her feet.

Another woman offers to hold the baby for her, but Elin's daughter's knuckles whiten on her grip on the child. "No."

"My dear." The woman who offered to help backs away a few steps. "What has happened? Why have you journeyed from your village to ours, with such a young child?"

Tears scar the daughter's face. Blotches mar her cheeks, the way they do mine when I've held in a good cry for far too long.

"The city"—her voice comes out scratchy, raw—"has been overtaken by Greeks."

I hold my breath until my lungs burn. The city we planned to visit tomorrow is overtaken.

"They took us by surprise. I know of no one else who was able to flee. Fortune had me on the city's border when I heard them attacking. So I fled."

Any hope of the magician still being alive shatters like my apple did against the courtyard stone.

She sinks to her knees again. This time, we hear her cry.

Chapter Fifteen
How Flight Perishes for the Shepherds

ELIN'S DAUGHTER PASSES OUT AS SOON as she gets to her bed.

She bleeds on the blankets. Apparently, during the birth, she split open, so a local town nurse had to administer stitches. But those came undone when she ran from her village to ours.

Elin sends me and Brisei out to get the nurse. We return with him, and he has us wait in the hearth room while he closes the wounds. Elin refused to leave her side.

Talith holds the baby and rocks him in her arms.

His little fingers tear my heart in two. No, I don't plan on having kids anytime soon. But the fragility of him, the weakness of his cries, causes itchiness to form behind my eyes.

"She is fortunate to have given birth to such a healthy boy," one of the women comments. The other females nod.

No kidding.

My mom got pregnant when I was younger.

One month later, she lost the baby.

I don't remember anyone doing much for her as she spent the next several weeks in bed, barely blinking at the TV. Once a lady from church stopped by with a casserole when she heard the news. The thing tasted like green beans and not much else. The women at that church didn't believe in spices or therapists.

She'd clapped my mother's shoulder in her bedroom. "It's better that your little baby didn't have to experience life in this cruel world. Isn't it an encouragement that he or she is in heaven now with Jesus?"

That caused my mom to stay in bed for another several weeks.

This caused my dad to start drinking.

He never stopped.

The woman who commented moments before runs upstairs with a cooling cloth. Although I wouldn't have chosen to stay in Palikari, the twenty-first century could take some pointers from this world.

How the women gather around Elin's daughter, squeeze her hand, press a cold cloth to her forehead, sing soothing tunes to her. We're lucky back home to get someone to sign our casts.

I also love the slower rhythm of life here. In this place, no one worries about missing assignments or SAT scores. Images of my cousin working three jobs before she met her husband flicker across my vision.

She would stumble into family gatherings with huge bags under her eyes and went straight to the couch where she'd pass out. Her hair began turning gray before she reached the age of twenty-five.

Soft footsteps descend the stairs behind us. Wrinkles burrow deep into Elin's forehead. "She is in and out of fitful bouts of sleep."

Elin's chin jerks to Talith, who has her finger buried in the baby's palm.

Light fills Talith's cheeks and smile. I tap her knee and motion to Elin. She spots her at the stairs, deflates, and rises from her seat. Brisei and I follow behind her to the daughter's room, mine just the night before.

The moment the door creaks, the daughter doubles over with a gasp. Her wide eyes reduce to slits and her face scrunches from the pain. She must feel the stitches now.

The nurse cleans off a wooden needle on a cloth. He nods once to Elin and exits the room.

Elin pries the child out of Talith's hands and places him on the bed beside his mother. Panic seizes my chest. What if she falls asleep and rolls onto her child? I wonder if that happened a lot before they invented cribs.

"Cylla." The daughter gasps, and blood drains from her cheeks. "Cylla."

"She is not here." Elin's voice comes out stern, like she has to scold a child.

The daughter blinks a glaze out of her eyes once, twice. Her head claps the pillow, and she goes out like a light.

"Cylla was a neighbor in her village." Elin appears to read my expression. "My daughter worries now if she made it out of the town alive. She awakes every few minutes and says a different name."

Needles pound against my temple.

I might have to do the same. Leave this town as soon as the Greeks invade, without being able to take anyone else with me. They might arrive when I find myself alone in the woods, or on the border without Homer.

Elin motions for us to follow her out into the hallway.

Once more I check over my shoulder to make sure the daughter doesn't roll over, onto the baby. A few inches of space separate the two.

I step into the hallway and shut the door behind me.

"We have another room in which you can stay." Elin's skirts drag up the next set of steps.

Although I never asked, I got the idea that Elin had a few daughters and one son. The son being the most important, of course, because he'll take Ulix's place as shepherd-of-the-people when Ulix retires or…dies. Brisei told me about the daughter who lived a town over—now with us—and one who married a man a few houses down. Elin often leaves the house to pay that one a visit.

But a third daughter…Elin never mentioned her. Maybe she moved across tribes.

We pace into the new room. Dust covers everything. If you made a candle of the place, you'd name the scent "Old & Forgotten."

When Elin notices the blanketing of dirt on the trunk by the bed, she calls in one of the females to wipe everything down. Five minutes later, the woman with the sponge leaves the room, and Elin flees to the doorway, as though she spotted a poltergeist near the windowsill.

A painting of a man slaying a serpent with a sword shows in weak beams of sunlight.

"I hope you will find this room adequate." Elin chokes on the words and sweeps herself back into the hallway.

The door to the room bangs shut.

She acted strange. I sit on the bed and cough as dust motes fill the air. After making a mental note to take all the blankets outside and give them a good flap, I rise and park on the trunk instead. "Brisei, you never told me about the daughter who stayed in this room."

Brisei clasps her elbows. She draws in a deep breath. "She was married two years ago. Gave birth last summer." Her eyelids shut. "Neither she nor the baby made it."

I wait until Elin has retired to her room to rest before I take the blankets down to the courtyard. Animal fur bristles tickle my arms all the way down to the bottom of the steps.

Yeesh, we have many more stairs to climb up on our way back to our bedroom.

A strange darkness and silence has fallen over the household. By this time, we'd usually eat our mid-afternoon meal. But the servants brought bread and cheese to our rooms and retreated to the garden to eat the leftovers.

Bedspreads fall to the stone courtyard in a heap. I grip the first one, an animal who had a sleek dark pelt, and slap it against the ground. The blanket makes a heavy thwack when it claps the rock.

A figure in my periphery sits on the wall between the cornices. When I spy Homer's curls glittering in the sunlight, I drop everything and amble toward him.

As I heave myself up, I make sure I'm plenty of yards away from him. Don't want someone in the house to pop out and spread the word all the way to the battlefront.

I tug my knee to my chest. "Hey."

"Sup."

I grin at his horrible attempt at a full-on American accent. "Hey, can we talk about what happened with you and Brisei and the spears in the cave?"

Images of Greeks holding Homer at spearpoint have plagued me ever since the wedding earlier this morning.

"Look, babe." I sigh and watch a dove flutter past and disappear into a neighbor's tree. "I know you're good at running—"

After all, as soon as he got the chance in England, he fled Uncle Laran's apartment. I tried to chase after him but couldn't keep up. He followed the stars when he wanted to return to us.

The only time Homer couldn't run happened when the archeologist pinned his legs down in a tub. Then and only then did Homer take the offensive and drown the guy.

I shudder at the memory.

"—but you and I both know with the Greeks preparing to invade the remaining Palikarian villages, and with our duel-happy *friend* Pandarus returning soon, that you're gonna end up with a spear at your nose at one point. What are you going to do then?"

Homer's ankles bounce off the wall. He leans on his palms and sighs. A warm, sweet-scented breeze strokes our nostrils.

"I wish I could say that I'd twist the spear out of their hands and turn the weapon on them." His shoulders concave. "But if I've learned anything at the temple and at your uncle's flat, it's to run and hide."

My stomach burns and I hunch into myself.

Really, Harp, that's your fault. Two summers ago, we spent the whole time on the run from the archeologist. We never taught Homer self-defense, and that ended in his brief capture, until I rescued him.

It would be ridiculous for me to expect him to turn into this macho warrior who stands his ground.

"Homer, I—"

"Do my eyes deceive me?" One of the youths emerges from behind the gate across the street. A group of men surge behind him. "Or is this the frail man who could not keep the ball in the air? Are you certain that you come from a noble family?"

A guffaw travels around the group. Beside me sounds a thump. Homer has thrown himself off the wall and has placed several more yards of distance between himself and me. Not that the youths notice. They don't pass me a single glance.

"A fisherman cannot be expected to also be an excellent woodsman or woolworker." Homer brushes an insect off his shoulder.

The youth with a constellation of freckles on his nose cocks his head. "Are you saying you excel in one of the events of the funeral games? Can prove your nobility?"

Funeral games? I wipe away the mental image of people sitting around a coffin, playing a round of Scrabble.

"A footrace." Homer gestures at the dirt road. "To the bottom and back. See if you can keep up with me." A strange confidence overtakes his voice. Like it did when I encouraged him to tell stories the night of the spear incident.

In the corner of my eye, someone takes Homer's place on the wall. I glance over my shoulder and spot Brisei.

"Very well." The freckled dude ambles beside Homer and hunches forward in a running position. "Let us see what you can do."

He winks at another boy in the group who lifts his hand, then swings down his arm to smack his thigh. They bolt off, clouds of dust trailing behind them.

"Brisei, what are the funeral games?"

Homer and the other runner vanish down the hill.

"A group of athletic events after a burial. Winners receive prizes."

"Think Homer could win one of those?"

She purses her lips. "If the funeral happens in a tribe that is not your own, you are not allowed to compete. Otherwise, Atro would have won all the prizes at the last funeral to take place here."

"Atro is good at athletic events?"

Her cheeks grow darker, and she smiles into her chest. Huh, must've missed her crushing on the dude.

Panting sounds to my right and I spy Homer charging back up the hill. He zooms toward the original starting line, marked by the streaks left from their sandals. He shoots past the spot and whirls around, in time to spot the other runner crest over the hill.

Even though Homer grips his sides, his spine has

straightened more than I've ever seen before. "You have your proof."

Red fills the other boy's face. He hocks a loogie and motions for the others to follow him back into his fenced area. They all have slumped into their shoulders like tortoises.

Homer turns to me and beams, quirks a brow.

"All right, all right." I roll my eyes. "That's the one time where running away is actually helpful."

"For the last time, Homer, Brisei only packed us so much wine to get through the journey. Now stop guzzling it before you get drunk and lose the way to the next village." The only nearby village not taken over by the Greeks yet.

We left at dawn. Brisei informed the kitchen staff she'd need supplies for an early laundry run, to wash the sheets that had gotten blood on them in Elin's daughter's room.

Homer sets down the wine flask in the cart that holds the blankets, and we venture off. We hope that by not returning, the household will assume the worst and not come looking for us.

"Trust me, they won't," Homer told me in the garden when we formed the plan to leave. "Elin may be giving us hospitality, but that doesn't mean she likes us. She'll probably be glad that there are fewer mouths to feed."

Rocks skitter past our sandals as we climb uphill.

Homer claimed to know a way off-road to get to the next village, so we won't arouse any suspicion by not going in the direction of the river. This forced us to plow through forests and itchy plants that stung us with their nettles. Let's hope none of them contained any poison, because I don't know the ancient cure for fixing that.

"Fine." Homer staggers, and I have to hold him up.

"You've already had too much," I hiss in English. "Like communion that one time."

I make him walk to my left, so I trudge closest to the cliff's edges. Above us lies a path that will lead to the next village, as long as we finish our uphill ascent.

"When do you think we shall reach the village?" Brisei asks, and Talith behind us massages her calves. I don't know how much we've walked, but long enough to see the sun turn from salmon pink to a whitish yellow. The star hides behind a shield of dark clouds.

"Let us hope before a storm hits." I keep my gaze pressed to the wheel on the cart before me. Our donkey glistens with sweat.

We've piled a few other items in the wagon, including some gold I stole from the storerooms downstairs. A woman guards the door to the household treasures, but with the servants round the clock taking care of Elin's daughter, I managed to find a window of five minutes when she didn't station herself in front of the door.

Along with the gold, we've packed some bread, fruit from the garden, and spare blankets, ones without blood on them. We have no idea what awaits us in the new village, or if they even have places left over to stay with so many people seeking refuge.

"How about we pass the time by telling stories?" Homer trips on a stone, and I catch him. "I'll start."

He begins with another scene from *The Iliad*, this time when Achilles throws a tantrum when Agamemnon, the war general, steals his war captive from him. Brisei winces as Homer continues the story, probably too drunk to understand the impact of the words.

I elbow him in the side. "How about something original, Homie?"

He palms his ribs and then his lips wriggle up his cheek. Oh no, I know that look. I've brought out the prankster. "Very well."

He rotates around and ambles backward up the path. I watch his footsteps to make sure he won't faceplant. "Let us tell the tale of Harper and the fig."

I halt. "Don't you dare," I hiss in English.

"When Harper and I talked daily, she was unfamiliar with some of the Palikarian traditions. Her uncle realized this and decided that we should pull a trick on her."

"Homer." I can't help it, laughter crawls into my voice, along with fire into my cheeks.

"We informed her that it was a Palikarian tradition to mash a fig into your hair when you spoke the language of our people. And that everyone did this on a daily basis. Much like the Egyptians with the scented wax cones that melt in their wigs."

"Unibrows are in fashion here. How was I supposed to know mashing fig in your hair was not normal?"

"To help make it believable, I and her uncle also put figs in our hair whenever Harper and I spoke."

Brisei has doubled over from laughter. "D-did she f-fall for it?"

"She wore figs in her hair for a month before we told her."

Loud laughter follows Brisei as she collapses to her knees. She draws a tear out of her eye with her index finger.

I jab Homer in the ribs again. "By the way, if we ever get back, Mom says y'all owe her hundreds of dollars. Figs don't come cheap."

In the corner of my eye, something glints. I turn around just in time to see a spear sticking inches away from my nose. The man holding the weapon wears armor like Pandarus's. Ahead, two other soldiers surround the wagon, which I didn't hear draw to a stop. My heartbeat throbs in my temples, in my clenched fists, in my shaking legs.

Ever so carefully, I glance over my shoulder and see a

soldier has jumped down from the cliffs above us and landed behind Brisei and Talith. He holds Brisei at spearpoint.

"Take the girl." The soldier before me, speaking Greek, gestures at me. "Kill the others."

Instinct takes over, and I spreadeagle my arms to shield Homer. "You will do no such thing." The words come out like a guttural growl.

"Machaon?" Brisei's voice quivers behind me.

The man in front of me lowers his spear. His face softens, eyebrows shoot up. "Brisei?"

She must know him somehow. The softness in his voice indicates a friend, maybe something more.

"Promise me you will not harm them. They simply seek safe passage into the nearest village."

Machaon motions his men out of the wagon. "It has been overtaken just this last night. We have been instructed to wait on the paths that lead into the city."

Overtaken. The word hits me like a stone so heavy it may throw me off the cliff.

"You were never here." Machaon dips his chin once at Brisei and his men plod up the hill. I wait until they disappear. Wobbling takes over my legs, and I crumple to my knees to make sure I don't topple over.

"Homer, please tell me we have another Palikarian village we can go to."

He firms his jaw, rolls his fists. All drunkenness has disappeared from his voice. "Our village is the only city of refuge left in Palikari. We have nowhere else to flee before the Greeks invade."

Chapter Sixteen
How the Kings Fall

HOW TO KNOW YOU'RE PREPARING FOR your city to fall under siege:

1. Your city has heavily increased the number of guards stationed on the city walls, especially at night, when the Greeks like to pull a sneak-a-roo.

2. Everyone stays in their household and keeps an eye on their possessions.

3. Meals become less extravagant because you don't know how long you'll have until the Greeks starve you out before they break through the city gates.

4. The guards' dogs bark all night because people keep trying to sneak onto your property to steal away some of your cattle.

I rub the bags under my eyes as Brisei and I head into town on the dirt road. Elin sent us—well, Brisei—on an errand to see what shops still sell any wares. We have a wagon loaded with small chests full of gold to see if we can exchange them for anything edible.

"What I do not understand"—I adjust the veil that tugs on my head—"is that when Mycenae collapsed, everyone saw each other as equals and helped one another. Why is everyone trying to steal from one another now?"

Word spread like Greek fire when we returned from our excursion with unwashed blankets. Elin interrogated Brisei and got out of her about the Greeks invading the next town over.

Well, gossip's gotta gossip.

By evening, every household knew.

"Ah." Brisei lifts a brow. "Not before they spent decades hoarding, starving, and fleeing from their cities. It always takes people a while to think about other people."

This unlocks a memory from my middle school days when my history teacher filled our classroom with balloons, one having a name of someone in our class. Thank goodness he checked beforehand to make sure no one had a latex allergy.

For the first round, he told us to find the balloon with our own name.

A lot of shoving and clogging of people between the desks happened. Someone stepped on another person's balloon and popped it on their way to the world map where a balloon had their name.

"Okay." The teacher had us stop after two minutes and reinflated a new balloon to replace the one that got deflated. "This time, find a balloon with someone else's name on it. Hand it to them."

Within thirty seconds, everyone had found and given the balloons to their owners.

"See what happens when everyone helps everyone else?"

I frown and my toes curl at the sand heaping into my sandals. Sunlight burns my left shoulder, where Talith often stands. She stayed behind at the household to feed Elin's daughter's baby. Elin's daughter has withdrawn to her room and spends the days sleeping and staring at an empty patch of wall beside the painting.

"Brisei, I thought breast milk dried after a few days. Where did Talith get that supply?"

She waves away a buzzing fly near her ear. "Talith had a

child before they took her. When she arrived here, she still had a fresh supply. Elin has a neighbor who does not produce enough. So she lends Talith most days to go to her house for an hour to provide the extra."

Brisei knuckles her lip. Sweat has brimmed on mine too. I lick off the salty taste.

"The woman, thinking Elin charged too much, found a wetnurse about a week later. But Talith stops by whenever she can to offer free milk. I think she misses her child back home."

A pang burns my abdomen.

That's horrible. I want to kick myself for misinterpreting Talith's baby gestures as wanting a kid. She really meant that she wished she could return home to her own baby.

Talith did mention the word baby about ten times on our hike toward the other city, before the Greeks stopped us.

The Greeks. "Brisei, how did that man know you yesterday?"

She fiddles with the tattered hem on her dress. "A childhood friend. We would have perhaps been a good pairing if I had not been born into a higher social standing." She pauses. "He reminds me a lot of Atro. Kind, quiet, loyal."

Huh, I hadn't realized Brisei came from the upper class before she arrived here. But she did mention her father was shepherd of the people, so that would translate as upper class. What an awful transition that must've been from a princess to a slave.

It does add up, why someone would take her. Homer had told me, on our way back to the city yesterday, that foreign nations tended to capture the wealthiest from cities.

Before we even reach the shops, I can tell that no one mans any of the stations.

Dried herbs have disappeared from one stall. No fish hang from the soothsayer's shop on hooks. What good would gold do here? Not like we can bribe the Greek army to send us food rations as they wait to starve us out.

By habit, I step into Cersei's shop to inhale the scent of clay and creativity.

To my surprise, she sits at the potter's wheel and runs her hands up and down a vase in the making. Her chin jerks up at us. Tears stain rivers down her cheeks.

"Cersei." I clap a hand on her shoulder.

"It helps to comfort me." She nods at the potter's wheel. Beside it, I spy several un-kilned pots and vases, made just this morning.

I get that.

Often, I would turn to my sketchbook whenever assignment stress would send a pounding headache to my temples. Something about smudging charcoal lines with the heel of my palm soothed me more than any of my classmates' cures from essential oil diffusers to, well, other scented items with questionable legality.

"What is wrong?"

She lifts her hands from the wheel, and the vase reduces to a deformed lump. "Last night, someone stole the last of our goats. We will have no milk or cheese to help us survive when the Greeks put the city under siege."

Cersei rubs her eyes, smudging clay onto her cheeks.

"Mother says they used up too much food at the wedding. Had we known, we would have postponed the event."

I lift myself and glance at Brisei. "Elin has plenty of goats."

Whites show in her eyes. "Elin will never agree to that."

"Why not? Elin has plenty. Perhaps people would not keep

trying to steal from her if she would be willing to help others not to starve during the siege." I crane my neck back at Cersei, who re-forms the clay in her hands. "What if I convince Elin to bring you a goat?"

Cersei's arms wobble so much, the top part of the vase goes crooked. "I—is it possible?"

"It is worth trying." I roll my fist and charge toward the road.

"My lady." A growl sounds from Brisei's voice, then a pant, as she catches up to me. "It will not work. You will invoke her wrath."

"Every life is worth trying for."

Images flash through my mind of my mom slumping onto the couch after returning from a job interview with my aunt for a secretarial position. Although she had a job lined up in England, after Dad passed, we had a few bills we couldn't keep up with. She'd hoped for something in the meantime to tide us over.

She read me the texts after my aunt didn't show for their interview at a Panera tabletop.

Pamela: Hey, Liv, sorry that I couldn't show today. Boss had me working into my lunch hour. Anyway, I don't think I can convince them to hire you on temporarily. They're really looking for someone who can commit for several years.

Pamela: I know the pay is $14/hour, a lot less than what that tour company is offering you, and since it's part-time, there aren't many benefits, per se. But he's also looking for some younger blood. No offense, LOL.

Pamela: I don't want to cross him. With upcoming wedding expenses—she FINALLY picked a venue—I just can't risk anything. Sorry, sis.

Pamela: Anyway, I hope you're not too disappointed. I'm sure there are tons of jobs that you could work in the meantime. There's a Chipotle near me that's hiring.

Chipotle also didn't want Mom. They claimed she had no food experience. Again they wanted "younger blood."

For the next few months, we subsisted off of a lot of meals involving ramen, mac and cheese, and toaster pastries. Finally, Mom managed to snag a temporary position at a call center for a craft store, which managed to pay for our plane tickets so she could work in England two summers ago.

Every time I spotted Aunt Pamela at a family gathering after that, I wanted to smash her nose right into the marshmallow frosting cake she bought from the store. Twenty dollars that could've gone toward a meal for her sister.

We arrive at the house and rush inside.

Right as Elin smacks the ear of a servant who holds a bundle of green herbs. "Be careful with that. You are getting it all over the floor."

My fist rolls, arm shakes, and I take a lunging step forward.

Clicking sounds behind me. I glance at Brisei, who mouths, "No."

It takes everything within me not to pop Elin in the jaw. What I should've done all those years ago with Dad when he and Mom would get into arguments that ended, well, like this.

Elin spots me and rests her hand on her hip. "Any luck?"

I relax my shoulders, which have hiked up two inches.

"There was nothing available in the market. Everyone is seeming to prepare themselves for the worst."

She makes a hybrid noise between a hiss and a grunt. "Should expect nothing less from those of inferior birth. Hoarding and keeping to themselves."

Then she grips the shoulder of the girl she just smacked and shoves her toward the basement. A woman stands guard.

During our tour, weeks ago, Elin had indicated she had placed this woman in front of the storerooms only at night, when thieves loved to roam most. But with the number of attempts of people scaling our wall yesterday, she has someone posted there every hour.

"Speaking of the people in the market." I swallow. "Elin, there is a little girl whose family lost everything last night. I was wondering—"

The burn of her gaze presses into my forehead. Yikes, that look could brand you.

"—if we could lend them a goat until the siege ends."

She squints at me and then a single laugh escapes her lips. "Why should I care for her? I do not know her."

"Because…" Man alive, should've practiced this on my way over here. I can feel Brisei shrinking behind me. "Because often the gods disguise themselves as mortals, and in sharing with her, you may heap blessings upon yourself."

No idea where those words came from. Maybe they drifted to my brain from memories of our first night here, and probably the only reason Elin took pity on me and Homer. Because she figured some sort of karma would repay her for feeding us.

Elin's face slackens. She squints at me again. "Perhaps you are right." She lifts and drops her shoulders. "Did you know Ulix said something similar to me before he gave me an apple?"

Again, with the ridiculous apples. What do they mean if not a proposal?

Elin continues her story, having received no answer. She paces the hearth floor. "He told me that I was likely a goddess who had roamed the earth to make sure mortals were behaving well. And that the best gift he could give me was one of marriage."

Her lips curve at the memory. She draws her hands together.

"Of course, it had already been arranged before he proposed. We were both of high standing, and he had been named shepherd of the people as his father had died in battle. An immediate marriage was required."

I didn't know that they had to wife themselves right away. Let's hope Ulix lives a loooong while. Long enough for Homer to formulate another plan to get us out of here.

She flicks her wrist, light disappearing from her cheeks. "Choose your goat and bring it to town. Before I change my mind."

We scurry outside into the warm sunlight and toward the grassy fields that smell of green and summer. With the backdrop of the brilliant blue sky and white cotton candy clouds, you could imagine yourself in a town years away from tragedy.

I glance over my shoulder and watch the men unload the cart of its gold. Turning back, I spot Brisei stroke a goat with a shiny black pelt and curly horns.

"This one gives a lot of milk."

"Perfect. I would not want anything less for Cersei." For that little girl, I'd give all the goats in the world.

"Thankyouthankyouthankyouthankyou." Cersei refuses to take a breath between words. She hugs the goat, then my legs, then Brisei's legs, then the goat again. It bleats when she squeezes its neck tighter.

I notice how her graying dress barely clings to her shoulders. Her collar bone juts out so much, you could put a stick of butter on it. How many meals has this girl gone without?

She strokes the goat's fur and grasps handfuls of it, eyes widening, like she can't believe it.

"This one is so young." She buries her face into the pelt and rubs her nose back and forth. "The one we had stolen from us was beginning to run dry."

The goat leans down to take a chunk out of something, a drying clay pot. I rush over and grab the vessel before it can get a strange lunch. Once I place the pot several feet away, Brisei and Cersei dissolve into giggles. They both pat the goat's back. Its yellow eyes flick toward the pot and back at me.

Nice try, my dude.

Footsteps thunder outside, and panic spasms in my chest. No, the Greeks couldn't have already invaded the city. Don't they like to attack at night? Then again, they ambushed Elin's daughter's town in the afternoon, or at the least, in the morning.

Brisei's and Cersei's faces slacken. I spot the clay mound in the corner of the room and motion for us to hide behind it.

They rush over, and I press my hands against the mound. Clay absorbs my palms, but I don't move from my spot.

I crane my neck out and watch colorful plumed helmets, in rows, flit past. Gray expressions fill the soldier's faces. Nope, that's definitely the Palikarian army. I could recognize that defeat anywhere.

Atro, placed in the farthest left of his row, snags my eye. He sidesteps into the shop and motions for me to come out from the clay mound with the beckon of his arm.

Cersei gasps. "Atro!" She shoves herself into a standing position and races forward to hug him. He doesn't return the gesture. Gray coats his legs now. Cersei turns to me. "He was one of the soldiers who stopped by and told me stories. The ones I painted onto the jars."

Atro's lips twitch and then fall into a thin line a second later.

Wrinkles burrow into his forehead when he glances at me again. "Come. Something terrible has happened."

Ice stings my temples. "What?"

Atro doesn't answer me. Instead, he disappears out the door and into the blur of soldiers marching past. The goat has reached the pot and has taken a bite out of the top. Brisei and I wait at the entrance until the last man has passed by. We join the crowd that surges behind the army on the upward ascent to the richer houses.

I try to eavesdrop on the crowd to get a hint at what happened, but everyone plods on in solemn silence. So I do the same. Except for my wheezing breaths when we near the top. You'd think after weeks, I'd finally manage to climb this hill without getting winded.

We reach Elin's house, and my stomach drops.

This can't be good.

The crowd clusters in the dirt streets, and I can't squeeze my way around them. Brisei tugs on my arm and motions to the wall. A few spaces remain to sit in between the cornices.

She heaves herself up and offers me an arm. Stones chaff my toes when I bustle to a spot. My backside presses between Brisei's and a nursing woman beside me.

A horrible wail pierces the air. Near the double doors, Elin collapses. Blood runs down her cheeks. Did she cut those by accident, or on purpose? Women who I've never seen before surround her. They beat their breasts and tear their dresses.

"Relatives?" I whisper to Brisei, and motion to the women.

"Professional mourners."

A stretcher lies before Elin with a white sheet covering the person it carries. We can only narrow that down to two men she knows on the war front—Ulix or Pandarus.

Elin lifts the sheet, shudders, and grabs a handful of ashes to heap on her head. Gray dirt spills down her face and sticks to her cheeks where the tears flow.

"Why"—this comes out like a growl—"was he stabbed from behind? He was nothing if not brave."

Brisei appears to notice my expression. "To be stabbed from behind means you ran away from battle. One of the most dishonorable things a man can do."

A soldier near Elin clasps his hands. "He was engaged in one-on-one combat. A foolish youth struck him from behind when he was engaged."

"The coward!" Elin beats her fists against the stone until scars form on the heels of her hands. Two of the servants grab her arms to restrain her from hurting herself anymore. "May he face the wrath of the gods."

"He already has. We have made sure that he did not receive a proper burial and that he perished in the most painful way."

Elin sniffs and growls at the servants holding onto her arms. "Release me."

They do, so fast it's as though she'd singed them. She then lifts the white sheet again and uncovers the dead man's face for all the crowd to see.

Even from the wall, I can spot Ulix's beard from a mile away.

The shepherd of the people is dead.

As the wails continue from the women, I spot Pandarus in the crowd of soldiers. He doesn't cry. Instead, he clenches his fists and shakes.

Part Three – Death

"There will be killing till the score is paid."

—Homer, *The Odyssey*

" 'Though you soar like the eagle and make your nest among the stars, from there I will bring you down,' declares the LORD."

—Obadiah 1:4

Chapter Seventeen
How the Shadows Enter the Valley

OF ALL THE SIGHTS YOU NEVER expect to see in the morning after the leader of a village dies—your boyfriend and best friend Brisei hiding behind a bush.

Homer spots me and beams at me. Dark circles form large bags under his eyes. He must not have gotten any sleep. "Morning, Harper," he says in English.

"Homie. What are you doing?"

"At the moment, nursing an incredible ache in my knees. I don't know how you ladies did this last time." He moves his fingers up and down his legs to massage out kinks. I notice a large walking stick lying beside him. Ahead on the road, two fresh pairs of footprints mark the path to and from somewhere off in the distance.

Did these two walk somewhere together? A strange burning sensation fills my gut. Is this jealousy? Why? Brisei didn't indicate she had any sort of crush on Homer.

I squat next to Brisei. Dew seeps into the fabric of my dress. "I meant, what are you doing behind this bush?"

"Oh." The grin slips off Homer's face. "They've called an assembly this morning."

"Palikarian, please." Brisei shields a yawn and then rests her temple against the bush's bristles.

"Assembly?" I ask in Palikarian.

"Yes." Brisei smacks her lips and shutters her eyelids. "To decide what to do with the wealthiest people of the city. The Greeks have given us nine days for funeral preparations before they invade."

A low whistle escapes my lips. Nine days. Most of the time in America, we squeeze in the calling hours and funeral within a week. Nothing could ever stamp out of my mind the chill in my lungs when I first walked into the room and saw Dad's corpse in a casket. Someone had stolen all the oxygen from the room.

Same happened yesterday when the ladies of the household washed Ulix's body in fragrant oil.

Someone had set out a table in the hearth room. Once they covered the body in white linen, I flew upstairs to my room, before the contents of that morning's meal could escape from my stomach.

At night, I couldn't blink away the images of my father, of the archeologist, of the story-stitcher, of Elin uncovering Ulix's face underneath the white sheet. I went into the hallway to ask for Brisei and Talith to sleep over in my new room. Brisei had abandoned her mat, going who knows where.

And Talith wouldn't stir. She's had to balance many hours doing her household duties and nursing the baby. Elin's daughter hardly touches him anymore. She hasn't eaten in over a day.

I wonder if anyone has broken the news to her about her dad.

Another yawn from Brisei pulls me back to the present. I point at the footsteps on the path. "What were you two up to this morning?"

Homer's cheeks darken. "Those belong to Atro."

Something about the way his voice goes up indicates he hasn't told me everything.

"Atro?"

Brisei smiles into her chest. "Homer told him his story as well as yours."

My heartbeat quicks.

"Homie," I hiss in English. I cross my fingers. "He and Pandarus are like this. What in the world, my dude?"

Homer shrugs. "He's really not the biggest fan of Pandarus, you know. Something tells me he's really on our side, and it doesn't hurt to have an ally in the Palikarian army. And besides, he shared his story with us. You should give it a listen if you have the time."

I pinch my nose and groan as Brisei reminds us once again to talk in Palikarian.

Footsteps approach the stone assembly. Homer presses a finger to his lips, and by instinct, I hunch down more, so the foliage can cover all of my face.

"Today is the first day Pandarus makes decisions as shepherd of the people." Homer shimmies until his stomach presses against the ground. "He will decide what happens to the people. If they will survive and escape the city or have to wait out the siege."

Yippee.

Based on Laran's history lessons, something tells me our homeboy won't make the right choice.

Conversation lulls a few minutes later. A hawk circles above us and screeches, but through the peephole I have in the bush, I can see that the soothsayer doesn't even survey the skies. Hawks must pale in comparison to eagles here.

The eldest man in the group quakes as he leans on the speaking stick. "Time is not on our side, so we must speak quickly. As you have been made aware, we have nine days for Ulix's funeral. Pandarus has graciously agreed to cut short the timing of the funeral games to give us more days to prepare against the Greeks."

Pandarus hunches into his seat, scowling at the floor.

"My father deserves a longer funeral. And his family, a longer period to grieve." Pandarus growls. "We must do what is best for the people."

I wonder who forced him to make that decision.

Can't blame the guy. Much as I despise him, friends and family members of Dad didn't handle the funeral all too well either. If I could saw off every hand that clapped my shoulder and, in the most condescending voice possible, said, "You need to be your mom's helper. She is going to have a tough time doing this on her own," I would have a refrigerator full of palms and fingers.

No wonder I lashed out so much in the months following. No one gave me a proper period of time to grieve.

The old man claps the stick against the stone. "Yes, thank you, Pandarus. May I remind you, as this is your first assembly, that only those who hold this staff may speak."

Pandarus glares at him.

"As I was saying"—the old man hacks a cough—"we must act quickly. The soothsayer had mentioned he saw some disturbing signs that indicate that if we do not make a wise decision, we may lose our city and all of Palikari."

He hands the rod to the soothsayer, who speaks now.

"Last night I peered outside my window and watched lightning flash on the left, an unlucky omen."

Oh, right, I forgot it rained last night. The only sound that soothed me to sleep.

Also, what if the soothsayer lived on the opposite side of town? The lightning would flash on his right side, instead of the left. Who comes up with the parameters for these signs?

"And I heard my son sneezing, an omen of death."

Okey dokey then. We just won't question that one.

"I believe the gods are not on our side. And when the Greeks invade, they will come after those of superior birth."

A.k.a., the rich dudes.

"Therefore, I suggest to the shepherd of the people that we

postpone any post-funeral events he had hoped for and evacuate the wealthiest members of our village with the secret paths, known only to us."

Pandarus rolls his fists and shakes again. He springs to his feet and wrestles the staff out of the soothsayer's hands. Whites show in the eyes of all the men, but no one jumps up to stop him.

Once he has the staff, Pandarus taps one end against the stone. "You would have me be king, but not experience all the benefits of the position?"

What kind of benefits? I thought the dude inherited his father's entire property already.

"Sir." A man two seats down from Pandarus lifts a hand. "We only mean to *postpone* some of the ceremonies until we are safe from the Greeks."

Pandarus growls and thrusts down the stick. "I do not know why you ask me, then. Since it appears the decision has already been made." He shakes his feet until some sand evicts from his sandals. Then he storms off toward the house.

What was that *all about?*

Brisei and I find Atro in the stables. Elin has sent us with the wagon to fetch him. They need all male hands on deck for some big pyre thing.

He wears a simple tunic today, and something about his lack of armor, and more displaying of his chest, has caused Brisei's cheeks to go darker than ever before.

"Atro."

Mid-oiling a horse's mane, he glances up at me, and his face softens. Something like recognition throws sparks into his pupils. I know that look. It's like being seen for the first time as you truly are. Homer shared a similar glance with me when I wore a crop top for the first time in England.

And he loved me, tiger stripe stretch marks and weird moles and all.

Maybe Homer was right. We can trust this guy with the truth.

"Elin needs you to load the wagon with wood for the fire."

"Right." He massages the oil left on his palm onto his arms and legs until he glistens. Be still, Brisei's heart. I think her legs are wobbling.

Hay jabs into my toes as we leave the stables. Seeing Brisei wilting from who knows how much sleep she got last night, I have her ride in the wagon. Atro and I walk alongside it. He strokes the donkey's neck as we follow the dirt road.

"You truly do love horses, Atro."

He pats the donkey's head and veers back onto the path, near me. "Ever since I was a boy, I wanted to compete in chariot races in funeral games."

"What stopped that dream?"

We veer toward a line of wagons that leads into a sparsely wooded forest. The noise of axes whacking at trees fills our silence for a moment.

"I was born into a family of goat herders. Only when I joined the army and manned a chariot did I have a chance to steer horses. Everyone here knows of my lineage and would not allow me to race."

Sad that they wouldn't let someone compete because of their lack of wealth. Then again, my school placed similar restrictions. In addition to paying an athletic fee, students had to purchase their own sports equipment and clothing.

Hence why I never joined sports.

Funny how colleges require extracurricular activities when so many students couldn't afford admission, let alone all the fees that came with joining some school club.

"Say you were wealthy. Would you compete in tomorrow's games?"

He clicks his tongue, nails gripping his arm until the skin turns white. "I am not from this tribe. They would not allow for it."

I chew on my lip when we draw to a halt. Men in the wagon ahead load their cart with wood. Man alive, we're about to have one heck of a bonfire.

"You know, Atro, change only happens if you take the first step." The wagon in front of us rolls away. Our turn. "I bet if you asked Pandarus, he would let you compete."

Our donkey parks in front of a freshly felled tree. Brisei hops off the cart and we all pile logs onto the wooden boards.

"Perhaps if you ask him, Harper." A twinkle ignites his pupils. "You have a certain way with words that could captivate every man, woman, and child."

Mind telling my speech teacher that? The one who wrote "lackluster" on my evaluation for my debate on the need for more skilled apprenticeships in America, rather than students taking four-year liberal arts degrees?

Atro whistles as Brisei double-times her load onto the cart. "My lady, what beautiful hands you have. They must be very skilled at labor."

Brisei hunches, maybe to hide her flushed face with her shoulders. "They are terribly thin, sir. Not like the lovely ones Harper has."

Atro keeps his eyes pressed on her. "Small hands are wonderful for holding, do you not think? In fact, I believe those hands would fit well into mine. Would you like to see if my belief is true?"

A giggle bobbles in Brisei's throat as they clasp hands. I roll my eyes but can't stop a smile from wriggling up my cheeks. Even a dark little cloud like me enjoys a good romance from time to time.

We finish loading up the pile before us and men tie down the stack with ropes. Then we roll our wagon back toward the dirt path. I make sure to keep several paces ahead of Atro and Brisei, so they can spend more time walking together.

Following the line, we head toward the temple where men stack more wood onto a huge rectangular pile. Yikes, you could fit several horses on that thing.

We reach the front and unload, then join the crowd that circles around the pyre on the left. The professional mourners claw at their hair and wail as stringed and wooden instruments blare a morose tune.

Once the men unload the last wagon's wood onto the pile, they leave the site and we wait.

Minutes later, the music kicks up tempo as a funeral procession marches onward. Wagons full of gold and food lead the line first. Shirtless men, bound by a train of ropes, stumble forward.

Brisei's lips tremble. "Those are Greeks. Soldiers they have captured from the battlefront."

"How can you tell?" Does she recognize some of their faces? Do they come from her tribe?

"Because Greek funerals all the same. You see those twelve men?"

I nod.

"They will follow Ulix into the afterlife."

Ice grips my calves and I feel myself growing faint. "Brisei, I need you to tell me when to look away."

"Believe me, my lady, I will. For I cannot watch such things either."

Following the twelve prisoners, Pandarus leads his family and a wagon that contains a sheeted bier. Soldiers in armor gather around Pandarus. I wonder why he hasn't asked Atro to join him. Maybe, like the funeral games, they reserve this for a their-tribe-only thing.

Several men lift the body up to the top of the wood stack.

Once they place Ulix onto the wood, the soldiers take daggers and slice off locks from their own hair. Some weep and wet Ulix's body with tears. Pandarus doesn't. He shaves a chunk off the side of his head near his ear, drops the hair onto his father, and clenches his jaw when he looks down at the corpse.

People grieve in different ways, Harper.

The soldiers load up items from the cart.

"Jars of honey." Brisei licks her lips. "Bread freshly made this morning. Wineskins."

All items this town desperately needs. How many hungry eyes feast on these items but will never get a chance to partake in them before the Greeks invade? They believe these souls need these items in the afterlife to sustain them.

Meanwhile, men place stones around the stacks of wood.

I glance around the area and notice several mounds heaped with stones. This must be where they buried all the shepherds of the people who came before Ulix.

Then comes the awful, the inevitable.

A man tugs on the string of ropes that binds the twelve prisoners of war. They stumble up the pyre. Many of them scrape their knees and shins on the way up until blood runs to their bare feet. Following them, a man leads a horse to the top.

No, no, don't tell me they're going to slaughter that animal too.

I watch Atro's expression. Sadness fills his eyes, but he must have grown used to this type of funeral format by now. He too believes Ulix needs a horse to go with him into the next world.

So I squeeze Brisei's hand. She shuts her eyes, and I tap Atro on the shoulder. "Let us know when we can look again."

I shut my eyelids and drive my fingers into my ears. My heartbeat soothes me for the next several moments. While I try to blot out my imagination of what's happening atop the pyre, I force myself to remember some of my happiest memories.

Of when Mom and I grabbed ice cream when I bombed the art show last semester.

Of Homer, learning some dance moves from me over a video call, and me slumping to the ground in a fit of laughter at how he bobbed that little booty up and down.

Of—

Heat inflames my face. I open my eyes and watch the whole stack of wood blaze, forcing myself to keep my gaze on the bottom, so I don't have to look at what became of the top.

Pandarus's back is to us. He watches the pile and continues to shake. Everyone around him wails, crumples to their knees. He doesn't move.

I picture a man to his side giving him a speaking stick and him thrusting it down, until the wood made a thwack against the stone flooring.

"He was upset at the assembly earlier," I tell Atro as the flames flicker in his eyes.

Wrinkles form on Atro's forehead when he lifts his eyebrows. "Oh, yes?"

"Said the elders had deprived him of some of the benefits of being a shepherd of the people." Sweat dews on my lip from the heat. "Who can blame him? I was upset about every little thing when my father died."

"Benefits." This doesn't come out like a question from Atro. Instead, he draws a circle in the dust that surrounds his feet with his toes. Lyre music kicks up behind me along with the wails of women.

Atro waits for them to die down and leans over to whisper to me. "I believe I know why Pandarus fell into a rage earlier."

"Because of his father's death?"

Atro frowns. "No. Because when one becomes a shepherd of the people, he must find a wife immediately. In fact, often he is married before he is crowned chief of the people."

My mouth goes dry. I try to swallow, but the spit sticks in the back of my throat.

"Harper, he is upset that he did not get to marry you before the Greeks invade."

Chapter Eighteen
How the Runner Gets Tangled in Thorns

I bury my toes into the cold sand and watch the pink sunrise stretch over the dark horizon.

Tugging my knees to my chest, I sigh.

"Couldn't sleep either?"

My spine jolts before I recognize Homer's voice. He sits beside me and his shadow props him up on his hands. Even though deodorant is all but a memory, I love his scent. Granted, he did use his allotted bath last night. Elin has cut us back to two baths a week, saving whatever oils she can for the coming siege.

"How did you find me here, Homie?"

"Had something else I needed to do earlier today."

Strange, he acted funny yesterday morning too. Did he need to go for a walk out here to clear his mind too? Had Brisei joined him yesterday?

Speaking of, I didn't find her outside my door this morning. So why didn't she follow Homer onto the beach?

I rest my chin on my knee. Damp, chilly sea air tickles my nostrils, and I breathe in the calming scent. "Homie, what did the apple mean? Because clearly the guy wanted to propose to me."

Thoughts plagued me all night of Pandarus's reaction at the assembly. He threw a fit because he wanted the whole town to stay behind and watch us get married. Ugh.

Since Pandarus hasn't indicated anything, everyone assumes that after the games, we'll get the rich folks out of town. Let's just hope he doesn't keep me under a watchful eye to make sure we get married as soon as we leave the village.

Wind rustles Homer's curls.

"The apple is like a promise. It tells all the other men not to make a move on the girl. Because he was off to war, I think he was worried someone else would swoop in and snag you when he was fighting on the battlefield, so he sort of reserved you."

"Gross."

Gotcha, the apple resembles an ancient promise ring.

My dress flutters against my calves.

"Thankfully, we won't have to worry about that. Right, Homie? They're going to be busy focusing on getting people out of here on the secret paths starting tomorrow."

Homer doesn't answer at first. He scratches an itch on his nose and his palm claps against the sand.

"Homie?"

"Laran never mentioned Herodotus saying anything about people attempting to sneak out of the city when the invasion took place." Weak pink sunlight highlights his wince. "And besides, as we learned on our day to the town over, the Greeks know where to hide."

Stones plummet into my stomach.

Great. Part of me had hoped we could take one of those paths and duck out of here right after the games. How in the world are we going to get out of here without ending up with a Greek sword in our backs?

Sure, we could head to the village the Greeks took over and run into Brisei's friend again. From what I can tell from how Brisei has described the Greeks pillaging towns, there would be nothing for us there. Or worse, they'd take all of us into captivity. Brisei doesn't know *everyone* in the Greek army, and men don't exactly listen to women here—unless they happen to be childhood crushes.

"In truth, Harper," Brisei had told me last night after the bath, "it would be far better for us to escape back to my village in Greece. They are rebuilding, and they know me as a noblewoman. They would welcome whoever I brought with me." Her face turned dark. "The journey is dangerous. Arduous. I do not know if we could make it."

My eyes rove the waters. Dark ships from the army rest on the shore.

"Why not steal one of those and sail to some faraway island?" I ask Homer.

"That's what I love about you, Harper. Your imagination." Homer's lips sag. "Unfortunately, even if any of us knew how to steer a ship—and keep in mind it takes dozens of men—the Greeks are way better out on the waters. They'll probably set fire to our boat, and we'll end up stranded on driftwood in the middle of the ocean, best case scenario."

Yeesh, so the ships *did* have burn marks when I spotted them come in last time.

I scan the shore for some sort of sign about what to do next.

Soon this beach will fill with men competing in the funeral games. After soldiers collected Ulix's bones and placed them in a golden jar filled with fat, Atro described the "games" to me on our walk back home.

Similar to the Olympics—or I guess a pre-Olympics, since those don't exist yet—men will show their prowess in several events from chariot races to boxing to discus and everything in between. Winners will take home prizes.

Atro told me what every man excelled at in the army. They would, in their down time when not busy slaughtering the enemy, practice the various sporting events in the army campground and on beaches.

"Every man of high standing must be good at something. If someone does not take home a prize, he brings dishonor to his family."

Man alive, thankfully I'm not a man. Because in this competition culture, I would get outed almost immediately for a lack of talent.

I sigh. "I'm sorry, Homer, that I'm super incompetent. Otherwise, I bet I could've come up with some way to get us out of here."

He tilts his head toward me, brows lifted in a "you serious?" look. "What brought this on?"

"I don't know." My knees, drawn to my chest, fall slack with my legs onto the sand. "Because I'm here and I'm useless. And back home I'm useless." I scrunch my shoulders. "Usually, heroes of stories come up with plans, are amazing at everything, and give epic speeches they apparently come up with on the spot."

Itchiness coats my eyes. I blink away a mist.

"Instead, you got some girl with a 2.5 GPA who couldn't get a college to say yes to her, traveling back to one of the most talent-based cultures of all time."

My knees jut back up to my chest and I bury my forehead into them.

"I just wish I could run away, Homie. That's all I want to do."

Silence fills the space between us.

His warm fingers lace themselves with mine. "First of all, Harper, I don't think it's a calling unless your immediate impulse is to run away. That's usually what heroes do first in stories."

He inches closer to me.

"Secondly, I wish you could see us as I do. As we all do. We don't love you for what you'll never be. After all, I couldn't keep the ball in the air to save my life."

I snigger and sniff away some moisture in my nose. "True."

"We love you as you are, and as you are becoming. And maybe one day you, too, can see yourself the way we do."

"Like an artist does."

He grins and leans into me. "Yeah, something like that."

Brisei and Talith reach the beach before the men do. It's the first time I've seen the latter in a while, what with the feeding of the newborn ten times a day.

Men filter onto the beach soon after, many shirtless. Thank God they have on loincloths or skirts of some sort, because all my classroom learning about the Olympics has taught me that men shed just about anything with cloth during these events.

Pandarus spots me and arches his back so I can get a good look at his abs. The man even oiled his belly, so every crevice shows.

I turn my face away so I can do the world's biggest eye roll. Not that they really roll their eyes in this culture. At least, not from what I can tell.

Atro, fully clothed, sidles beside Brisei. Neither says anything.

A man in a loincloth calls the crowd over. I notice that no other women, except for Talith, Brisei, and me, stand on the beach. Should I go home? A vague memory of a book in elementary school mentioning women not being allowed at the Ancient Greek Olympics floats across my brain.

Pandarus won't keep his gaze off me.

Maybe he made an exception for the event. Typical him, ignoring the customs of his people.

"The first event will be the boxing match," Damas says. He

holds up palms he's wrapped in leather strips. "Any man from this tribe of noble standing may compete. If they dare come against the bronze-armed Damas."

A guffaw passes through a select group of men nearby. Either because they know of Damas's incredible boxing abilities or that he's full of it.

A "referee" pokes a finger in the sand and draws a rectangle around Damas and a man with a scruffy beard who has challenged him. The crowd surges around the border the referee has created.

"Winner will receive two donkeys and a fresh white mantle." The referee slaps his thighs, and the match commences.

Tall men block my view. I catch sight of some undercut swings from Damas between the heads of two soldiers. Huh, so he actually *can* box. Good to know the man does more than just steal clothes off dead bodies on the battlefield.

Sweat drips from Damas's forehead when the other player yields. The other has received a nice shiner to his left eye and some bloody welts on his cheek.

"Atro, what troubles you?"

Brisei cocks her head when she asks this. Atro, although smiling, winces around the eyes. Like someone who took a punch to the stomach but can't show the pain.

"You are wishing to compete." Brisei thumbs her chin, peering at him. In all my time with her, I've discovered she has an inexplicable way of seeing people. Like, actually *seeing* them.

He lifts and drops his shoulders. "It matters not."

"You *do* wish it."

"I am not of this tribe."

Images from yesterday surge into my brain. Atro had mentioned that they wouldn't let him do the chariot race because he came from another place in Palikari. But what had he said about how I could help?

I squeeze my eyelids shut and retrace the words. *"Perhaps if you ask him, Harper. You have a certain way with words that could captivate every man, woman, and child."*

Brisei looks at me, eyes softening, pleading. Like she knows the secret about me too.

Well, might as well make myself useful.

Two more men step into the ring and swing arms at each other. I weave my way through the crowd, avoiding fists that pump up and down as the Palikarians cheer on the competitors. At last, I find myself near Pandarus. I try hard to ignore the worms wriggling inside of me.

Men around us catch on and form a pocket of air for us two.

"Enjoying the event, Harper?" He squinches his eyelids at me. Oh Lord, help me not to give this dude a black eye.

"Yes." I blink several times and clasp my hands behind my back. Ugh, I hate myself. "I was wondering if you would be willing to do me a favor?"

"Anything for you, my star."

Eww, I am not *your anything.* "Right. I was wondering if you would let Atro compete in the chariot races. I have heard he is quite good."

Shadows cover Pandarus's face. Sweat from within the ring flicks up like the boxers have turned themselves into human sprinklers.

"He is from another tribe. I do not know if that has been done before."

"Surely you can make an exception for him? He is your friend. And." I bobble my heels back and forth like I'm some stupid rocking horse. "You are the shepherd of the people."

"Therefore, I could change the rules." His eyes alight. The embers reduce to coals moments later. "I would have to make an exception for everyone who does not come from this tribe." He smirks at Homer, who stands on the opposite end of the ring. "To be fair."

Fire fills my cheeks. He still hasn't seen Homie race and wants to watch him faceplant or make a fool of himself.

"Put him in the footrace. You will not be disappointed."

Pandarus lifts a brow but doesn't answer. The boxing match ends. Damas takes home the donkeys, a laurel wreath on his head, and a thumb that doesn't bend the right way. Talith leaves and mentions something about the baby. Her legs shuffle up the beach and all of her sags. Much as she loves that child, she's stayed up all hours to nurse and care for him in the night.

I should know. Found her downstairs this morning with him when I left for the beach.

A bounce fills Atro's steps when a referee announces the next event, and Pandarus adds the addendum that anyone who is Palikarian may compete. Chariots roll up on the beach. Unlike the laundry day wagons, these ones gleam in metal and have various designs carved into the sides.

Atro climbs into one with a gorgon head.

He drives his two horses to the starting line and blows a kiss to Brisei from behind. She dips her chin to her chest and shakes so much that I swear she'll explode.

A referee slaps his thigh and a whistle from the horse whips fill the air.

I cringe at the noise and can only imagine the pain the animals feel with those leather strips flicking on their backs every few seconds. Thundering hooves disappear down the beach. I squint and catch the chariots whirling around a wooden post someone has stuck into the ground.

Atro's horses pull into the lead, and Brisei lets out a

shrieking cheer. She claps her hands to her mouth. "Sorry." She probably thinks she drew too much attention to herself.

I whoop even louder than her, so much that a man nearby hunches over and glares at me.

Brisei's shoulders relax, and we attempt to compete with each other for who can shout the loudest. Atro's chariot flies past the finish line and his wheels get stuck in the mud on shore when his horses veer toward the ocean.

He jumps out of the cart and receives the laurel wreath and his prizes—two tripods and a racehorse.

"Well done, Atro." The referee rubs some sand off his legs that the horses kicked up when they flew past. "Our next event is—"

"The footrace," Pandarus calls through cupped hands. "And it would be my honor to invite Homer to compete in this race, as he has received high praise from the Lady Harper, for this event."

Homer passes me a wide-eyed glance as the referee retraces the starting line that the horses have blurred into oblivion. I cringe. *Sorry, Homie.*

Maybe Pandarus thinks I was joking and that Homer is actually terrible at this event. Barefoot, Homer approaches the line of runners, the only one with his tunic covering his whole chest.

Someone sidles beside me. One short laugh trails from his lips. "This ought to be entertaining."

Red ants crawl up and down my arms at the sound of Pandarus's voice. Confirmed, he thought I wanted Homer to do this event to humiliate him. "What do you mean?" Saying this through my teeth, I fail to disguise the seethe in my tone.

Pandarus's spine slackens at these words. In my periphery, I watch light die from his cheeks. "Well, perhaps not the *most* entertaining footrace I have ever witnessed. That happened at the temple to Leinos."

I freeze.

Leinos's temple, the same place Homer worked before he time-traveled himself to me. Where he mentioned winning running competitions back in the day.

One of the runners has asked to un-sheath the sandals from his feet. Says he thinks he'll run faster barefoot.

"What do you mean?" This time a quake has entered my throat. All hostility has left me as I feel the blood drain into my toes.

Sunlight bounces off his teeth. He displays them in a smile, almost a snarl. "I was taking a sacrifice to Leinos to ask him to let us vanquish our enemies on the battlefield. I had gone to the temple during an unusual hour, to avoid the crowds of soldiers who liked to visit in the mornings."

The runner has discarded his shoes. Another asks to do the same.

"The slaves at the temple had not anticipated me and were competing in a footrace. The winner…" He sniggers. "He had the strangest running form I have ever seen."

He mock-imitates it by kicking his feet up and down like a mix between a Leprechaun and a turkey who has legs for days.

Oh man alive, didn't Homer have a strange style of running when the youths in the neighborhood challenged him to a race? I didn't do track in school, but I've never seen an Olympic runner do anything like that.

"Granted." Pandarus stills. "The form helped him to win, but it made me collapse to the floor of the temple and double over to contain my laughter."

The other runner has shed his shoes, and the referee raises

his arm. They lift their butts in the air to take their marks.

Pandarus sniffs and flicks a tear out of his eye with his middle finger. "Funny. Without a beard, Homer reminds me a lot of him."

Panic constricts my chest until I can't breathe. I need to get Homer out of the race.

At the same time I screech Homer's name, the referee slaps his thighs and the runners kick up sand. Sure enough, Homer frog-legs himself down the beach, pulling ahead of the pack.

I refuse to watch Panadarus's expression. In the corner of my eye, his eyebrows narrow more and more. Oh no, no, no.

Homer rounds the post and dashes—well, waggles—back toward the finish line. I try to focus on the gentle lapping of the waves, the seagulls screeching above, anything but my racing heart.

He passes the finish line, meters ahead of the other runners.

Pandarus marches forward and snatches the olive branch crown out of the referee's hand. He shoves the wreath onto a panting Homer's head. "Congratulations on a race well run." Pandarus glances back at me and winks. "And for conjuring up so many pleasant memories."

He moves back toward a cluster of soldiers, but not before shoving his shoulder into Homer, who collapses onto the sand.

Oh man, he knows.

He knows.

Chapter Nineteen
How to Untie a Cord of Three Strands

I RACE OFF THE BEACH AFTER the archery event.

Homer left after the footrace, and Brisei followed soon after, mentioning something about household chores. Not wanting to arouse any suspicion from Pandarus, I waited one event longer before fleeing from the sands that have grown burning hot.

I crumple to my knees near a pile of horse dung and finally inhale. During all of archery, I held my breath so much, dizziness filled my skull and black film formed over my eyes.

Every part of me wants to run away.

My muscles twitch with an electricity to flee in any direction.

If I do, I'll run into the Greeks who'll take me captive. Or worse, if I manage to evade them, I have no idea how to survive the wilderness or where to go.

If I don't, I have to stick around and find out what Pandarus will do to Homer when the two encounter each other again.

I can't do this. I can't do this. I can't do this. I can't...

Well, *chica*, you're gonna have to. You don't have many options.

For the time being, I breathe into my knees until I go from hyperventilation to a breath per second.

I unwind myself and bolt to my feet as a small brown snake slithers past me. Funny, in one omen the snake represented Palikari and the eagle symbolized Greece. In another, both countries were eagles. I wonder who creates the rules for soothsayers. Or if they make it up on the spot for funzies.

Dusting the sand off my calves, I set off in no direction in particular.

Already the sun cooks me like an oven. Although the humidity isn't as bad here as in England, the metal loops that hold the fabric on my shoulders brand my skin.

Dryness coats my tongue. I need to head somewhere cool.

The image of the cave pops into my head. Perfect. I swivel around and head toward the path.

Bleariness fills my vision on the way up the rocky pathway, until I feel myself float away on a mist.

A thwack pulls me back to the present.

Inside the cave, two figures lunge at each other with sticks. Coldness blows onto my cheeks and calves as I enter the mouth and step inside. My eyesight adjusts as Homer throws one end of his staff toward Brisei's calves.

She stumbles back and lands on her backside. He presses his rod to her sternum. "Yield."

"Hello?"

Both of their chins snap up at me as I step over the dried creek in the cave. Even in these moist conditions, the summer heat has swallowed up some of the water in here.

"Harper!" Homer pumps his staff up and down like a senior classman who just got the spirit stick from homecoming week. His arm drops. "We were hoping this would be a surprise."

"Surprise?"

Brisei rises and shields a yawn behind her palm. "Homer has asked me to teach him how to wield a spear these past few nights. We have had to pilfer a tripod from the house so we can see in the darkness."

She gestures to a torch staked in the ground near the dried stream. I scan the top of the cave for the usual cluster of bats, but they've disappeared. Maybe they've hung farther in where the temperatures get cooler.

"You have been practicing?" Warmth spreads in my chest.

"After we found ourselves face to face with a Greek spear, I figured it would not hurt." Homer shrugs.

I lean my head back against the wall. Brisei cringes. Maybe at the rocky sludge I feel falling onto the veil behind me. But I don't care. Anything to cool down the dewy sweat on my neck.

"Brisei, where did you learn to fight?"

Her face softens. "From my brother. He needed someone to train with before he joined the army. I"—she slumps—"I was able to hold off some of the Palikarian men when they invaded my village. But not Pandarus." A quake has entered her voice. "I am afraid that I am not the best person to train Homer against him."

Man, this girl's far more hardcore than I give her credit for. I can't even do the full ten pushups they ask us to do in gym.

"The hope is that we just need to use this in emergencies," Homer adds and plods over to me.

"Homer is quite good at quick footwork." Brisei perks up on her fake spear when she says this, like the rod is holding her up. She pants and palms a sheen of sweat off her forehead. "If he ever ended up toe-to-toe with Pandarus, he could exhaust him and strike when he got sloppy."

I chew on my lip until I tear off skin. "Bad news, it may come to that."

Water drips on the stone behind me. Brisei and Homer's eyes go wide.

"How do you k—"

"Pandarus knows about you, Homer."

I explain to him the story Pandarus told me right before the footrace, and how Homer's running form matched the description of the slave.

"That explains how he congratulated me after the race." Homer massages his shoulder, then his backside.

My eyelids crinkle. "How are you feeling?"

"Like running away." He snickers. "That is obviously not an option. At least, not for now." He nods at Brisei. "We are hoping to have a plan on how to leave the city in the next seven days. For now…"

He lifts himself on his spear and plods toward the back of the cave.

"We continue to fight."

Brisei pants but pulls herself into a straight line.

I rise from my stone. "Brisei, I can take a turn. Something tells me that if I get the chance to poke a spear in Pandarus's face, I am going to take it."

Aches form in my arms when I leave the cave. Brisei left a few fights in, claiming that this time she *really* needed to return to the house before Elin got suspicious.

"I will tell her that I attempted to find more fare in the markets, but without luck. Besides, she is so withdrawn, perhaps she will not notice or care to ask me."

True, Elin has become as pale as her daughter. Although she ventures out of her room more than the latter, her voice, her hunched spine, and her slow, staggering footsteps all reminded me of shattered glass.

Although Brisei said she couldn't defeat Pandarus, Homer *has* improved. A lot.

He sometimes even went on the offensive. *Which reminds me.* I knead the kinks in my backside. Butt landings somehow hurt way more than you would think.

Perhaps if they go toe-to-toe, he might stand a chance. Let's hope Pandarus gets winded fast.

On my descent from the cave, moisture clings to my legs along with the itchy insect bites I can feel forming. What I wouldn't give for some bug spray right now.

I reach the town and by habit scan the stalls. No inhabitants.

The only life forms I see scurrying here and there are people who rush out of their houses to grab something in the courtyards or fields, and then back in. Even the cattle from most of the fields have disappeared. I swear I hear bleats coming from some of the houses nearest to the marketplace.

Another bleat sounds from Cersei's shop. I see her silhouette feeding the goat something and I step into the cool shade.

She's handed her goat a handful of grass. Dirt clumps fall to the shop floor like confetti.

"I love you, dearest Phauno." Cersei buries her nose into Phauno's black pelt as the goat's jaw works from side to side.

"She loves you too."

Cersei snaps up when she hears my voice and her eyes light up. "Harper!" She springs away from the goat and collapses into me with a hug. "Father has asked me to watch her in here, for safekeeping, as he prepares the house for the siege. Too many family members have indicated they may steal her away, so we are hiding her in here."

So I *had* heard bleating from one of the huts near the shops.

She grabs my hand and leads me over to the goat. Together we stroke Phauno's pelt. Coarse fur runs through my fingertips.

"What I do not understand"—I sit, knees crackling—"is why only those of higher standing get to leave the city via the secret paths."

Not that the secret paths would do the townsfolk any good if the Greeks know about them.

Cersei works her fingers around Phauno's ears, which flick away flies. "If too many people take the paths at once, the Greeks may suspect that we are taking advantage, and they will invade early. Father says that it will be tricky enough to get all the wealthiest out of the city in seven days without causing alarm."

Huh, I hadn't considered that.

The Greeks expect us to spend this time doing a funeral. If I were them, I would also attack if I felt like someone used the grace period to escape.

"Besides, when the Greeks invade, they will loot the finest treasures. They care not for the poorest men."

A sudden idea flashes in my brain.

What if we disguise ourselves as poor people and hide in Cersei's house until the Greeks leave the city? Sure, they might Hellenize the place and stick around for a while, but they won't touch us because we don't have anything to offer.

They only capture the richest people, after all.

"Does it give you comfort knowing that they only want wealth?"

Cersei frowns at her clay-covered fingers. "Well, when I said men, I meant *men*. Women are not safe during such invasions. Who knows if the Greeks will get blood-hungry and slaughter all men as well?"

Heaviness fills my chest.

Why hadn't I considered that either? I've read enough books about pirates and pillaging Vikings to know this.

I mentally scratch out some of the plans I've formulated on how to escape Palikari.

~~Plan One: Use the Secret Paths~~

Greeks probably have themselves stationed and waiting on these already. After all, we ran into Brisei's childhood friend on a route supposedly only Homer knew about.

~~Plan Two: Disguise Ourselves as Lower Class~~

Depending on the Greeks' mood that day, sure, they won't take us into captivity. That won't stop them from killing us. Or something worse…

Back to the drawing board. Or, with luck, more spear practices with Homer and Brisei.

My chest tightens, and my temples pound from an oncoming headache.

"Created anything new?" Maybe some of her artwork can take my mind off the inevitable that will come in seven days.

Cersei pats Phauno on the back and motions for me to follow her to the rows of jars at the front of the shop. I squint as we enter a patch of sunlight. She displays her newest creation for me, a bowl with Phauno painted in the center. A girl, in the painting, pets the place in between the horns.

Horse hooves clip clop outside. I blink at the sun's beams and make out Atro. My finger reaches to my waterline to clear away some tears from the brightness.

"Atro, congratulations on winning the chariot race."

He steps inside. His horse remains on the road and bucks its head up and down. Wrinkles form on Atro's forehead. "Pandarus is about to do something foolish."

What else is new? Needles prickle my skull. What if he tries to kill Homer?

I swallow, but my throat has gone dry. "Shall I convince him to do otherwise?"

A growl lodges in Atro's throat. "I do not believe you can persuade him away from making this decision."

"Then why—"

"Sometimes it helps to know when a storm is coming, even if you cannot hide from its gales."

My lungs burn. I try to force myself to exhale. Great, here's hoping Homer's few spear lessons can help him withstand a man who trained in the army for several years.

Without another word, Atro exits the shop.

Images from the chariot race earlier flash through my brain. Maybe if I turn up the charm, Pandarus will calm down and let Homer go.

Sure enough, a minute passes before the cluster of soldiers from the beach pass in front of Cersei's shop. Pandarus, to the far left of the crowd, spots me and swaggers in our direction. Sweat drips off his curls and his laurel wreath. He clutches a tripod in his hand, no doubt from one of the events. I wonder which competition he won.

"Harper, you are without your attendants." He eyes Cersei, who spies him and inches toward the clay mound to hide. Maybe everyone in this town knows Pandarus is bad news.

"Talith had to nurse your sister's child. Brisei has duties back at the house."

"It is dangerous for a woman to be alone." His smirk sends a shudder up my spine. "Nevertheless, you will be safe by my side. Walk with me."

Irritation prickles my skin.

Before I can launch the first comment that comes to mind— which includes several Palikari insults I finagled out of Homer on one video call— I think of Homer, and clamp my jaw shut. Time to sweet talk this sucker.

I force a smile. "Of course."

Sunlight scorches my shoulders again when I step onto the road. We plod uphill, me making sure to keep a healthy few feet of distance away from him, him inching closer with each step.

"Harper, how did you enjoy the funeral games?"

"Oh, they were quite lovely." My voice goes up so high that it scratches my throat. "Everyone did a wonderful job."

"It is not often that a woman is allowed to see the events. They are usually reserved for men only."

I take a step to the side and scrunch my nose at him, the way I see some couples do in the hallway at school. "I am grateful you made an exception for me."

"Well, it is as you said. I am shepherd of the people. I can make changes to the rules."

Like not stabbing someone if they disguise themselves as a rich person and live in your house for a few months?

I wince but take one step closer to him. Maybe if I close the gap, it'll get his mind off Homie and onto…other things.

We reach the top of the hill, and he leads me out into the field full of goats. His family is one of the few not hiding them within the household. Likely because they've hired a few more men with guard dogs to protect all fields, stables, and pens.

"Harper." Pandarus pats the back of a long-horned goat. "Are you sure that you have no living relatives?"

Wait a few thousand years, pal, and I can accommodate you. "Not currently."

"That is unfortunate. Nevertheless, would you pick ten goats that you like the most? Make sure to choose ones without blemish and ones to your liking."

…Okay?

What a strange request. Again, I don't understand all the

customs here. Maybe he wants me to choose some for funeral games prizes. Although, I'm rather sure they ended the funeral games early today to get the people out of Palikari.

How to pick a goat…. Do you slap them like my dad did with watermelons in the store?

I thumb my chin and choose ten random ones. He has the goat herder move them to the side. The goatherder takes wet clay and stamps a handprint on the backs of each of the ones I "pick."

Once we finish our game of pick-a-goat, Pandarus has me follow him toward the stables where we play a variation, choose-a-horsie. I roam the stalls up and down and scan the pelts of these beautiful creatures. Maybe, if Pandarus gives me a horse as a gift, I can re-gift it to Atro. He'll appreciate the new addition to his ever-growing collection of equestrian friends.

I halt at the stall of a beautiful mare with a sleek dark coat. Something about her dark eyes draws me in and makes me want to cry. My shaky hand reaches out and pats her neck. "This one."

"Wonderful, we shall take her and the goats with us after the wedding."

I freeze.

Time stills.

My heartbeat throbs in my eardrums.

"Wedding?"

"Ordinarily, I would give your father a bride-price, but seeing that you have no living relatives, we had to adjust. I will take the animals you have chosen with us after we are married, through the secret paths, and to a city of refuge."

"Wedding," I repeat. My throat has gone so dry that I can feel the words forming blisters on my esophagus.

"Why, yes. I figured that we have seven more days before the Greeks invade. The next few should give you plenty of time for the pre-wedding bridal rites. We should have enough days to spare to wed." He licks his lips. "We will have to ask the village inhabitants to stay for the next few days, of course. Surely four days will be enough time for them and us to leave."

"Pandarus is about to do something foolish."

Stupid, stupid, stupid. Why did I think that meant he'd kill Homer? This boy's gone and stooped even lower by postponing when people can get out of this town.

"But"—my legs and lips tremble—"what about what the elders said? In—" I stop myself short before saying "in the assembly." He doesn't know I eavesdropped on that meeting. "About people needing as much time as possible to escape? About putting duty of country before our own wants?"

"Well, it is as you said on the beach. I am shepherd of the people." A twinkle ignites his pupils. "I can change the rules."

Chapter Twenty
How the Giver Finds Their Gift

Senior Year, Spring Semester
Art Show

"Okay, okay, chica, breathe." I blow out a breath and glance behind me at the makeshift white wall covered in paintings. I promised myself I wouldn't let myself look at the other displays, but here I find myself glancing across the way at photos from one of the girls who *did* make yearbook the previous year.

She's chosen to do everything in black and white, with some color pops. A little girl in the rain, maybe her little sister, wears red rubber boots covered in polka dots in one of the photos.

Never could I snap something so beautiful in a million years. She must've spent hours retouching.

Itchiness crawls up and down my arms, and I force myself to stay still. To not flee immediately from the small gym premises, where we set up our artwork for the competition.

The freshmen girls' basketball team put up a stink about it. Literally. The place smells like sweat and a mixture of some dubious contents in someone's gym bag.

Nails dig into my palms. I unclench my fists, my jaw.

Breathe.

Chill, girl. You just need this to fulfill the credit that college lady talked about.

She said I need to participate in an extracurricular club or a school event. And this was one of the few without a fee attached.

High marks from judges wouldn't hurt.

They haven't made an appearance yet. According to the schedule stamped on neon orange paper they handed us at the entrance before we started setting up, they don't roam around the displays until seven thirty. I check my phone for the time. 7:16.

"Look who it is!"

My neck snaps up to see my mom traveling toward me, cradling a laptop in her palms. Homer gazes at me through the screen, beaming and shielding a yawn behind his palm. Mom's new boyfriend sidles beside her. He doesn't say much, hands in his pockets.

"Homie, what are you doing awake? Isn't it like three in the morning over there?"

He scrunches his eyelids and forces them as wide as they can go, a wake-up tactic that never seems to work. "And miss this? You've been working on it for months."

Thanks to Juliana. After her encouragement at the art museum, I signed up for my slot at the show. Maybe I could help the world see things as they could be, like she mentioned all those months ago.

"Want to give Homer a tour of your display?" Mom bobs the laptop up and down to make Homer nod.

I roll my eyes. "Sure." I whirl around and face the paintings and photos, fighting the urge to rip everything down. "Here's a photo of Homie in Hyde Park with a bird on his finger." My voice attempts a casual tone. No biggie. I only spent two hours in Photoshop agonizing and deleting edits with the dodge and burn tools.

"Beautiful." My mom gasps behind me. In my periphery, I watch her fish a tear out of her eye with her index finger.

Hope sends beams bursting into my chest. *Maybe it's not that bad.*

I shake the thought away. *Settle down, Harp. Mom probably cried over the scribbles you did when you were two.*

"And here's a painting of sparrows. Sensing the bird theme?"

"Brilliant." Homer's voice behind me sends tingles down my ears all the way to my toes.

"And a girl whose arms transform into wings. Used coffee grounds to paint this one."

"Wow. That's really cool."

Alas, the Mom's Boyfriend™ talks.

Warmth spreads into my gut. *Huh, if a near-stranger thinks the artwork is interesting, maybe so will the judges.* I wince. Nah, Mom probably told him "no kissies" if he didn't say something nice.

I turn back to face the screen and shake the nerves out of my fingertips. "Y'all should see the other artwork. This is nothing."

"I'm sure yours measures up, Harper." Mom's arms shake underneath the weight of the laptop.

"Why don't we head out into the hallway? Judges are supposed to get started soon. There's a chair where you can set Homie down, Mom." Something tells me that I won't be able to stand watching the judges when they reach my display.

We sally out into the hallway. Homie and I talk in Palikarian while Mom and her boyfriend find another pair of chairs farther down.

Engrossed in a discussion about some weird British sitcom Laran made Homer watch earlier that day—much harder to talk about in Palikarian than you'd think—I hardly hear the adult who pops her head out of the gym door to alert us that the judges have made the rounds and left their score sheets on the display cases.

Although they won't announce the first-place winner until

tomorrow, we can get immediate feedback in the form of pink score sheets stapled together.

Shakiness filled my calves when I approach my booth.

Mom, who shadows me, appears to take notice. "Harper, whatever they say, you already told that woman at the college about this event, right? Showed her the signup sheet and everything?"

I breathe, shoulders dropping.

True, because the deadline to apply fell before the event, I emailed my application in with plenty of screenshots of the upcoming events signup forms and some of my artwork. Even had the event coordinator CC'd to confirm I hadn't made up the whole thing.

At the end of the day, it doesn't matter what the judges said. As long as I check the box for an extracurricular, and pull up my grades, which I did, I can land a spot at that college.

We reach my booth and flick through the score sheets. My eyes flit straight to the judges' comments section, where they provided a few sentences of overall thoughts.

Score Sheet One Comments

Feels a little contrived. Student could use some more tips on editing software for retouching for the photos. I'm not sure what grade she's in but may be helpful to take one of the Photoshop classes if she's in a younger grade.

Score Sheet Two Comments

I think there's a lot of potential in some of the artwork, but it feels very surface level. Birds are overdone. We passed quite a few boards with bird subjects before we got to this one.

Score Sheet Three Comments

Not bad! She seems to know what she's doing in a lot of these. Just not particularly inspiring. I don't know if when I go to bed tonight this one will stick out clearly in my mind like some of the others.

Score Sheet Four Comments

Pretty lackluster. Doesn't really say anything. A pass for me.

My arms quiver. Every inch of me wants to tear the sheets into pieces. Instead, I clap the papers down onto the table that holds some of my 3-D clay bird displays and force a smile at Homer. "Well, I guess you can't please everyone." My voice cracks on the last word. Gave myself away.

Mom rushes forward and snatches the papers off the table. She leafs through them, blood draining from her face, then clears her throat. "I'm sure they went tough on everyone, sweetheart. That's their job."

Doubt pools in my stomach. "For sure."

I scan the faces of others reading their packets. One girl with ringlet curls beams and shows one page to a woman behind her, probably her mom.

My phone buzzes in my pocket, and I spot another email from the admissions lady on my screen. Wow, she got back fast. I emailed her last week with the application.

I swipe open the message and read. Hope swells in my ribcage.

Harper,

I was so pleased to see your application come in this past week. Thanks for sending along the artwork as well. Always great to see young minds exercising their creativity. I certainly hope the waived application fee code worked. Let me know if it did not.

I'm afraid I must be the bearer of bad news.

Although I thought I could pull a few strings with the boost in GPA and the extracurricular participation, I'm actually stepping down from my position as of today. Actually, I'd made the decision about a month ago and have been training my replacement for these past few weeks. Otherwise, we would have sent out the notice sooner.

Unfortunately, my replacement has a different vision on how to do things. He's a by-the-rulebook kind of person. So he wasn't terribly keen on making any exceptions. However, I am pleased to see you apply yourself more in your studies. That attitude will take you far in life.

Please don't see this as a rejection, but perhaps, a redirection to something else. As mentioned in our previous correspondence, I do believe that taking some classes at a community college and reapplying a few semesters later may be beneficial in your application process.

Best of luck to you in all your future endeavors, and I am sorry I could not be of more help.

Regards,

Bella Demos, Former Director of Admissions

All those months of hard work. Of staying up late and incurring migraines to study harder for tests. Of spending hour upon hour on those paintings and photos, hoping someone would see something in me. For nothing.

Itchiness forms behind my eyes. I shove my phone into my pocket and dart into the hallway. I spot an unlocked classroom and bolt inside, throw myself into the teacher's rolling chair stationed at a desk, and sob into my arms.

Lights flick on, and the irritating touch of my mother's bony fingertips grazes my shoulder. "Sweetheart, what's wrong?"

She must've set the laptop down somewhere.

"Mom." Snot dribbles out of my nostrils. I wipe them on my long sleeve shirt. "I'm never going to amount to anything."

Her hand hovers over my shoulder again. I flinch, and she withdraws her arm.

"Harper." Her voice comes out softer this time. "Why do you believe this about yourself?" Tears glaze her eyes.

"Because I can't get into a college. I can't get good grades. My artwork is awful, and the judges hated it. If I was the hero in some book or movie, people would be rooting for the villain. Because I'm the worst hero in the world."

She doesn't respond for a few seconds.

"Sweetheart, some people are born to be inspired, and some are born to inspire. Both are heroes in my book."

I frown at a water stain in the ceiling that reminds me of a snake. "What do you mean?"

"Honey, you're, as the kids say, a hype man."

Oh Mom, always the boomer.

"Please don't ever use that terminology again." I snicker into my sleeve. "And no, I'm not."

"Sure, you are. Your photo at the museum inspired Juliana to go into modeling."

Juliana signed up for a bridal runway show a few weeks after that field trip. After that, she spent her weekends doing gigs for local magazines and wedding venues.

"And in England, your artwork, and you just being you, helped Homer to see that he had value and that he deserves a fulfilling life, just like everyone else."

Homer *did* transform during our time together there. He became more of himself…because of me?

"I mean, you got Dave to talk. Do you know how hard it is to get him to give me more than one-word answers to questions on dates?"

I wondered where Dave, Mom's boyfriend, had gone off to. Maybe holding the laptop somewhere else.

"You inspire, sweetheart. And that drives heroes to become heroes." She squeezes me in a side hug and plants a kiss on my hair. "I can think of no higher calling."

Palikari, 800 BCE
The Temple to Leinos, God of Death

I place my girdle on the steps that lead up to the statue of the god of death.

Often a bride and her family head on a journey to the goddess of fertility a town over. Because of the Greeks invading and sacking that place and all, we had to make an exception and hope Leinos passes along the info to the fertility chick.

Behind me, Elin chants something that sounds depressing. A jar of incense sits beside her. Every so often, she waves her hand through the smelly smoke.

Beside her, a pool sits in front of the statue. I don't remember seeing this my first night when we arrived in Palikari. Elin explains that it brings moisture to the metal on the statue. I thought that sort of thing is what turned the Statue of Liberty green, but this is why I didn't go into architecture.

Slaves weave through the forest of columns.

I can't help but stitch Homer's face onto each of them. Did

he sprinkle water onto the altar from a bowl, like one of them does now? Did someone have to hoist him up on the world's tallest ladder to polish the statues we spotted on reliefs on the sides of the temple?

Elin made us march around the temple seven times for luck before we entered. On each round, she talked about the different reliefs.

"That one was our war with the Amazons."

"And that one was our war with the gorgons."

"And this was the war against the giants."

Yeesh, a lot of fights. We get it.

Elin stops her chanting and sinks to her knees. She lifts her arms up to the air. All color has drained from her voice. Life has not come back into it ever since Ulix arrived at her doorstep in a sheet.

"Oh, Leinos. Harper has presented the girdle of youth before you. May you accept her offering and bless her fruitfully during the bridal rites to come within the next few days."

Ugh, don't remind me.

All of this is my fault.

If I hadn't told Pandarus about how he could change the rules so he could let Atro compete at the games… If I hadn't acted all sweet to prevent him from killing Homie, making him mistake that to mean I had come on to him…

Speaking of Homie, Pandarus hasn't breathed a single word to him since. At dinner last night, after news spread throughout the town about the surprise wedding—and the surprise that none of y'all are allowed to leave, by the way—they chewed on their meat in silence.

Maybe he won't act on anything if he gets his way. A.k.a.— I shudder—a honeymoon.

Elin finishes her prayer and motions for me to follow her out of the temple. Brisei and Talith flank her side. Talith cradles the baby in her arms. Elin's daughter begged her this morning to take him out of the house and on a walk, so she could sleep in peace.

The baby slept through the whole girdle ceremony.

First, we do this, and tomorrow, we have Elin's family over for a Palikarian bachelorette party. And the day after that…

Saliva sticks in my throat. *Homie, I hope you're working on something, because I either end up in Pandarus's hands or the Greek army's in any scenario I've run through in my head.*

In silence, Elin and I head toward town. Every once in a while, the baby lets out a weak cry and then quiets. Huh, they must get louder as time goes on.

Near where the town border meets the shops, I spot a cluster of people surrounding a cart full of piles of laundry. The family, I presume, of two adults and several children, gathers around the wagon wearing soiled rags. No doubt they can't afford that thing. Maybe some master has sent them on a laundry task, but do they work kids as young as what looks like three years old?

I spy Atro speaking with the woman of the crowd. Wait a second. Draw a unibrow on her, and I swear I spotted her at one of Pandarus's parties. She wore jewelry at the time.

Atro meets my gaze, and his eyes widen when he notices Elin. They swerve back to me. *"Help,"* they say.

Got it, divert Elin.

I inch to her side, hoping my head blocks her periphery. "Elin, I might go visit a friend in a shop, so you go ahead without me. I believe I spotted your daughter walking up the hill just now."

Color fills Elin's skin again.

Guilt gnaws at my gut, but Atro needs this family to do

laundry unnoticed for some reason. Elin's pace picks up and she almost races up the hill. For the first time, her arms sprawl out like wings. I could've sworn they've gotten clipped ever since the funeral.

I turn to Atro. "Please tell me my lie was worth it."

"This is a wealthy family. Because Pandarus is making everyone stay in town for the wedding…" He spits on the ground. Got it. He and Pandarus are no longer friends. "He risks the lives of these people. Who knows how many can leave this village without the Greeks taking notice?"

Atro walks to the cart and lifts up a sheet on one of the baskets. Bread and fruit are piled to the brim. "They have provisions. This should more than last them on the journey. We will see how many other families we can sneak out of the city before Pandarus senses something amiss."

The woman flicks her eyes back and forth at me, lip quivering. I reach forward and squeeze her hand.

"I will tell no one."

She mouths "thank you" and clicks her tongue. The donkey, carrying the cart, rolls up the hill. The family follows behind and vanishes.

"They are not the only ones who shall leave this city before the wedding." Atro jerks his chin toward the shops and plods in the direction of Cersei's pottery hut. "Come. Homer has formed a plan to help you escape."

Chapter Twenty-One
How the Cheater Gets Pummeled with Stones

"Homie, tell me you have a spankin' plan that can get me out of having to go on a honeymoon with—" I pause when I spot Cersei molding a vase neck on the potter's wheel.

Atro, Talith, and Brisei crowd around the mound of clay in the corner of the room. The baby has awoken and cried, so Talith crouches down to feed him.

"I do," Homer says in Palikarian. He waves his arms to get Brisei's attention. She pulls her gaze away from Atro. "May I explain it to Harper in her language?"

She dips her chin. "Yes. Atro is telling me the plan."

"Brilliant." Homer slaps his palms and rubs them together. "Now, to be on the same page, we've established that we need to get you out of here by tomorrow, because the day after tomorrow is when you…" He taps his ring finger.

Blush ignites my cheeks. I've tried so hard not to think about what all the wedding would entail.

Two years ago, that Harper would've refused. Stomped on Pandarus's sandaled toes. Tried to run away.

Knowing Pandarus, that would've gotten me killed.

Strange how I've only lived eighteen years and have met so many Harpers. I can't decide which one I like the most yet.

"We've also discovered that we're probably going to end up running into Greeks at one point. We need to bolster our chances of getting past them without them, you know, killing us."

"Or worse," I breathe.

"Right, so Cersei gave me the first idea for the plan. I

stopped by her shop earlier. Moving clay with my hands helps me think."

"Same."

The art teachers, bless them, would often open their classrooms to students after school. They had to stay behind to grade papers anyway and would lock up around five. Some days, I would ask Homer if we could cancel or postpone our video calls so I could go to those rooms and sketch something on paper, mold something in my hands.

He always understood and said yes.

"First part of the plan, you dress up in Brisei's clothes, or the clothes of one of the servants." Homer points to his curls. "You have the hair for it. Most richer women grow it out."

I scrunch my nose and park on the dirt floor, brushing off some of the dust particles from my dress. "That's not going to stop the Greeks from doing something. Even if I look poor, I'm still a woman, Homie."

"Notice how I said you're going to wear the poor clothing."

He jabs an arm at Brisei.

"I saw a Palikarian family, of great wealth, hiding over there."

He says this in Greek. Brisei breaks away from her conversation with Atro and beams at Homer. "Perfect."

Homer turns back to me. "I've been practicing all day, in between spear practices. She says they have different dialects and accents, depending on the region."

I scrunch my brows.

"Confused?"

I nod. "Are you trying to say that you're going to impersonate a Greek?"

"A Greek soldier, yes."

"Homie."

"Yes?"

"We don't have Greek armor."

He thumbs his nose. His legs bobble up and down. "Ah, but we do. You remember the tour Elin gave you of the storehouses the first night?"

"Yes, but—"

"How amongst the jars of spices and chests of clothing they have plenty of Greek armor down there, whatever they didn't choose to display above the hearth?"

During the tour, I had thought about how Mom changes the wreath on the door every season. Did that work the same with the Greek armor? Did they switch out breastplates and shields for different holidays, or just when they got too covered in soot?

"Yes, but, Homie, those rooms are guarded. Especially after people kept trying to rob the property."

"That, my darling, is where you step in."

During the bachelorette party tomorrow, Homer is going to find ways to get the other lady servants to make themselves scarce. I will "have an emergency" which will require the female servant guarding the door to carry me to another room, with the party attendees swooning and trying to help me. During that time, Homer will sneak down to the storehouses to get the armor.

"And maybe some provisions if there's time. It's going to be a long journey for four of us."

Four. He means me, him, Talith, and Brisei.

"What about Cersei?" I glance at the potter's wheel and realize she's gone missing. My chin owls over my shoulder, and I spy her at the gray clay pools with her new goat friend. She keeps trying to get her to stop drinking from the dirty water.

"We can try to grab her if there is time. With Atro leading a lot of families on the secret paths this morning, I don't know how long we have before the Greeks get suspicious."

I make a mental note to tell Cersei to visit me tomorrow. Maybe to bring a gift for the party. Elin will make her stay outside of the gates, like she did the other day with a beggar who asked for food. I can grab Cersei and go.

Speaking of Atro—

"What about him?"

Atro seems to recognize he's being talked about, even in English, and he cranes his neck toward me.

"It is my duty to stay here and help as many families as possible escape."

Brisei's eyes soften, lips sag, but she doesn't say anything.

I clench my fist. "Your duty? Atro, these people are not from your village."

"They are still people, are they not?"

Sadness wells in the back of my throat. I attempt to swallow it but wind up feeling like I'm drowning. They should've made Atro the shepherd of the people. He deserves the title way more.

My shoulders slump, and I swivel back to Homer. "Fine. What's my 'emergency'?" I toss up air quotes.

He grins. "You're not going to believe me when I tell you."

Wandering womb.

What in the actual world?

Apparently, the Palikarians believe that the womb likes to travel throughout the body when a girl gets older, up to her throat where it'll choke her, and she dies.

The only cure? To put a baby in there to weigh the womb down.

Or in the case of a bachelorette party, carry the girl to her bed and sit on her stomach, to trap the organ.

Homer was right. It's tomorrow, and I still don't believe him.

Downstairs, Elin shoos Pandarus out of the house and says he cannot return until dinnertime. He growls, grabs a spear off the wall, and mutters something about killing a few animals in the woods.

Right before he leaves, he winks at me. "Care for stew again tonight?"

I grimace. When can I get the time to tell Brisei to switch out the soups again? What with Homer having her on a "laundry emergency."

Homer has also convinced Elin that in his region of Palikari, all the brides have their bachelorette party with the richest of the rich.

"Having more than one servant there is in bad taste," he said at dinner last night, over a large bite of goat cheese. "People in town will say that you could not convince the wealthiest of your friends to come over, so you had to make it look like there are more people with servants."

Elin, wanting to save face, also shooed away the servants this morning with "urgent tasks." Like Homer predicted, she kept behind the woman who guards the storeroom. In case one of the partygoers wants to get their grubby little hands on the gold and fancy dresses downstairs.

One servant places plates full of custards, cheeses, and fruits in the hearth room. Most of the time, we eat out in the courtyard. In Palikari, they conduct this party indoors to remind the woman that her duties lie at home, in the kitchen, and in the ordering of the household affairs.

Other fun rituals before the wedding, according to Elin this morning, include a boy who has both his parents sleeping in the same bed as the bride the night before the wedding. This reminds a bride that her duty, also, is to pop out lots of little ones.

So yeah, let's hope Homer gets me out of here before that.

Elin spots a servant and waves at her, clicking her tongue. "Back outdoors. There is pruning in the garden to do."

Wonder if she'll spot Homer out there picking fruit and putting it in baskets. If all else fails, we'll have that for our journey. Brisei informed the kitchen about the surprise laundry day, so they've packed her some cheeses, bread, and wineskins. Not enough to last four people more than two meals, but it would have to do.

They rolled the cart to the stalls where Atro was grooming horses. He'll bring the cart back once Homer has changed into Greek garb, and me, into that of a servant. We convinced one of the older servants to switch clothes with me.

"I nursed Pandarus," she told me. "If he kills me, his milk and blood is on his hands."

Guilt clenched my gut like a fist when she said this. Would we really risk this old woman's life for her clothes? I made sure to emphasize over and over to her to say that we forced her to do it and wouldn't say why. I doubt that will make much of a difference.

I want to bring her. If we take anyone in our party who looks rich, the Greeks will stop us, and she will be wearing my rich people clothing.

Speaking of, memories reel from yesterday about what our journey will look like today.

"Where are we going to again, Homie?" I'd asked him this after I told Cersei to bring me a gift to the bachelorette party. No way we'll leave this town without that *muchacha*.

"Brisei's tribe. It's a three-day journey, but hers is one of the closest to the Palikarian border. And they are rebuilding. No doubt they'll welcome back the daughter of the shepherd of the people with open arms. They won't question whoever she brings with her in her entourage."

The trick—getting there without getting captured.

The servant Elin yelled at zooms through the double doors, and I perch in the chair she's placed for me at one end of the table, the most important spot.

Women from Elin's extended family and wealthier neighbors filter through the entrance to the house minutes later. Amber beads and dangling earrings glitter from their necks and ears. They've put on their most spotless garments and carry baskets full of gifts in their arms. When they spot no servants, they place them at the feet of the one guarding the storeroom door.

I glimpse the dulled armor over the mantle.

"Why can't we use the armor over the hearth, Homie?"

"Like they wouldn't notice that's gone missing?"

True. If someone pilfered my Christmas tree, I would spot the difference right away. No, we have to go through with Operation Wandering Womb.

Once the chatter from the ladies settles and they each have a chance to cram some briny olive relish down their throats, Elin lifts herself from her seat and stands in front of the hearth.

"Ladies, as you may be aware, this *aulia* will be different than the usual format. Harper, having escaped from her home, did not have a chance to bring any childhood memories with her. We have asked that you bring one toy from your children in place of her dedicating all her toys to the goddess of childbirth, Lú."

They rise from their chairs, the wood groaning beneath them, and amble over to their baskets.

One by one, they lift the childhood objects. A black horse, a doll made of clay, a carved wooden sparrow. They place them in a sad pile in the hearth.

Elin lifts her arms to the heavens. "Oh, Lú, accept this offering as Harper is to leave the days of her childhood and pursue the great duty of bringing children into the world herself."

As she continues the prayer, sadness wells in my throat again.

Cersei, if she doesn't escape with us, and survives the invasion, will have to do this in three years. Give up her childhood early for the sake of a man.

When she molds clay, when she plays with other children, does she do so with a pang of sadness in her chest? Knowing, dreading? Like me right now?

Elin finishes the prayer and motions for the servant guarding the storerooms to ignite the hearth. She does so and returns to her post right after. Flames from across the room form sweat above my lips. I can't tear my gaze away from the toys crisping and charring in the fire.

"For the next part of the *aulia,* we dedicate hair on Harper's head to the goddess of love, Oditi. That in doing so, the goddess of love may bless her marriage." Elin draws a knife from her belt. Why didn't I notice her wearing it before? She looks so much cooler with that.

She pinches a lock of my hair and saws off the strands. Then she casts the hair into the flames.

Homer said I need to cause a scene somewhere between the hair burning and prayer about the hair burning. Most of the bachelorette party festivities fizzle after that.

So I shove my forearm into my gut and let out a guttural groan, loud enough for Homer to hear me out in the garden.

"Oh. Oh!"

"Harper!" Elin's voice quivers, maybe worried she committed some serious voodoo with my hair by accident. "Tell me what is the matter."

"I feel something below floating. I cannot stop it, and I fear it will not stop rising."

"*Hyster*," Elin mutters. She clicks her tongue in the direction of the storeroom. "You, carry her upstairs and weigh her down." Then her voice travels back to me. "I had wondered if this would happen. You are far too old to be unwed."

The fire in my cheeks travels to my neck. *Excuse me?*

Before I have a chance to glare at Elin, someone flops me on my back and a cluster of ladies carry me up the steps. At one point, I feel myself slipping backward from the upward angle and worry they'll drop me, and I'll crack my skull on the steps.

They reach my room and plop me on the bed. Sure enough, the servant who helped carry me lands on my stomach. I let out an "oof" and grimace at the sudden weight on my abdomen. Good thing I relieved myself before the party.

Ladies around me click their tongues and pass me sorrowful glances. A few share stories of their "harrowing" experiences with the wandering womb.

Scrunched in the corner of the room nearest to the door, Elin watches me. Perhaps for a sign that my womb has calmed down and returned to its proper place. I need to give Homer plenty of time to grab the armor and other supplies. So I ask the women to tell me more stories about their flighty wombs.

They pat my hands. One tells me, "Not to worry. The line of Pandarus is quite fertile. He shall sow a seed within you soon and weigh down your womb."

Yikes, did not want to hear that sentence, like, ever.

After several more ladies inform me about what I can "look forward to" tomorrow, I've had enough. If Homer hasn't gotten the goods, he never will.

I pat my abdomen. "It has settled for now. Thank you."

Elin motions for the servant to rise. She bounces off my stomach and flees downstairs. The others bid me adieu and tell me to stay in my bed until morning, so I can make it harder for the womb to shimmy up my body into my throat.

Once they exit, I wait.

Moments later, Brisei appears with the older woman in tow. I recognize her from laundry day. She didn't trust me on the shore, and I can't blame her, after the danger we're about to put her in.

"Are you sure you want to do this?" I rise from the bed.

"I fear not Elin. For she has other matters on her mind." With shaky arms the woman pulls the rags over her head. "Her son Pandarus. Even though I nursed him, I do not know what he will do."

My fingers falter on the hem of my dress. "Brisei, are you certain we cannot take her with us?"

"Not in your clothes. Sorry." She chews on her bottom lip. "If Pandarus has respect for any of the servants in the house, it is her. She breastfed him, raised him. When she agreed to this, I knew he would hesitate to do her any harm."

If only they gave the slaves more than one outfit. During laundry day, many of them had stripped and washed their attire. Probably get that chance just once a month.

I shimmy out of my billowing dress and tug on the older woman's. Sweat and some other mysterious stench wafts from the fabric. The dress comes up to my knees and has frayed in almost every area.

In my dress, the older woman looks radiant. I squeeze her shoulder. "Thank you."

She points her chin at Brisei and then back at me. "Keep her safe."

"I promise, on my life." By instinct, I clasp the dress to hoist it up, and the fabric goes up to my thighs. Brisei, behind me, tears the veil out of my hair. Once she discards it, she goes into Elin's daughter's room to retrieve Talith. All three of us pop out the bedroom window and climb down the ladder.

In the courtyard, I spy Homer at the gate in Greek armor. His thin shoulders are swallowed by the breastplate, but dang, he looks *fine.* The guardsman and his dogs have evacuated the area. He probably left for the midday meal. Good timing, considering the dogs wouldn't have taken too well to a man in foreign armor.

Homer must've planned for that.

"Atro has the cart ready at the stables." Homer jabs a thumb over his shoulder. "Ready to go?"

Shakiness fills my arms and legs. Everything moved so fast, and now that I've had time to think about it…

Homer must see my lip quivering because he cups my chin and says in English, "We're going to be okay, okay?"

"Okay."

"Find your brave like you helped all of us to do."

I suck in a breath. "You are my brave, Homie."

"And you, mine." He plants a kiss on my lips, perhaps the last one we'll have a chance to share. Who knows what will happen in the next seventy-two hours?

We break apart and something glitters in my periphery.

I turn my neck and flinch.

Pandarus, five feet away, glowers at us. And then he throws down his spear onto the courtyard.

Chapter Twenty-Two
How the Eagle Dies

"Pick up the spear." Spit flies from Pandarus's lips.

Every curse word I know flies through my head—English and Palikarian ones I made up since Homer refused to teach me any. Of course the man who challenges anyone who so much as looks at him wrong would catch his bride-to-be kissing a temple slave outside the gates.

From the corner of my eye, I see Homer shaking. I'm betting all of his spear training with Brisei has fled him now. Totally get it. Same happens to me when faced with a multiple-choice test.

I step in front of Homer and throw up my arms. I keep my voice as smooth as possible. "Pandarus, this is not what you think. You do not need to—"

His eyes flash at me, and his hand flies up. I half expect the back of it to meet my cheek. "I will deal with you once the fight is over. Be silent, woman."

My shoulders jut up to my ears. Oh yikes. Yikes, yikes, yikes. I fight away the memories of Dad when he'd get into similar moods. Completely sober right now, Pandarus hasn't even touched a bottle of booze. I thought he'd gone hunting.

He must notice how my eyebrows narrow because he lifts his chin at the house across the street. "I asked one of the youths if they would like to accompany me. For some reason, they were not home. Their whole estate, deserted. Only servants milled about the place."

Part of me wonders if Atro got to the house yesterday or early this morning. Tons of people dressed in rags headed to the river this morning with carts full of laundry. Strange how no one seemed to catch on, but maybe the Greeks operate a lot like the Palikarians. They don't notice the poor, the slaves, the invisible.

"When I turned around, I noticed Homer sneaking into the house. So I hid in the bush over there to investigate. After all, my mother shooed me out of the house for the *bridal* rites."

More spit flies on the word "bridal." I shrink into Brisei's and Talith's shoulders that flank me now.

"He emerged from the household wearing Greek armor that I rightfully won from the battle. It is clear to me now." He gestures at Homer's garb. "You intend to rob me of my war spoils and of my future wife. I cannot let that stand. Now pick up the spear."

Homer clenches his jaw, and I hear his teeth click from two yards away. "Pandarus, as Harper said, this is not as this appears. I implore you to remember the rules of *xenia* and hospitality. As your guest, I have no wish to fight you. As that would go against all Palikarian laws."

My heartbeat leaps into my throat. By technical standards, they shouldn't fight. Even if they were sworn enemies from other countries, they can't touch each other.

That might mean I have to go through with the wedding, but at least Homer walks out of here alive.

Pandarus slaps his palm against his stomach and bellows a string of laughter that prickles my ears. Then he cocks his head. "You know, Homer, I am in two minds. One mind says to stone you for pretending to be a man of high standing, when I know you used to work as a slave in the temple of Leinos."

He stoops to the courtyard and picks up a loose stone.

"After all, cowards who return from the battlefield receive a death by stoning. Why should you be any different?"

Pandarus tosses the rock and catches it.

"My other mind says that since you have acted with cowardice that I can ignore the laws of *xenia*. We can therefore engage in a duel of spears. So I give you the choice. Pick it up, or—" He cuts a glance to the rock and smiles.

Great, so either my boyfriend can get pummeled to a pulp with stones or have a spear sunk into his gut. Excellent options.

Homer's knees crack as he bends to the ground and grips the spear with shaky hands.

"Good choice." Pandarus glances at Homer's armor up and down. "Now, are we to fight like cowards in armor or like men?"

Are you kidding me right now? Homer needs those shin guards to block against Pandarus's favorite move, "let's stab the guy in the legs until he puts his shield down".

"Like men." Homer places both of his hands on his helmet and thrusts it onto the courtyard. Metal dings against the stones.

A smirk cuts up Pandarus's cheek. Without another word, he jogs toward the house to get his own spear.

"Homie," I hiss in English, "what are you doing? You need that armor."

He shimmies out of the breastplate. "Most of the moves Brisei taught me go for the breastplate area. If Pandarus isn't in armor, I have the best chance at striking." The breastplate clatters on the ground. "And besides, I'm fast, and that armor was weighing me down."

"You can't go through with this."

"Harper, I'm not going to convince him any differently." He kneels to unbuckle the shin guards. "And neither are you."

True. If I'd found my betrothed kissing some random dude in my driveway, I might want to commit some light murder too.

Wind whips in my hair, and I crane my sweaty face toward

the breeze, in the direction of the stables. Wait a second, Atro. He and Pandarus were very good friends on the battlefield. Maybe if Pandarus's girlfriend can't convince him, then maybe his roommate…

I point a finger at Homer. "Don't you dare fight until I get back. Stall him. Say that Harper needs to see him in his full glory. Whatever."

"Harper, what are you—?"

My dress bunches underneath my fingertips as I sprint toward the barns. I can't tell if Brisei or Talith have followed behind me, because my wheezing breaths take up most of my hearing until I reach the entrance.

The scent of hay punches me in the nostrils. "Atro!"

I clasp my knees and exhale, inhale heavy breaths.

Atro un-noses himself from one of the horses. I've seen some cat owners do that, placing their forehead and nose against the snout of their kittens. "Harper, what is it?"

"I need—you stop—fight."

"What?"

"Follow me." I flick my wrist and unbend myself. Here's to hoping that Pandarus will take his sweet ol' time deciding which spear would look best when it put puncture wounds in my boyfriend. I blink away images from the night of the soothsayer.

Too bad Brisei and Talith can't tell me to look away.

"What fight?" Atro reaches my side and we half-jog on the way to the courtyard.

"Between Homer and"—*wheeze*—"Pandarus."

I spy the courtyard, and Pandarus has not emerged from the house yet. Calmness fills my lungs that still have fiery thorns wrapped around them. My pace slows to a walk.

Sunlight burns my periphery on the path ahead, but I spy a

small figure running toward me. Cersei un-blurs and holds up something glittering in the sunlight. She flashes all her teeth when she recognizes me.

"Harper! I did not know if the rites had ended, but I wanted to bring you a gift." She lifts up the same crown her sister wore on her wedding day. "A family heirloom. I figure, if the Greeks invade, I may not have a chance to wear it when my time comes."

Something like relief spills into her voice. Either happy to see me or grateful not to have to go through with any sort of future marriage.

"Cersei, it is lovely, but now is not the ti—"

"Why are you wearing this clothing?" She pinches the frayed hem of my dress.

"I shall enjoy decorating the courtyard with your blood." Pandarus flies out of the house with a shiny spear. Yup, the dude definitely took his time in the storehouses deciding on the perfect one, because it doesn't have soot covering it like the one he handed Homie.

I wonder if Homer's weapon has a dulled edge, like the other armor over the hearth, to give Pandarus an extra advantage in the duel.

Atro seems to get the picture because he strides past me, into the courtyard, and in front of the un-armored Homer. "Pandarus, this is foolish. I ask you to stop immediately."

The flames in Pandarus's eyes extinguish and he slackens. Then he hunches over again. "Atro, step aside."

"Are you not to marry tomorrow?"

He clicks his jaw and glares at me. "I am."

"Could you not ask Homer to flee the city as penalty for any erroneous actions on his part?"

Pandarus's knuckles whiten on his spear. "I could."

"Then why all this senseless violence? Have you not had your fair share on the battlefield?" Atro's legs wobble. "Do not the same nightmares plague you at night as they do to me now?"

Whimpers and screams from Pandarus's room had gotten worse ever since his father's funeral.

Pandarus clamps his eyelids shut and dips his chin to the courtyard. An image of a scene we read in class from *The Odyssey* flashes through my brain. Athena stepped in when Odysseus went on a rampage and killed the suitors who had come onto his wife— because he'd been gone for twenty years and all, and one would reasonably assume a guy had died after all that time.

She asked Odysseus to stop fighting, or the bloodshed would never end.

Maybe Atro will have similar luck here.

Pandarus's eyes fly open. The flames have returned. "Atro, you are not shepherd of the people." He shoves Atro to the side and stands a foot away from Homer. "I can change the rules."

Pandarus's spear angles at Homer's nose as Pandarus crouches. "Atro, give us the marks to begin."

"Pandarus, please."

"Give us them, or I will start without warning."

Atro hesitates, then steps back. He raises his palms and slaps his thighs.

Pandarus lunges as Homer, who ducks out of the way. Cersei appears to have gotten up to speed because she hides behind me. I tell her to shut her eyes until the boys have finished.

I, on the other hand, can't tear my gaze away no matter how hard I try.

Like the night with the soothsayer, Pandarus aims his spear over and over again at Homer's exposed shins. Homer seems to anticipate this, and after the third jab-and-jump-out-of-the-way maneuver, Homer grazes his spearhead into Pandarus's arm.

Pandarus roars as a stream of blood drips down his triceps.

Man alive, Homie, Brisei taught you well.

Off-balance from someone anticipating his favorite move, Pandarus drips with sweat and wobbles back into position. This time he aims his spear at Homer's head. Homer ducks, but not before the spearhead gashes his cheek on the downswing.

Yikes, Pandarus has caught on to Homer's tactics as well.

"I thought you said we would fight like men." Pandarus swings his staff repeatedly over Homer's head and forces him toward the courtyard wall to the left.

Homer pants and continues to back away from the swipes.

My eyes go wide, and I glance back at Brisei. "He is going to back him into the wall."

She chews on her lip and keeps her eyes pressed on the fight. "I know. Homer and I have practiced this, backing him into the cave wall. Notice how winded Pandarus has become as they journey over there. That means—"

He's getting sloppy. Something tells me fights with his opponents haven't usually lasted this long. Because he always got them on the shin-swipe move.

I glance back and notice that with every swing from Pandarus, Homer uses his frog-leg running move to avoid the thrust. Pandarus glistens with sweat now as Homer has dodged his last few blows and aimed a few more at Pandarus's shins.

Brisei behind me lets out one laugh. "Figured it might be helpful to try Pandarus's favorite moves on him."

Veins pop out of Pandarus's neck when Homer does this. He roars and strikes his spear down at Homer again and again. Pandarus's arms wobble, his swipes getting more and more crooked and weak.

Homer backs into the wall and lands on his butt when

ducking from one of the downward strikes. Shoot, Brisei probably didn't teach Homer how to fight from this position.

My heartbeat throbs in my throat. I catch Cersei watching and I tell her to shut her eyes now.

Pandarus aims his spearhead downward. "Nowhere left to—"

Homer shoves his spear into Pandarus's gut.

Strikes true. Black blood pools at the spot of the wound and spreads throughout the white fabric. Pandarus sinks to his knees and coughs up blood. Now's my turn to look away. Vomit surges at the back of my throat, but this time I swallow the bile down.

He—I relax my shoulders—actually did it.

"Brisei," I whisper, not daring to open my eyes with the gurgling noises coming from the courtyard. "How did you know to teach him that?"

"I did not. There is something to be said about an underestimated opponent."

Someone taps my shoulder, and I open my eyes. Pandarus now lies in the middle of the courtyard in a pool of dark blood. Atro crouches beside him and shuts Pandarus's eyelids with his fingertips.

Tears form in Atro's waterline, and a pang of sadness strikes my chest once my heartbeat has slowed.

My eyes flick back to the household, and I blink away the memories of the archeologist's backyard two summers ago. Even though Henry had kidnapped Homer and tried to kill us, part of me then wished we waited around to see his daughter find him. So we could understand, fully, what we had done.

Should I run inside and let Elin know?

With how she reacted to her husband passing, who knows what she'll do if she finds out about her son?

My legs carry me to Atro, and I place a hand on his back. The gesture feels awkward.

"You must have cared a lot about him."

He sniffs and shields his face with his cloak. Lots of men did this at Ulix's funeral. Must not be acceptable to show emotions in this world. "That is not why I weep."

"Why then?"

"As you do, I saw him as what he could have been."

Water blurs my eyes, and hot streams pool down my cheeks. I imagine Homer as I first found him in England, insecure, afraid, always running away. Brisei and Talith, wounded by slave traders and soldiers who took them. Atro, on the sidelines of the funeral games, wishing to compete, and Cersei in the wedding crown that glitters in her fingertips.

If they had not been seen, they would've stayed that way.

And if they had not seen me, I would still be huddled in the temple to Leinos when I first arrived here.

What could Pandarus have been like if he knew what he could become? Visions swim behind my eyes of him ruling as a kind shepherd of peace who cares about his people, of him using those impulsive actions to fight against the invading Greeks and saving vulnerable villagers.

"I see him now as you do, Atro." I release my palm from his back. "And I am truly sorry."

Atro doesn't say anything. Instead, he rises and steps into the house.

Homer, still sitting, leans his head against the courtyard wall. He, too, cries. I go to him and tear off some cloth at the bottom of my dress. I press the fabric against the slash on his cheek. How it must burn to mix his tears with that blood.

"He's going to join my nightmares, along with Henry." He whispers this in English and claps his forehead against my shoulder.

"You had no choice." My voice shakes in my throat. I lace my fingers with his, and neither of us says anything. We just stare at the scene before us and blink rivers down our cheeks.

Atro emerges from the double doors with a white sheet. He places the shroud over Pandarus's body and lifts a prayer to the heavens. Near the gate, the three girls hug one another, each shaking. I have no idea if they feel relief, sadness, or what, but the blood has left their faces. Any death, no matter to whom it belongs, leaves the living shaken.

Once he finishes his prayer, Atro rises and turns to Homer and me.

"We must hope that someone sees him soon and gives him a proper burial." He cuts a glance at the house. "Homer, it would be best if you put your armor back on. You have a long journey ahead of you."

"Ahead of *us*." Brisei breaks from her huddle and steps into the courtyard. "Atro, I will not be able to stand it if you stay behind."

"What of the people?"

Homer has risen from his spot and wiggles into his breastplate. I go with him and help clip on the shin guards.

"The rest will leave tomorrow, like they had planned to do after the wedding." Brisei reaches him and clasps his arm.

"What of duty?"

"What of this?" She pulls him down and plants a kiss on his lips. Then she tugs at his arm to follow her onto the dirt road. "Come."

Screams from the streets interrupt Atro's protest.

I fasten the right shin guard, and Homer and I race to where the group has clustered. I peer down the road, past the shops, and toward the blur of white city gates in the distance. Smoke plumes from one of them, and people in the houses ahead have fled from their doors onto the street, in our direction.

My throat has gone dry. "Please tell me that my eyes are deceiving me right now."

"They are not, my lady." Brisei's lip quivers. "The Greeks have begun the invasion early."

Chapter Twenty-Three
How the City Walls Crumble

"WHY ARE THEY ATTACKING EARLY?"

My legs wobble so much that I have to hold on to the courtyard fence to stabilize myself. Maybe this is why Herodotus never documented the people escaping. They didn't have time to.

"They must have stopped one of the people we helped to leave early." Atro turns to us, cheeks drained of color. "We must go now."

Cersei cries into my skirt and mutters the word family over and over again. I glance up in the direction of the smoke. Her home is close to the fires that seem to spread from building to building. We won't be able to get to them in time.

"Can we help no one else?" I glimpse the house behind me, but not before my eyes snag on the sheeted body of Pandarus. "What about Elin? Her daughter?"

Elin had sent most of the servants into town for various errands to avoid them attending the bachelorette party. Otherwise, I'd suggest them as well. Something tells me, hopes within me, that the Greeks will ignore them as Homer said they would anyone poor in this village.

Atro grips Brisei's hand and releases. "We can try."

Homer and I dash into the house. I feel the shadows of Brisei and Talith behind me. Ever with me, even during an invasion.

I motion for Talith and Homer to head into Elin's daughter's room. "Split up," I tell Homer in English. "We don't have time to go all together to each."

He nods and tugs Talith's arm up the stairs and into my own

room. Brisei and I dash into the one across the hallway and find Elin in her bed. Her grayed face stares out of the window, blankets drawn up to her chest.

"Elin, the Greeks are invading. If you wish to escape, we must do so now."

She doesn't move.

"Elin, please."

I reach for her arm and tug, but Brisei clicks her tongue behind me. I release my grip. "What?"

"My lady, we cannot *force* her to go." She passes me a significant look.

My shoulders drop and I turn back to the bed. Dust collects on some of the nooks and crannies of the wooden bedpost. A snake pattern crawls across the footboard.

The room smells of staleness and something rancid. I wonder if she has had anyone clean in here these past few days.

"Please, I do not have time to ask again. Think of your daughter. Think of—" I can't mention Pandarus. Will we have to go out the back doors, through the garden, to avoid her seeing his body?

Does she already know?

"Think of your grandchild. They need you."

Elin firms her jaw. "There is nothing for me. Not without my husband. Go."

She hisses the last word and refuses to look in our direction. Arms band around mine and pull me back to the door. Elin's made her decision. We can't do anything about it. If we dragged her onto the cart and rode to Greece, how would that make us any better than the people who did the same to Brisei and Talith?

Speaking of, when we reach Elin's daughter, Talith saying "Greeks" over and over again, while Homer interjects about how they need to go, hasn't moved the wilted figure in the bed. Like her mother, she refuses to lift her gaze away from the window.

Homer passes me a sad glance. "She will not come."

Her baby, nestled by her side, scrunches his eyelids, somewhere deep in sleep.

I wonder about the dream he has. Is it wonderful, and can we step inside it for a moment?

"What about the baby, Homer?" I clasp his shoulder and feel the tremble in my fingertips.

"If she does not come with us, and he is left behind, they will take him as a slave. He may work in one of their temples like I did." His voice cracks on the final words.

I squeeze tighter, to steady him. "We cannot allow that to happen."

"Harper," he hisses in English, "we can't simply rip the baby away from her. That would make us monst—"

"Take him." The daughter turns her chin to us, lips trembling. "Please." She whispers the last word and cranes her neck back to the window. I wish we could drag her out of bed, talk some sense into her.

Homer cradles the baby in his arms and hands him to Talith. Somehow, in the exchange, the child doesn't wake. Homer palms my back and I head toward the door. It hits me, halfway down the stairs, that Elin's daughter had a perfect view of the duel that went down between Homer and Pandarus minutes before now.

Did she love her brother? Did the duel set her over the edge?

I try to wipe away the thoughts. She deteriorated long before today, and Elin didn't even have a view of the courtyard. Grief about their husbands and their cities must've kept them glued to their sheets.

Brisei has something bundled under her arms. A fur blanket.

"For the child." She hugs the wad tighter to her chest. "It

had fallen to the floor of Elin's bedroom. I assumed she would not miss it."

Based on how the screams outside have grown louder, the Greeks have weaved their way up the houses on the hill. They'll get here within minutes.

Bright sunlight burns my eyes when I step into the courtyard. When my vision returns, I see Cersei kneeling over Pandarus's body. She places something metallic on his belly, the wedding crown she had gifted to me. Neither of us will wear it now.

She rises, spine stiff as it can go. "I have decided to go with you. Atro has convinced me."

Atro has a cluster of baskets by his feet. Someone has covered them in a white cloth.

"We cannot take the cart with us." He jabs his chin in the direction of the stalls. "The horse will slow us down and make us more susceptible to the Greek armies and robbers. We grabbed what we could."

I pick up a woven one that weighs my arms down. My fingers pinch the cloth and I spot the wineskins stuffed inside. Great, this won't last all of us the whole journey.

"To the river." Atro grabs a basket, and Brisei picks up the remaining one. Homer scoops up his shield and spear into his arms. I realize, now, that he had to have pulled the spear shaft out of Pandarus after the fight.

My memory from those minutes ago feels blurry and distant. I wonder if the details will come back to me later.

We shuffle up the road past the horse stalls. Atro passes one longing glance at them before double-timing his steps. He had to leave behind his prize horse from the games. Cersei shuffles close beside me and sniffs, muttering something about her goat. Although screams sound behind me and the scent of smoke clogs my nostrils, I refuse to look behind.

Brisei wails beside me and gestures at the shadows from the woods. Soldiers in glittering armor advance toward us. Guess "ahead" ain't all that great to look at either.

We huddle together and wait for the inevitable. I shield Cersei with my body and turn my back to the soldiers, and I force Brisei and Talith to seek shelter underneath my wings. If we go out, I do so first.

Funny how two summers back I couldn't stand the sight of people.

Now I have found some blessed ones worth dying for.

My heartbeat roars in my ears.

"I saw a Palikarian family, of great wealth, hiding over there."

I crane my neck over my shoulder. Homer, having spoken perfect Greek, gestures at the empty neighbor's house, across the street from Elin's estate. We can only hope they didn't run into an army when they escaped the city.

A soldier with a blue horsehair crest helmet squints at Homer. "Well done." He claps a hand on Homer's shoulder, which has all but shrunk underneath the huge breastplate. "You shall receive your reward in due time."

Horsehair dude gestures with his chin for the other soldiers to follow him. They charge in the direction of the house. Homer waits until they've disappeared from our view and glances at me. "Run."

I drop my arms from around my friends, as does Atro. He's formed the other flank in our "protect the others" circle. Liquid in my basket jiggles and sloshes as we sprint toward a wooded area ahead.

Acid fills my lungs and I wheeze, but we continue into the shadows of trees. Homer runs next to me and grips one handle of the basket, so I only have to hold the other end with one arm. He must've discarded his shield but still carries his spear.

We continue to run until we reach the river. Sand fills our shoes as we stop, drop the baskets, and flick our flushed faces with water. Birdsong drowns away the sound of my racing heart.

The baby in Talith's arms has awoken and lets out a weak cry. She lifts him to her breast, but he refuses to eat.

Brisei clasps her sides and pants. "Friends, we must continue. I am afraid we will not like the next three days." She retrieves her basket and splashes into the water.

We follow. Not sure whether to feel relief or dread.

Dread, definitely dread.

The first day, we continue to make our way through no man's land, a place between civilizations. Apparently between Brisei's tribe in Greece and Homer's village in Palikari, a stretch of forests and mountainous terrain bridges the two. Which means lots of blisters, lots of thigh chafing, and lots of sore arms from carrying baskets and babies the whole time. We alternate who handles the child every so often. At night we find a cave that has a few dry spots we can lie on. We turtle ourselves into our rags and set out the blanket on the floor for Talith and the baby. He finally eats, and so do we. Half our rations.

That night, some animal sneaks into the cave at night and steals half our bread and cheeses. Come morning, we have enough for one more meal, so we decide we'll eat it around evening and hope for the best. Thankfully, we drank quite a bit of the wine as Homer recounted stories from *The Iliad* for us. He would tell us more on the journey, but we pass the hours in silence, in case any Greek soldiers have decided to lurk nearby and might hear us. And besides, with all our panting and wheezing, we couldn't get out a "once upon a time" if we wanted. Brisei has given up on humming the "Song of Linus" to herself a few miles in. I leave tonight's meal with a burning stomach. Man alive, I will regret waking up in the morning. If I can stop shivering. I press myself into Homer's back for warmth.

On day three, I wake up with a horrible emptiness and achiness that goes all the way down to my toes.

Back when I was ten, my church did a thirty-hour famine to raise money for a mission in the Dominican Republic, and I had awoken sore and grouchy then too. We cheated for that and guzzled soda and chewed on gum the whole night to help us through.

Now, as I force myself to sit up along with the others, dizziness fills my skull.

We've discarded the baskets at the back of the cave near a moss-coated wall, so at least we don't have to carry anything other than the baby. Brisei lifts up a cracked-lip prayer to some river goddess that we'll find water along the way.

I chew off skin on my lip and wait until it bleeds, so I can taste something before the journey.

Doesn't help that Homer and I both awoke in sweats from nightmares about Pandarus's body. We cuddled and tried to soothe the other to sleep each time it happened. For some reason, this conjured up images for me of Elin and her daughter. I hate to think of what became of them.

During today's hike, with no cloud cover whatsoever, I force myself to focus on anything but the needle-sharp pain in the soles of my feet. Not a clue how many miles we hiked, but I can guess dozens by this point.

Every song I can recollect runs through my head as my legs wobble. Black film must coat the eyes of everyone else, because on more than one occasion Cersei bonks into a tree, and Atro starts to head down the wrong path until we call him back.

Everyone here, except for me, has experience with long stretches of hunger, but not while taking a lengthy journey.

We reach a river and dunk our faces into it. Hesitation doesn't exist in this moment.

If the giardia and other waterborne parasites want to take me down, this is how I'll go. Cersei locates a clay deposit, and she and I distract ourselves by molding a dolphin on the shore while Talith breastfeeds the baby. She must not have much left in her because the baby cries when she lifts him to her shoulder to burp him.

I massage my feet underneath the waters and wince at how the blisters and scabs sting.

Without a moment to spare, once Talith finishes burping the baby, we re-lace our sandals and set out again. I've run out of songs and angry prayers to God. So I hold in breaths and let them out in moans through my nostrils, hoping the burn in my lungs can distract me from the aches in my toes.

No luck, that made me way more lightheaded. I have to cling to a cliffside for support. The rest of the group continues ahead. Homer, the only person behind me, stops.

"Homie, I can't—"

"What? Do this?" He pants each word. We have to keep talking and extraneous movements to a minimum. Homer doesn't look irritated, but his voice comes out that way. All of ours do. A side effect of not having food in our bellies.

"It feels like there are needles in my"—gasp—"feet."

Sunbeams burn my cheeks from above. I pray for clouds again, but nothing comes.

"You know, Harper." He lifts his arm as if to wipe sweat from his face. He must think the movement will take too much energy, because he drops his arm. "This is the most important part in a hero's journey."

"What? Where their feet fall off?"

"No, the boring parts. The parts people skip"—breath—"over, because they want to see the good stuff about the hero winning, and not the long journey it takes to get there."

I shut my eyelids to keep the world from spinning. The water that sloshes in my empty stomach does nothing to help me stay conscious. Already my lips have gone desert dry again. "What do you mean?"

"When a hero gets a rejection slip from a college. When they receive horrendous feedback from judges. When their feet feel like someone has placed hot coals under them."

I open my eyes and see him with his eyebrows lifted.

"That's what makes them the hero, Harper." He takes a step in the direction of the group. "Because they take a step." Again. "And another. And another."

Pains shoot through my soles, but I ignore them as I tread forward toward him. He holds out an arm, far enough away from me so I have to keep walking. At last, I strain my hand enough and grip his fingers.

"And that, Harper." Breath. "Is why you're my hero."

The group has vanished behind a cliffside. Brisei pops her head back around and motions with a churning hand for us to race to her. We pick up our pace and almost bump into her when we turn the corner. Rocks skitter past our sandals and down the cliff.

"Friends."

Brisei gestures at a city in the distance. Whitewashed buildings crawl up an open hillside, without a single forest in sight. Some of the buildings have scorch marks from a previous invasion, but like everyone had said…they were rebuilding.

"Welcome home."

Chapter Twenty-Four
How the Pilgrims Find Their Country

Two Months Later
Athens, 800 BCE

Rosy-fingered dawn appears this morning.

I watch the sunrise from the front steps of the estate with a slice of bread, dipped in wine, in my hands. One of Brisei's hired hands pours a bucket of acorns into a trough for the pigs in her ancestral home. It surprises me that the architecture looks so similar to the houses in Palikari.

It also seems that a few of her sisters survived and made it back to the home. Perhaps their own servants hid with them in the invasion and returned with them. I don't ask many questions. Those will come with time. It seems like a touchy subject around Brisei.

When we returned to her home two months ago, she released all the servants and told them they could stay if they would accept payment.

According to Homie, coins won't show up in Greece for another few centuries. For now, they accept gold and cattle for their hard work. We've spent the last two months building houses behind our estate for them if they chose to stay.

As for the rest of the work, the six of us who arrived here handle it. I help with the weaving, sweeping, and of course, the laundry.

I catch sight of a smaller figure racing up the dirt road. In the burn of pink sunlight, Cersei beams at me when she enters through the gate, carrying an amphora in her palms.

"You were up early." I still can't speak in Greek yet. Brisei has taught all of us words in our spare moments, and I try my best to repeat what I can when in her presence.

She says we can go with her to parties once we know enough phrases to get by. Based on my calculations, we can do so in the fall.

"What did you sculpt?"

Cersei pads up the stone courtyard in bare feet. No matter how hard we try, after that long hike to Athens, we haven't been able to convince her to wear sandals for more than a few hours. She lifts up the jar, which has some sort of lettering at the bottom.

"It is for Alcmaeon."

She runs her fingers up and down the name she's inscribed at the bottom of the vase. Sure enough, in Greek letters, it reads, Ἀλκμαίων

Ever since we got here, Cersei has spent every moment learning the Phoenician letters from Talith. She says some of them don't translate easily into the Greek language, so she changed them up to match the sounds that came from her throat.

Two weeks into our stay, Cersei had created all the letters.

"I had to get up early." She sets the jar onto the steps and rubs the heel of her hand against her eyes. "So many people in town want their names on pottery."

With trade routes opening up with other nations these past few months, everyone has gotten a little excited about all things foreign. Who knows? Maybe, in a few years, people will read and write in the Greek alphabet Cersei's developed from the Phoenician one she learned from Talith.

Speaking of. I shove the rest of my bread into my mouth and scoop Cersei's latest creation into my palms. "I will take this to Talith to give to Alcmaeon. Breakfast is on the table."

It was my turn to grind grain and make bread this morning. My knees ache, but I don't mind the soreness as much as I did the first few weeks I had to complete this task.

I step inside and heat burns my cheeks. Takes forever for those wood ovens to cool down. Up the stairs I go into Talith's room. She sleeps with the baby Alcmaeon by her side.

Elin's daughter never told us his name. In Palikari, they don't christen their children until the ninth or tenth day after birth, since so many babies die within the first few days of life. It was the one name she never woke up and screamed.

So Talith came up with the name for the child, after Brisei's late husband. She's caught onto the Greek language far faster than us, because the other day, she told Brisei, "I hope he can do assembly, just as your husband did."

I set the jar on the trunk in front of the bed. A smile plays on Talith's lips, I assume from a pleasant dream. Good, this poor thing deserves something sweet after all this time.

My tiptoes lead me out of the room and I almost bump straight into Homer, who has emerged from his bedroom. I shut the door behind me and let him head down the stairs after we both exchange a "sorry."

"Did I miss the sunrise?"

"It's a beautiful one." We seldom speak in English unless we've found ourselves alone. I've lost a lot of words, and imagine in a few months, will forget a great many of them. No wonder Homer had me speak with him in Palikarian an hour each day.

We step into the hearth room and find Atro and Brisei chatting on chairs draped in animal furs. Atro props his feet onto a footstool, unaware of our presence.

"The assembly does not seem keen on allowing for those of lesser wealth."

Since the assembly was also not "keen" on a woman joining, Brisei has Atro going in her place. She announced her engagement to him a month in. As daughter of the shepherd of the people, and with the rest of her family seized or killed during the invasion, she needed a husband. Her father is no longer alive, so her time is limited on when she can keep the estate—per the rules of her city.

Atro now brings her ideas about politics to the assembly.

Brisei shrugs and chews on her bread, swallows. "Alas, well, we can only hope that with time they will allow for new changes. At least they seem to be excited about your suggestion to have the other villages participate in sports competitions, outside of funerals."

Atro's lips twitch. "Sparta was definitely enthusiastic."

Huh, I know the Olympics get started sometime in this century. I wonder if Atro and Brisei play a part in that happening.

Homer presses his hand to the small of my back and we sweep ourselves outside to watch the rest of the sunrise. I place my head on his shoulder and let out a long sigh. Silence fills the space between us until rosy dawn turns orange.

"Brisei says you can start telling stories at parties once you get your Greek down. Think you'll be ready by fall?"

A quick breath shoots out of his nostrils. "Maybe autumn of *next* year. There's no chance I can recite *The Iliad* and *The Odyssey* in perfect Greek within a few months."

"Fair."

Still, he does practice on me every night. He's gotten the intro to the first book of *The Odyssey* down pat. *"Tell me, O Muse, of the man of many devices, who wandered full many ways after he had sacked the sacred citadel of Troy…"*

Homer lifts himself and paces to the end of the front porch.

His fingers pinch the leaves of a nearby apple tree that grows by the house. Brisei tore down most of the garden to make room for the homes in the backyard. At least we have this guy and a tamarisk bush, stationed near the pigsty.

"What were you doing in Talith's room this morning?"

"Oh, just dropping off some pottery. Cersei spelled out Alcmaeon's name on the bottom of a vase. Whole town's wanting stuff like that. Soon they'll be able to tell apart their Alphas from their Betas."

"Hmm." Homer plucks a leaf and spins the stem in his fingertips. "I think I read a name like that in one of Laran's books. Something about the guy being in the lineage of whoever came up with democracy."

A sharp breath flies into my nose.

Huh, I wonder… Democracy doesn't get to Greece for another few centuries. Someone had to be a grandfather of the guy who invented it, right? What if we rescued that same baby from a life of slavery?

With Brisei's track record of loving politics, I'll bet that the world's greatest "aunt" will teach Alc a thing or two about government.

"Speaking of pottery, I ran into a local magician in Cersei's shop the other day." Homer returns to the tree and buries his face inside the branches. "We could always—"

"Nah. I think I'm okay with sticking around for a while. I feel like we're on the verge of something like a…" I search the clouds for the words I've lost in English. Found 'em. "New age."

College can wait.

Something tells me I have far more exciting things to look forward to than gen eds and crippling student debt.

Homer pokes his head out of the leaves and grins. "I do like the sound of that. So what you're saying is you're ready for any kind of adventure, whatever is thrown your way?"

"I *can* handle it." After all, I survived a Greek invasion, time travel, and may or may not have brought the right people into Greece to usher in the Archaic Age.

"I like the sound of that can."

His arms whip out from the tree, and he lobs something the size of a baseball at me.

I catch the apple, and my heart thunderclaps in my chest.

"Well, Harper, how about a new adventure?"

ACKNOWLEDGMENTS

To my Lord and Savior, Jesus Christ, who thankfully never expects me to be the very best at everything. You've imbued us with gifts and talents that I hope to use to bring people your hope, joy, and encouragement.

To my friends who never let me give up on this book. Especially to Sonya, Alyssa, Carlee, James, Jess, Ellen, and David. I was so daunted by this, but your excitement spurred me on to complete it.

To Miralee and Tessa for believing in this book. We received so many rejections on this, and so it was such a blessing to receive your "yes," your amazing feedback, and your willingness to usher this story into the world.

To my encouragement squads: The Cyle Group (or whatever the heck you're called by the time this book releases in 2024), PWR Group, and Goon Squad.

To my family who have been supportive, even when I was battling a tangle of emotions from the past few years.

To the cover revealers, reviewers, endorsers, beta readers, editors, and everyone who helped to polish or get the word out about this book. I appreciate you more than you could ever know.

And of course, to the readers. Thank you for taking a chance on me. I get nervous before every book release, worried that no one will even read it. Thank you for following me on this journey.

A PERSONAL NOTE FROM THE AUTHOR

It's not common for me to wait so long to write the second book in the series. By this timeframe, I may have forgotten important details or will have lost the original vigor that accompanied the first book.

I thought it important to provide a timeline of what happened in between *Sparrow* and *Eagle*, and why I think I needed a little extra time to form the right words for the second.

I remember vividly writing chapter nineteen of the last book in February of 2018 when I got a phone call from my dad.

As far as my family went, I usually was the one to initiate calls in college. So I knew he had something important to tell me.

"I have some bad news—"

I already knew what he was going to say. "Dad, this is really not a good time." Fresh into our second semester, our professors had piled on the coursework. I had lines to memorize in a play I was in and was working as an assistant stage manager for another production.

"Hope, I'm sorry—"

Then I hung up. I didn't want to hear about the divorce. The unspoken word my parents had stretched out over months of a separation, dangling the possibility of them getting back together. The word I didn't want to hear a week away from my birthday.

So I hyperventilated/sobbed into my pillow. And then I set out to finish the book.

I poured every emotion, every heartache into Harper. Yes, then I finally found my writing voice, but it was after twenty years of wondering if my parents' relationship would last. Flash forward to the incredibly quick timeline of the past few years.

February 2018: My parents announce their divorce. They actually divorced in January, but didn't want to tell us until February, because a family member had suffered a loss.

March 2018: My dad gets a girlfriend.

May 2018: I got my first book contract.

Summer 2018: My mom gets a boyfriend.

Fall 2018: Some whack and spiritually dark stuff happens on my campus. Won't dive into details, but it did traumatize me. I still get flashbacks.

November 2018: My dad proposes.

January 2019: My mom is engaged.

February 2019: I graduate from Taylor University and move into my mom's.

March 2019: Dad is married and lives in Florida for eight months of the year.

March-June 2019: Experience the most heavy, suicidal depression in my life. I work an $8.50/hour job, after applying to 200+ jobs with no luck. Try out the dating scene and get stalked.

June 2019: My first book is published.

July-November 2019: I house-sit for my dad while he is in Florida.

December 2019: Anxious to sell the house, my dad and stepmom insist I buy a new house and take their cat Twix with me.

February 2020: I move into the new house, with a mortgage and a very fat cat.

March 2020: My grandma passes away, and lockdown for the pandemic begins.

March-July 2020: One third of my income is knocked out, and I'm living paycheck to paycheck. Try out the dating scene and get ghosted a lot.

July-October 2020: We start to see contracts for other books roll in, including *Why the Sparrow Cries*, after years of rejections.

November 2020: I get a full-time job and no longer have to worry about living paycheck to paycheck.

December 2020-June 2021 (June is when I started writing this book): Working on a lot of deadlines. Since fourteen books got contracted for 2021-2024, there's a lot of catch-up to do.

December 2021: Twix sadly dies.

Edit from Hope in 2023: A lot more happened in two more years, but as you can imagine, I got slammed with a lot.

It seems that things have finally slowed down, now that I've had a chance to process everything. So much happened in such a short period of time that I didn't have a moment to breathe.

Now, with more time on my hands, and more time to heal, I've let wounds scar. I've dipped into some metaphorical peroxide.

So now I have the opportunity to write a Harper who had two years to reflect and cauterize.

I wanted to choose the right words for her. For a girl who has been battered and bruised, but who also has a bright future ahead. Full of forgiveness, full of life, and full of love.

A HISTORICAL-ISH NOTE FROM THE AUTHOR

I want to start this thing off by clarifying I probably got a lot of details wrong. In fact, I know I got a lot of details wrong.

I know this because I chose one of the most obscure historical periods to write on, and to make matters worse for myself, most historians don't agree on much from the time period.

Often, when I read other books of historical fiction, I can get down on myself. It seems as though these authors have lived through the Regency period or Revolutionary War from the sheer amount of details they include in their stories.

Then I have to remind myself that most historical books take place from the 1700s onwards, periods for which we have an embarrassing amount of information.

Whereas the Greek Dark Ages moving into the early Archaic Period has next to nothing.

No writings, very few archeological findings, and some sketchy stories from a blind bard to go off of.

That said, I decided to research this period as much as possible to get all the details right that I could. Although I can't include everything below, as I have (literally) hundreds of pages of notes and annotations, I'd love for you to take a peek into this time period and the research to back it up.

My Research Process

I've spent about four years researching this book. Research has included, but is not limited to:

- Undergraduate classes specifically geared toward this time period

- Lectures from experts in the field of Archaic and Dark Age Greece

- Up-to-date historical books on the subject and analysis of the way of living in both the Greek Dark Ages and Archaic Greece

- Archeological finds from the Greek Dark Ages and Archaic Greece

- Comparisons of how people of various people groups lived and acted during this period

- Homer's works and other Greek works of antiquity that discuss the time period

- Commentaries on Homer's works, one of my favorites being the translation of the Odyssey by Emily Mills

- An Ancient Greek cookbook…literally (they ate some weird stuff)

- A wonderfully delightful YouTube channel called Tasting History (there were actually a ton of other YouTube channels, but I'd be remiss not to include this one)

I could go on. Needless to say, I had a ton of fun researching for this, but I definitely had my work cut out for me. Let's dive into a few of the major hallmarks of the period and how it played a role in the emergence of Archaic Greece.

The Fall into the Dark Ages

No one seems to agree on what led to the fall of the Mycenaeans (a sort of pre-Greek civilization). When Mycenae collapsed, the collapse rippled outward to the surrounding Mediterranean countries for several hundred years. Kind of like what happened when Rome bit the dust.

For the longest time, people thought a group known as the Sea Peoples did Mycenae dirty and sacked their city.

Now most historians have speculated a combination of events led to the collapse such as civil wars, environmental disasters, etc. In either case, by the time we get to the 800s BCE, the Greeks probably didn't have a great idea of what caused the Dark Ages. They passed everything down through oral tradition, since writing went out of style until the 700s.

Writing

Before Mycanae's collapse, people wrote in something known as Linear B. Once the Dark Ages started, writing stopped. Probably due to scarcity of resources or little time devoted to art or the need for writing, penmanship didn't come back into style until the 700s, when the Greeks adopted the Phoenician alphabet due to increased trading relations with foreign nations.

So they passed down their history via oral tradition, often through bards or "song-stitchers." Hence where the historical Homer steps in.

Historians have argued if Homer even existed. Many don't think a blind bard could've done *The Iliad* and *The Odyssey* all by himself. The consensus seems to be that there may have been multiple bards taking up the mantle or people revising and adding to the stories over time.

Stories had a huge importance during this period. Stories reminded them of the past, of better times. Most of what we find in the *Iliad* and *Odyssey* were probably glorious *"nostos,"* nostalgia for the Greek peoples.

Art

Art really declined in this period. What little we have of it is simple geometric shapes, unlike some of the ornate and complex art works from before the Bronze Age collapse.

Pottery continued, but we don't see it getting more complicated until we enter the Archaic Age in Greece. Along with the emergence of the polis, the Greek people appear to experiment more as they get closer to that 700s mark. We have various pottery designs that get more intricate in shape, and even fun little 3-D models, like a centaur found in Lefkandi.

The Polis

The Greek polis—a city-state—such as Athens or Sparta, sorta kinda didn't exist during the Greek Dark Ages. At least, the polis really hits the ground running around 750 BCE. This book takes place in the 800s BCE.

Most people probably would've identified more with their tribe rather than Greece as a whole. The term Hellas (Greece) didn't really exist in the Greek Dark Ages.

We do see, in works like *The Iliad*, various tribes banding together to defeat a greater enemy. In this case, the city of Troy.

Why it's important to dive into the polis is because the Greeks go on a colonizing binge in the 700s onwards. They Hellenize areas around them (turn them Greek). Part of me thought back to the Etruscans and how the Romans essentially did the same thing to them. It took historians forever to figure out the Etruscans were really their own people.

I wanted to do the same with Palikari, a made-up country. A land shaped by Dark Age Greek customs but not quite colonized and Hellenized yet.

Olympics

Olympics started in the Archaic period. I find the funeral games a really interesting precursor to this.

When you died, people apparently mourned you. Then they wrestled and boxed for prizes after they cremated you. Fun stuff.

Like the Olympics, victors would receive various prizes. And it appears many of the funeral games transferred to sports activities later, such as the footrace, boxing, and wrestling.

Temples and Gods

Gods pop up in stories all the time in the Greek Dark Ages. They often cause woes for human subjects and literally start and get in the middle of wars.

Unlike Palikari, most Greek sites pre-Archaic Period didn't have elaborate temples and such. I wanted Palikari to be slightly better off than Greece, until Greece gains enough strength and colonizes it. I modeled the Palikarian temple off of the famous Minoan temple found in Crete.

Many Greek temples do seem to follow that template, and I wanted to give Palikari something a little "other" than what existed in Greece at the time.

Greeks would have continued ritual sacrifices, celebrations, and libations to deities into the Greek Dark Ages and onwards.

Treatment of Slaves and Women

I remember in one of my history classes we learned that the Greek Dark Ages sort of leveled the playing field for men and women.

Yeah, not really.

Sure, the restrictions probably weren't as tight on women as they later got in the Classical Period. Women had very little say, had to travel with a party of people at all times, had to defer to their father's judgment as to who they could marry, were expected to produce ample offspring, and were encouraged to be silent.

Slaves had it far worse.

They had no say in whether a man in the house wanted to do illicit activities with them. And any slave who showed defiance often received some kind of punishment that would have resulted in a painful death. We see this happen at the end of *The Odyssey* when Odysseus slaughters the female slaves in the house because the male suitors slept with them.

These females probably had little say in the matter, as far as the male suitors go.

Slavery also would've been on the forefront of the minds of everyone in Greece. If another nation attacked your town, they would either kill you or sell you into slavery. For men, this meant either working in coal mines (a horrible, horrible way to go) or working in a household as a meat carver, horse groomer, or other type of slave. Women typically became house slaves.

Homer, in our story, was born in Palikari, but his mother sells him into slavery at the temple. Not atypical during the time period.

Leadership Hierarchy

They appear to have had warrior-kings, otherwise known as the Shepherds of the People. Odysseus serves as one in *The Odyssey*.

Men also decided everything by council. They would meet in the town square, and whoever had the talking stick could, well, talk. They would often allow the oldest to speak first. In Ancient Greece, they had a high reverence and respect for elders.

Women, of course, were not allowed at such meetings.

In the Army

Although this solidified later on, many Greeks joined the army at an early age, often tweens or early teens. In many polis city-states, men didn't completely exit their time at war until the age of thirty.

Women, on the other hand, married very young, again tweens or teens. Many died in childbirth, both infants and mothers. By the time they reached Harper's age, they probably had at least one or two kids, if not more.

The Very Best

From what we can ascertain from Classical works, everyone in Dark Age Greece strove to excel at something. Everyone always had an epithet that preceded their name. "God-like," "master of the battle cry," "horse tamer," etc.

People often equated wealth with such positions. Although they allowed for beggars to eat food from their tables, they certainly wouldn't want to lose to a homeless man in a footrace.

If you didn't excel at something, someone may question your heritage. Or worse, overtake it. We see something similar happen to Telemachus in *The Odyssey* when he can't seem to stand up for himself. The suitors vow to dispose of what they viewed as a weakling and take over the estate themselves.

Xenia and Hospitality

Familiar with the fae? And how if they give you a gift, they expect one in return?

Welcome to Dark Ages Greece hospitality. They treated strangers well and allowed them to bathe, dress, and eat before stating their business. Often, in stories, they would talk about how gods or great men could very well arrive at your house dressed as a beggar, and you were to show them kindness. They expected politeness from the foreigner, and they expected something in return.

Sometimes this meant an alliance. At other times, it meant that if they visit your hometown, they expect the same hospitality.

The Afterlife

In Ancient Greece, and many other civilizations, if you didn't get a proper burial, you didn't make it into the underworld. We see this in *The Iliad* when Patroclus begs Achilles to stop taking his sweet ol' time in getting Patroclus's funeral together.

In this particular time period, they cremated the dead. Often this also involved burning pets, prisoners of war from foreign nations, and household goods so these items could travel with the person into the afterlife.

Then they'd wrap the bones in fat and place them in a jar, and they constructed the burial mound for the bones of the warrior, as well as (in the future) his wife, armor, and other precious goods which would be buried with him.

If a man of the house died, his firstborn son took over. Unless, in the case of *The Odyssey*, the suitors managed to marry the recently widowed wife.

Conclusion

I could go on, but this essentially summarizes some of the most important hallmarks of the Greek Dark Ages, especially as it transitioned into the Archaic period.

Although I may not have gotten every detail right, I hope my four years of research have helped to paint a picture of life during this obscure time period.